# Intervals of Hope

## Christopher Canniff

*Intervals of Hope*
Copyright © 2021 Christopher Canniff
All rights reserved
Published by Blue Denim Press Inc.
First Edition
ISBN 978-1-927882-67-2

Cover & Interior Design—Shane Joseph
Typeset in Cambria and Georgia

Library and Archives Canada Cataloguing in Publication

Title: Intervals of hope / Christopher Canniff.
Names: Canniff, Christopher, author.
Identifiers: Canadiana (print) 20210269553 | Canadiana (ebook) 20210269561 | ISBN 9781927882672
  (softcover) | ISBN 9781927882689 (Kindle) | ISBN 9781927882696 (EPUB)
Classification: LCC PS8605.A574 I58 2021 | DDC C813/.6—dc23

"In the chaos of sentiments and passions which defend a barricade, there is something of everything; there is bravery, youth, honor, enthusiasm, the ideal, conviction, the eager fury of the gamester, and above all, intervals of hope."
-Victor Hugo

"And the word 'Family' implies much more than a collection of people tied by relationship. Differences of character and opinion, the stress of poverty, bits of success, days of fun, accidents and illness, long and heart-rending separations, even death itself—all serve to bind its members closer, and charge the word with lovelier meaning as life grows sterner."
-From *A London Family Between the Wars*, M. Vivian Hughes, 1940

## Other Works by Christopher Canniff

### Novels

*Poor Man's Galapagos* (Blue Denim Press, 2015)

*Abundance of the Infinite* (Quattro Books, 2012)

### Short Stories

*The Russian Soldier* (Descant Magazine)

*Solitude* (Tightrope Books)

*Clean Conscience* (LWOT, Montreal)

*Soli Deo Gloria*

For Gordon Schottlander, whose bravery, courage and service to his country is an inspiration to us all

and

For my great–grandfather Wilfred Littlejohn who fought with the First Battalion, First Canadian Regiment in the trenches of the Great War.

# 1

September 18, 1934
London, England

Crouching behind my bedroom door and peering downstairs past the painted wisteria paper lining the walls, I was a jungle cat ready to pounce. My pa, Wilfrid Lionel Dixon, was not supposed to be here; yet there he was, leaning on the kitchen door frame with a newspaper under his arm. His hat was askew, casting an outline along his grey, grubby face. A scarecrow among the shadows, that's what he was. The only sounds came from the sputtering kitchen stove and the infuriating navy blue cuckoo clock in the upstairs hallway. Maybe Pa was coming home to London to live, to get a job here, and this was not simply another visit. My mum, Doreen, would have a husband, and we would finally have a father again.

Or, more likely, this was only another sham.

Dressed in her old white housecoat and stumbling upon Pa's sinewy figure outlined beneath an iron cross, Mum suddenly stopped. She shuffled beneath his arm, I'm sure, wincing at the stench as she moved toward a kettle heating between a pile of glowing bricks and a copper hood, waiting in silence now for the water to boil, her hands uselessly clenched together.

Verbalizing my thoughts, with each word more emphatic than the last, she started their chewing match:

"Ya here to stay?"

When he didn't respond, she moved beneath his arm again into the darkened drawing room, sitting on the lilac-flowered couch that looked like a girl giant's deformed shoulders. Opening my bedroom door wider to hear his answer, as though I didn't already know, I repositioned myself in the dark beside hinges I had cleverly lubricated with bicycle grease to avoid detection in an instance such as this. There was a clattering of knitting needles as Mum nestled into the comfort of the girl's hulking arms.

"No," Pa replied softly.

"I could have told you this, Mum," I said. "And you wouldn't have had to bother asking."

A shrieking noise caused my heart to flip. The kettle was boiling.

Relieved, perhaps, to hear the vessel calling out to her, Mum walked back into the kitchen and set to work. They moved together, out of sight, and I shifted to listen. I needed to move downstairs, to know why this scarecrow had left his fields unprotected to come here, what had changed, what other deceptions he had planned. There were no simple visits. He was after something.

A kitchen chair grazed across the linoleum floor; a single cup and saucer were removed from the cupboard and clanked onto the table.

"What're you here for, then?" she asked, moving out of view.

"Right," I said aloud. "I was wondering that, too. And ask him if he's afraid of catching fire with the heat under the kettle."

The clock snapped rhythmically. Pondering now if they had heard me, they began speaking again a moment later. The echo of their voices was subdued.

Descending the creaking stairs, with the subterfuge of a spy, was the only way.

As I began, Ian began snoring behind me and I rolled one of my socks, tossing the ball his way. The mass bounced neatly off his face, hushing him. Recalling my mental map, bypassing the creaky parts of the top stairs, I carried on with my descent. Five steps later, the infernal cuckoo clock chimed and then erupted into its odious song before returning to unremitting ticks. I continued down, my drop easier now.

At the bottom of the stairs, separated from Wilfrid and Doreen only by a thin wall, there was no escape. In the glass of the window, Mum's reflection flashed by. Pa was seated, so I could only see the image of his emaciated back.

I was certain Pa said the word "luggage." Glancing around, there were no bags that I could see; but maybe he was planning to take the bulky green suitcase, our only piece of luggage, to return here with all his stuff.

The last I had seen that suitcase, years before, was after we had relocated to the Middleton Colliery in South Leeds. We had been in the mining town for only a short time when Mum suddenly announced that she had been swindled and that we were not, in fact, losing our London home to the bank as Pa had led her to believe. She strained to carry her suitcase as we made our way down the dusty road, her two young boys on either side holding her arms as we gazed back at our father. I had wanted him to take us by the hand and lead us back to our row house, demonstrating what a man should do when confronted with the impending loss of his children. And each morning after such a dream, one that I'm sure we shared, I envisioned him awakening to begin the day and mourning his inaction so many years before over a slice of oily bacon, an egg, dry bread and black tea hastily prepared by his elderly landlady. A pitiful consolation.

Mum, her reflection clutching on to the kettle's wooden handle, turned back toward her husband.

"Your sons," she said. "Why, they need a father."

"Right, Mum, stick it to him," I said quietly. "Fathers are supposed to show sons what they're to become. If fathers are nowhere to be found, well then—"

But there was no response from him.

"Nicholas is fourteen years old," she continued. "Almost a man."

"I *am* a man now," I clarified. "The man of this house, anyway."

Confusion flashed in her sea-green eyes and from the intensity of previous fights, and the rarer tender moments, I wondered whether she might suddenly hurl scalding water, or simply set the pressure vessel aside and embrace him.

"I miss the lads," he said.

"I haven't heard you utter that one before, Pa," I said quietly. "Good line for whatever you're up to."

"The boys are upstairs, asleep," she said. "They're always after me, asking when you'll be home next. Good heavens, I'd like to give them some idea."

Retrieving another cup and saucer, she set them on the table. Moving to sit down, she stopped and gazed upward. For a moment, I thought she might have caught a glimpse of me. But then, she glanced away as I put my back to the wall to reveal nothing of this clandestine spy but a covert shadow.

Pouring herself a cup of tea from a blue and white flowered teapot, she invited her husband to do the same. His voice, garbled with an echo resonating on the walls, muttered something about a job. She did not reply, perhaps surmising the details he had not yet divulged.

This could be the start of a new era for all of us.

"Your new job, it's at the colliery then?" she asked.

"A promotion, and a new house," he said before elaborating further, now presenting his plan for all of us to move to the mining town where Pa's chum Edward had died of the "lung" and another chap Reginald was almost buried alive in a cavern, the doctors and the miners considering it a miracle that Reginald had even survived.

"You must've questioned your decision till now," Pa continued, "which is good for not one of us, staying here in London with the boys. It's against our upbringing, our morality, and even against God's will that a married couple with children should be living apart."

"Who fed you that line?" she asked. "I passed a gift onto the boys, being here. They'll not be trained by their father to work in the mines."

She had said before that without her resolution to stay in London, Ian and I would, one after the other from the age of fifteen, slowly become this man before her now: a man hardened and beaten by the underground and by drink, with thick, calloused hands ingrained with the soot of the earth that would not fully wash away and that kept him securely within its confines. Still, she had the power to impart another gift, that of a father for Ian and me, and a husband for herself.

"Albert sent me letters," she said. "Doings in the mines and such. I don't want him writing about an accident involving you, or some illness you have from always inhaling dust. We want you here."

"Dreadful," I said. "I told you before, Mum, that he won't move here unless some place like Beckton Gas Works is hiring."

Evidently, they were not, as Pa said nothing in reply.

I could not recall the last time I had seen her smile, but there must have been a period when she smiled often, a time when that was all my father thought about. After meeting her and her father, a retired Lieutenant, at the bar of the Cecil Hotel during the war, Pa must have fought with her image in his mind. Her visage had surely changed little since, her waved auburn hair cropped short, and her lips curling toward the dimples drawn on her cheeks when she smiled. In his idle moments in the trenches, Pa must have deliberated about his homecoming and their life together after the war, having some conception of a life he was fighting for, his image of their future nothing like this.

The legs of his chair dragged across the floor, and he raised his voice.

"I don't know what is the problem with you," he said.

His voice trailed off, and she did not reply. She must have known that what he had said about morality and God's will was true. The reflection of Pa simply stared across the table, his image cloudy with the steam rising above the pot.

"You're keeping the family apart," she said, "not me."

"You're both to blame," I said, far too loud. "No giving in. More his fault than hers, though."

The jig was up.

Pa walked into the next room. Finding me leaning against the wall, he jumped.

"Go upstairs," he said.

I stood there as Mum lit some lamps to illuminate the white and gold drawing room. She sat down in her rocker and began knitting a blue sweater. The fireplace glowed with blue and white decorative tiles and an iron hood, the wavering illumination adding to the light from a tasseled table lamp. Black fur shone from the cat Minnaloushe, now sleeping on the floor beside her.

"I'm not so tired," I said, casually moving away from the wall, peering into his eyes. "But maybe, based on the look of you, I should be. Why're you home?"

"Brasher than ever, I see," he replied. "What did you overhear?"

"You said you're not here to stay, and then you said something about luggage I guess, which is confusing if you're not moving back here. Then you said you missed us. You have a promotion and you're looking for a new row house in South Leeds, where we can live together as a family."

"So, after all that, I'm to blame for keeping the family apart?"

"Mum doesn't want to be in South Leeds, and you don't want to be here…so, when you were in the war, what were you fighting for?"

He paused before answering, squinting at me and shaking his head: "What claptrap are you on about?"

"I mean…why aren't you living here? Don't you want us?"

There was no response until, clenching his right fist in his left hand, he raised his arms and shoved me back. Losing my grip on the floor, my contorted body spilled down, and he slinked through the front door without a word. Minnaloushe darted after him. Mum threw her knitting needles to the side, the drumsticks clattering to rest. She embraced me there on the wooden floor, squeezing out tears.

He would not be back for months this time, maybe longer.

I wanted to run after him. But I had not challenged his departures before. And I certainly wasn't going to oppose him further, a soldier who, without contemplating desertion had risked his life so often over a four-year duration of service to his country. Yet running away seemed easy to him now.

In bed, I tried to calm myself by reading Pa's war journal that I had recently found, while listening to the sputtering and crackling of coal in the drawing room fireplace. I lay awake for a long time before I was able to fall asleep.

I crawled on my hands and knees, first though pouring rain, then up to a German front line trench and over the edge, the blade of my bayonet plunging into the blackness. Pa led the way through underground tunnels and I had the notion that my father, the war hero, had never been so pleased with me. A smile creased my lips.

My subconscious led me to dodge the crags and low ceilings of the tunnels, peeking up to see a sea of rocks suddenly pouring down from above. I was not hurt, but my father was no longer there. My initial shock was accompanied by a sort of panged relief; as though acknowledging that Mum's troubles, all of which seemed to stem from the man now buried beneath blackness and ash, were over.

My father had faced the German Army for nearly four years in the trenches of France. And ever since examining his wartime journal, a longing for his approval and stress in defying him had become more poignant, more palpable. I knew of his being gassed and awarded medals during the war, tangible yet reticent depictions of courage and valour.

*"We're not going anywhere,"* Mum yelled, which shocked me into consciousness and awareness of an ignominious shame. The darkness of my dreams had transformed into an ethereal bedroom, Ian snoring beside me.

After rubbing my eyes, I sat up, climbed out of bed, opened the door slightly and crouched down at the top of the stairs, waiting. Mum was in the next room, yapping in her sleep again.

Maybe my lack of action was keeping the family apart. My parents may have been responsible, but perhaps I was also somehow to blame.

I lay back down in my bed with thoughts of my recent fights in the schoolyard where I had not been hurt, except for bruises easily concealed beneath my clothes; my gambling at Pitch and Toss; and my recent discovery that I could talk back to teachers and even my own mother without reprisal. Yet Wilfrid was previously impervious to such vehemence from either of his two sons.

He was not used to any nonsense from me, and maybe now he would only stay away longer as a result.

My stomach ached, my head sweated, and this kept me awake for seemingly interminable hours as I stared first at the candy-striped wallpaper of my bedroom, the uninspired paintings of a windblown meadow and another of a pond replete with lily pads, and then up to the wavering shadows on the ceiling. Mum mumbled until she had nothing more to say. The cracks on the ceiling oscillated like moving rivers from the moonlight reflecting off the trees outside, and my eyes wound down the length of the rivers carefully before I was finally able to sleep once more.

---

*Christopher Canniff*

The next morning, I resolved to bring the family together. Since no one else would do so, I would have to invent a scheme.

I soon learned, over a breakfast of black bread and marmalade, that what I had suspected was true: my father had left for South Leeds as unexpectedly as he had arrived.

A war hero in retreat.

8

# 2

After Pa had left for the mines once, I discovered a pile of his love letters beside the fireplace, written to Mum before they were married. Some were composed in the trenches of the Great War. One even had a tuft of Pa's brown hair taped to the page, making me jump, expecting that a rat had chewed through the page and was staring up at me. The day after, before I had the chance to read them, the letters were gone.

"Some of my stuff got pinched," Pa said the next time he was home. "Where is it?"

"I thought you weren't coming home again," she replied.

"Well," he alleged, "maybe you wanted things that way."

So, when I heard Mum in the attic now in the early morning, where she stored old Tiffany lamps and lampshades, metal tins, hatboxes, photographs, Dinky Toys, dress patterns and scrapbooks, my stomach soured. I knew she was searching. Not cleaning, shuffling or organizing, but rummaging for any of my father's possessions that, in an act of defiance and empowerment, she could toss away.

She was dodgy and could not be trusted, anymore than he could.

"Mum!" I yelled toward the ceiling. "Make a list for the market, and then I'll be off!"

I heard her descend the ladder, squeaking down the stairs with her characteristic shuffle. She was certainly taking a break from her foraging to itemize what she needed.

From under my pillow, I retrieved Pa's faded brown journal with Canadian, British, and French flags on the front, as well as the tattered letters written on all types of parchment: the collected scribblings of my displaced father that now offered me suggestions, advice and admonitions.

I ascended the ladder to the attic.

In the corner over Mum's room, beneath a model airplane Pa must have built as a child, some newspapers collected over the years and a coin collection handed down from Pa's grandfather, I found a large wood and metal trunk. Opening the dusty trunk revealed a welcome glimpse of blue, the colour of the sky that accompanied the morning sun. The shoebox was still here. Opening the box and stuffing the letters and the journal inside, I carefully descended the ladder, then the stairs, finding Mum in the kitchen.

"Here," she said, handing me a list along with some coins. "Some vegetables for soup is all for today. What's that?"

Underneath her eyes, the skin was dark and wrinkled in this early morning light. The frayed white nightgown fell from her shoulders as her darting eyes locked on the blue box under my arm. She pulled up on the straps of her gown.

"Some refuse from my room," I said.

"I'll burn it for you," she said, reaching eagerly for this fragment of sky. "Hand it here."

"No," I said, turning away with the box. "You're too busy rummaging. I'll take care of this, don't fuss for me."

"Leave it by the fireplace."

She ascended the stairs before continuing up to the attic.

By taking the contents of this box with the war letters and securing them somewhere away from Mum's indiscriminate tidiness, I could avoid having Pa's wartime experiences discarded as though they had not occurred, as if he had been at home like his friend Art Maunders, who was unable to pass the physical as he "had some fingers off" from a carpentry accident. Pa, like Art, might have spent his time listening to news of the war and working at the grocery store by day and chasing women by night.

Pa, a normally private and quiet man, would surely have preferred that the shoebox remain tucked away into a corner of the attic, away from Mum's touch, but still unacknowledged and unknown.

I forced down hard on the pedals of my rusty bicycle, which I had named after my Aunt Betsy, who died of stubbornness by refusing to see a doctor for what might have been consumption. With the box tight under my arm, I bullied Betsy to the busy market booths of Whitechapel where I shopped most afternoons. After perusing the assortment of vegetables set out in front of the hanging poultry and beef swarming with flies, I grabbed a bunch of carrots, a head of cabbage, and some Turkish Delight and Marzipan for myself, placing some coins in a plump old woman's sweaty palm and taking my purchases away in Betsy's basket. I held my breath past the stinking fishmongers, ready with their cleavers and marble slabs to cut the heads from an assortment of filthy fish, and then pedalled past Trafalgar Square to the multicoloured trees lining Great Russell Street. Church bells chimed in the distance. The street was lined with autumn leaves, and the cold wind bit into my face and penetrated through the holes in my jacket.

All I would keep was a few letters and Pa's diary, which would constantly tug on the stitching of an oversized pocket I had sewn into my coat.

Then, while chewing on some Turkish Delight, I saw the place.

I dismounted the bicycle after stopping swiftly and stealthily, without falling, passing through the heavy iron gates of the British Museum.

Arriving at a set of twelve wide Portland steps leading to the main entrance, I pushed my bicycle aside. The rusty frame clattered to the ground, and I retrieved the cabbage that made a mad dash and the carrots that flopped lazily to the earth. I returned the root vegetables to their cage to thwart their attempted escape.

The elderly guard was distracted briefly from his copy of the *Daily Mirror* newspaper.

I was crafty, even cunning at times, but regrettably not so discrete as to avoid detection. Mum couldn't do any better, and this guard could certainly take her down, tackling her frail form easily if she showed up to reclaim her husband's belongings.

"Here you are, for your museum," I said, setting the box on his desk with a thump, opening the door further. "You're quite welcome."

Folding his daily and setting it aside, the crinkly man glared up at me with a furrowed expression, lowering his rounded glasses.

"What are you on about?" he asked. "You can't leave that here."

"What, my bicycle, or this box?" I asked.

"Both. And don't be daft."

"This is my father's letters and things from the Great War. Now your museum will have some real stuff, instead of drab learning out of encyclopedias and history books and such. Pa wouldn't like his personal items here, but better here than in the fire, that's what I say."

"You talk some sort of nonsense, you do. There's a process to follow. Make an appointment with the curator. And move that bicycle aside."

"No time for an appointment, not with Mum lurking about the house. I'll take it inside, myself. Betsy, I'll put her over by that tree."

The guard waved me away dismissively before returning to his newspaper.

The colossal Roman columns on each side of the entryway resembled an ancient acropolis from one of Mum's travel magazines. Leafing through those journals after dinner, we would often examine the photographs and read articles detailing elaborate trips we could not afford. The enormous cruise ships, palm-treed islands, vivid white-azure beaches and historic tours of European capitals elicited within me more than a simple fantasy of travel to discover faraway lands. We would all voyage from Montmartre and Montparnasse in Paris to the ruins and museums of Rome, to the art and architecture of Spain to the jungles and exotic spices of the Orient, and across the ocean to America and to Canada, the land where Pa was born. And within these grand journeys was the reciprocated amity and conception of my father, previously unknown, as a man who was kind, generous, and interesting instead of the dreary, miserable chap we all knew.

The words of poet Laurence Binyon adorned a memorial here to sixteen men who, once employed by the museum, had not returned from the battlefields of the Great War. As their bodies do not age as ours, the poet proclaimed, so their memory, too, would not tarnish.

I checked my pockets. Nothing but some empty candy wrappers, an old shoelace, and a broken pencil. There was only one method I could concoct for getting in without paying. An appropriate opportunity, a duplicitous performance, and I would be inside. If properly executed, no one would know. If not, everyone would.

Walking to the front of the queue, I lingered near the counter watching the ticket seller, a young woman with dark eyelashes and thick lips. Standing to the side and out of her view, but still near the entrance, I awaited my chance.

A short time passed before an elderly woman began counting small coins on the counter. Not only was she old, but she had shaking hands, too.

As they said in America, Showtime.

I bumped into the woman, almost dropping my shoebox as the coins clattered to the floor on both sides of the desk. The ticket seller disappeared to recover the money, and some people in queue bent to the floor to assist. Shimmying alongside a plump man wearing a hefty trench coat and a bowler hat, I passed into the foyer unnoticed as the commotion ensued.

I spent a while searching, sometimes in circles. Past enormous stacks containing endless volumes in the reading area of the Great Room, at the end of the hall before some Parthenon sculptures, I finally located an exhibit where I could deposit Pa's belongings.

There it was, lit up like Christmas: a display of British involvement in trench warfare.

There was a collection of newspaper articles, handwritten letters and an assortment of various artefacts such as compasses, maps, rifles, revolvers, and an assortment of ammunition from the Crimean War, the Boer War, and the Great War. Along a portion of the wall in a section on the Great War, seeing no one around, I opened my shoebox and tacked one of the letters to the wall.

This letter to Pa's cousin Arthur made me chuckle again. Arthur had asked Pa to send him a shell, which I understood to be a projectile with explosives. Pa wrote back that he didn't know what size Arthur wanted, so he had better come over and get one for himself.

I placed a photograph of Pa in his army uniform near a collection of similar photographs. He stared back at me with a sombre expression as I found a section on recruitment, tacking his signed enlistment papers to the wall.

Opening the shoebox revealed his three gleaming war medals. There was the bronze 1914 Mons Star, a crown atop a laurel wreath crossed with two swords; the silver British War Medal depicting a naked St George on a horse trampling a Prussian shield; and the lacquered bronze Victory Medal, with the winged and robed Victory extending one hand while holding a palm branch in the other. One of the display cases was not locked, and I removed a pin holding the case closed, moving other less important items aside and placing Pa's medals inside, then adding a nameplate I had fabricated from a piece of wood I found on the street. While not like the others, the nameplate still appeared good enough to pass muster.

Sitting on the floor, I opened the shoebox which had some German buttons and Austrian, German, and French currency Pa had mailed home during the war, as well as several letters addressed to his mother, father, and brother written from the trenches and during times of leave. A letter to his father with a YMCA header was folded and tucked in a corner, and opening the letter revealed, in rounded and left-slanted script, my pa's life in the war.

*On July 18th, 1915, I joined the "Bomb Throwers," or what some called the "Suicide Club," figuring that if we had the chance to use bombs instead of artillery, we should certainly do so.*

*After a while, I began leading the Bombers. I chewed the fat with one of the Bombing Officers, William, for a long time one day when we were sitting in the trenches waiting for nothing. William told me that overseeing men meant double duty. You must look out for yourself, he said, and make sure your men survive. You must go with your gut because so many situations you are in are not planned. Your reaction must be instinctual and emotional too. You want to charge a machine gun nest when you see your men being killed, or because you see a section of the army being held up somewhere. It is your reflex to go and get them. You don't think a lot about anything. Just like when you are* bullied as a boy and forced to fight back. Everything the Bombing Officer said that day was true.

And then, near the end of May, there was another battle, and it was pretty hot. A regular hell for the first 24 hours. After a day's bombardment, we couldn't take it anymore and all of us in the First Contingent made a charge in the pouring rain. When we started, we found a bunch of Germans in a front-line trench. We bayoneted some and shot others, taking about forty prisoners and capturing three machine guns and all kinds of bombs and starlight, too.

The Third Battalion charged next, and we in the First Contingent supported them. After we reached the first hill, Fritz gave us an awful bombardment. Fritz didn't let up and neither did the rain. We were all mud from head to foot. The mud was so deep that lots of fellows had to be pulled out as the First and the Third advanced.

The Third Division was lost, but the First took back some of our trenches and artillery and levelled Fritz's trenches. Fritz's losses were heavy and the prisoners were glad to get out of the fighting. We were certainly happy to get out too.

I didn't have anything to eat till we got out; over 28 hours after the battle began. But then I made up for lost time. I found some rum and had a pretty good swig of it. It helped to calm my nerves. The papers said Fritz was running short of grub, but we found all kinds. There was butter and lots of other stuff like sausage and bread.

The First Division had been in one of the hottest places on this front for longer than any of us cared to remember. An English artilleryman told me that there were more guns on both sides here than at the eight-mile front at Verdun. At Verdun, Fritz was using flame throwers and poison gas. So, it gave a little idea what we had put up with, and what we might be in for.

George Carson, from my battalion, is missing. He was one of the Highgate Boys that joined the Army at the same time as I did. George has either been killed, wounded, or taken prisoner. That's the way when someone goes missing.

*Out of the old boys that came over to France with the 1st Battalion, I know, from talk in the tents, that there are only about seventy of us left out of 1,000.*

A thin shadow blocked my light and my head rose to see a scrawny man with a moustache in a suit and bowler hat, staring at my open shoebox. Pointing to a corner of the room by one of the display cases, I began explaining what this man now saw before him.

"I found this shoebox, over there," I said. "I was sorting through, to find what belongs where. To put things in their proper place."

He did not respond, his gaunt face unmoving, and I attempted to wave him away as the guard outside had done to me.

"You can move on," I continued. "Shimmy along, now."

"Shimmy along?" he replied.

"Yes," I said, waving my hand. "Now shoo."

"Where is your admittance?"

I began sifting through the box, which might be described by my math instructor as less of a box and more of an oblong, irregular trapezoid.

"I admit it is in this confounded trapezoid somewhere, to be sure," I said. "You can help me sort through, if you'd like."

Seizing the letter I was holding, nearly tearing the page, he grabbed the shoebox and stuffed the letter inside. Taking my arms with his skeleton hands, he helped me up and began leading me toward the front entrance.

"You will see those items are given to the curator, to be put where they belong?" I asked.

"Your concern for the tidiness of our museum is both touching and perplexing."

I broke free from this man's skeletal grip a moment later and ran back to the exhibit, long enough to bid goodbye to one of the letters on the wall that Pa had written while still in training in Quebec, before he was sent overseas to the trenches and battlefields. The letter was written at YMCA Camp, Valcartier, Quebec, September 5, 1914 and described his camp, the 25,000 soldiers there, and the doctor's examination of his bum leg which he figured would send him home before the end of the war, now expected to be over by Christmas, the war that would last another four years.

The guard outside shook his head now as he saw me being callously and unjustifiably pushed toward the heavy iron gates of the British Museum, old Betsy's rusty chain drooping on her meager frame nearby. With birds singing and a gentle wind blowing, I sat down on a bench and felt for my father's journal in my coat.

Living through the details of his early life in the war, by reading and re-reading his journal, the old drunken man with a blackened face and hands who came home for brief visits to scold and bully Ian and me and deride his wife seemed to vanish into the handwriting. A lifetime of conflict that had begun over a few dollars and a shoelace at the Valcartier camp in 1914 had extended to years of fighting against the Germans to expel them from France, and continued until today as he quarrelled with his wife to get his family back.

Extending my leg to reach into my pocket, I produced an envelope I had intercepted at the post office. Such letters from South Leeds, written by Albert, a man living with my pa in his small tenement and who had taken an intense interest in Mum over the 18 days we had all lived there together, would often make her cry for days. From my bedroom in South Leeds, through the thin walls, and likely when they thought I was asleep, I overheard Albert's promise to send her such letters. While Pa's sporadic letters detailed how much money he was sending home and menial particulars of intact families in South Leeds, Albert's regular letters contained whatever absurdities came into his mind, including wild fantasies about him being married to my mother. So, without telling anyone, not even my younger brother Ian, I had begun collecting as many of these letters as I could, reading some and disposing of them all.

I tore the envelope open and unfolded the pages. This specific letter described a "death stoppage," for which they apparently had a rubber stamp due to the frequency of such events. The investigators of this stop-work order had determined that the Safety Officer had gone for his "snap," a short break, when Pa, who had recently been promoted to a supervisor, was left in charge of the Davy Safety Lamp. He had evidently dropped the lamp and triggered an explosion underground. Part of Wilfrid's sleeve had caught on fire as a worker standing only a few feet away was buried beneath the collapsed ceiling. Emerging from the pit completely blackened from coal dust, there was now the smell of burning flesh. The cause of the incident was later determined to be accidental.

Albert's arm was amputated, and Pa had almost died from the extent of the burns to his body.

Pa's promotion had been "rescinded" as quickly as it had been bestowed. This was the same job he had come to London to tell Mum about, sham employment that would bring us all together to live in South Leeds.

The doctor said that those who survived were indeed fortunate, that God's favour must have been upon them, the same reason I attributed to Pa's survival during the Great War. But I wondered why Albert would have sent such a letter to Mum, except to mourn, for pages and pages, the loss of his arm, without mentioning the loss of his fellow miner except in passing.

As I shifted my weight on the bench, I wondered how the family would be different if my father, and not the other worker, had died. Peering at the words of this letter, I chastised myself for such thoughts; but still, I couldn't help speculating how the family would change. Unable to afford our London home, we would have to move to my paternal Uncle Devon's house in the country. My unmarried uncle would become a surrogate father for this displaced family. We would be back to the place I wanted to be, where some of our best summers were spent, at my uncle's house in medieval Northaw with its church, bakery, shops, and a national school. I was drawn to the openness of that place and enjoyed sitting in the tall grass next to Ian, surrounded by a sea of sky. We would categorize the different characteristics of oaks, poplars, willows, jasmine, and crab apple trees, and write them down in notebooks. There were robins, starlings, magpies, and sparrows, and we counted cows, sheep, pigs, foxes, and pheasants. Ian had renewed energy outside of the city, his perpetual sickness abated in that place away from the smog of industry and automobiles on busy streets.

But in my memories of those summers in Northaw, my father, much of the time, was there. Ian and I had passed the days fishing together with him, hunting for pheasants, or taking long walks. In our extended periods of time outdoors we only actually caught a few small fish, and didn't shoot any birds, but we discussed at length who would roast the pheasant (always Pa), which accompaniments were best (bacon was my choice over Pa's rice and Ian's potatoes), and the anticipated taste and texture of the game (which none of us could answer, but a tougher chicken meat seemed reasonable). Pa answered our unending stream of questions, some well thought out and some not, with intelligent and detailed answers and without ever seeming to tire of our inquisitiveness that annoyed even us. He showed us not only that he had a good heart, but that he had the potential to be a great father.

We were together there more than we ever were in London, or anywhere else, and these were the best reminiscences I had, not only of Pa, but also of my brother—in recent memory.

My eyes wandered now to a lacquered plaque, perched on the wall above poet Laurence Binyon's memorial to sixteen men from the museum who died in the Great War. Written on the plaque were the words *Dulce et decorum est pro patria mori*, [1] Horace's ode to it being a "sweet and seemly thing" to die for one's country (or, I thought, to fight each day facing the prospect of death for one's family). Pa almost died many times in the war, and continued to take such risks today, although unnecessarily—surrounded by coal dust, cigarette smoke, groaning conveyors, and the smell of body sweat, stale air, earth, and the prospect of his own demise.

I produced a photograph of Pa in uniform, which I kept with me between the pages of his journal. The man in this photograph had dug trenches and set out barbed wire in the pouring rain of France and then, years later, pulled away at rocks where a mine worker had stood only seconds before. His culpability in the death of a fellow worker must have revived memories of helplessness during the war, having survived with around seventy others from a battalion once numbering a thousand soldiers. He was a hardened authority on the probabilities of existence and extinction and the familiarity that, in an instant of a bomb blast or a bullet whining through the air, or a Davy Lamp crashing to the ground, either outcome was feasible.

In the years of shells exploding and bullets whizzing nearby in the war, and in the brief flash when he must have first seen that Davy Lamp ignite, it was only in the moments following those ephemera that he would have become suddenly aware that he was alive.

And in my dreams, rocks poured down to bury Pa as I crawled with him on our hands and knees through the underground mine tunnels, providing me with a sense of liberation from the source of Mum's troubles. The guard beside my bicycle lowered his newspaper and turned toward me in one final sigh of exasperation as I voiced these words into Pa's monotone, expressionless eyes.

"I'm sorry, Pa," I said, "I'm sorry."

# 3

Occasional political rallies by the British Union of Fascists took place in and around London. My classmates said their fathers attended these events, but I said nothing. They didn't need to know that my father was absent during those years, or that we had begun assembling matchbooks at home to try supplementing what little money Pa was sending. Mum said that the mortgage payments were falling behind and, at the age of 15, my schooling would be done. I would have to find work for more money than the pittance of assembling matchbooks would provide. My days of playing cricket, tennis and football, cross-country running, reading comics and Hardy Boys novels, learning about Latin and German, being good at but not interested in math, being chosen in my more obedient days as a Prefect in charge of classes below me and not only failing to discipline the younger boys for their games of Pitch and Toss, but actually participating in the games—all of this would be over shortly. I didn't know where I would work any more than I knew when I would start. A job in the mines may have been the easiest for me to get, but Mum wouldn't allow this. And moving away from my mother and brother to be with my father wasn't any way to reunite the family.

At night, Ian's snores no longer lulled me to sleep; they combined with images of crawling on my hands and knees through blackened trenches and underground tunnels with Pa, rocks piling on us from above. Sleep eluded me and I couldn't catch any, except briefly, for the first time in recent memory.

One night, despite the convection oven created by the brick Mum had heated in the fireplace and left between my sheets in the usually cold bedroom, a move intended to bribe me into the warmth of sleep, I rose up without rousing my brother and glimpsed out through our bedroom window. Spirals of smoke filled the city. There were lights in the distance, and nearby.

Betsy was below, glowing like a streetlamp with astonishing potential in a world of drunks and fellow insomniacs wandering the streets; a promise of adventure where I would travel down the Champs Elysées or the streets of Sao Paolo, Shanghai or Bangkok, a spy working for the government or a courier delivering an urgent message to a consulate of a certain troubled country; or, a Samaritan on the road from Jerusalem to Jericho; or Don Quixote de la Mancha fighting giant windmills. I anticipated what would happen: encountering a beautiful, troubled woman wandering the streets in search of love, as happened in so many stories I had read from Mum's bookshelf; engaging in a fight in which I could intervene to save some helpless victim; befriending a group of boys who met late at night and wreaked havoc in the empty city wherever they could; or the discovery of a new place, somewhere, that might give purpose to senseless wandering by giving me an eventual destination.

Opening the window, I held on tight and began shimmying down a drainpipe attached to the house. Hand over hand, I descended. Then, as I was almost there, a few decrepit bolts broke loose from their supports. I fell to the ground, backward, descending on one of the bushes with a muffled ruckus, the branches attacking my back from all angles.

My presence was announced in the silent darkness by Betsy's pedal-powered light and clattering chain. This was the same path I took by day, from the now-closed markets of Whitechapel to Piccadilly, through Hyde Park past the winding Serpentine Lake, and then in a loop back home again. But on this path there were enemies hiding around every corner or in subterranean dwellings, laying out barbed wire, landmines and sending up starlight to light up the battlefield. All of them were eager to see me shot. I fancied myself an officer at Bustard Camp surveying the operational preparedness of my troops for the battlefield, or a British fighter pilot flying between hundreds of searchlights and guns and anti-aircraft fire, ready to bring down German airships.

On this particularly foggy evening, a pea-souper, I made a sudden turn to avoid what was either a German military truck or an approaching streetcar—which I hadn't seen until I was within a dangerously close distance. The tram driver frantically rang his bell even as I rode off in a new direction. His signal was gradually replaced by church bells, the reverberations of which I didn't recognize, and I made several more turns before being delighted to realize that I was no longer lost among starlight in the sky above the fields of France. This was a new city with a less opaque soup, maybe a dense chicken broth or a watery tomato, permeating the air.

Between a street corner and a group of run-down houses, in a stinking alleyway leading away from the train tracks of the main street, I stopped and dismounted amidst an array of hazy yellow lights. As I approached the glow, the words "Duke and Duchess" beckoned me, running up the side of a ruddy grey brick building beside a pasted advertisement for a currently running play entitled "The Barricade."

Walking my bicycle over, the words "Duke and Duchess Theatre" became apparent, although half of the letters were not illuminated. An arched overhang sat above a set of wooden doors, the portico curving up to illuminated flower petals on an otherwise unimposing edifice. The sign for the "Savoy Brothel for Lonely Travellers" was still legible beside it, the paint flaking in places.

If Mum knew that I was travelling throughout the city at night and had turned up in a place like this, she would bar the window and put a lock on the door. Pa, too, would prohibit me from riding my bike in the evening—if he was here to do so, that is. Defiance toward my mother, and now my father, instilled in me the conceited smugness of newfound manhood; or at least, that of being more than a mere boy. I could make decisions and would be liable to no one else.

These were the thoughts that motivated and accompanied me inside.

In the foyer, the ticket booth was dark, and no one was behind the counter. A poster touted this production as the first of a series of four plays about soldiers of the Great War.

"Sounds fine to me," I said to the empty booth, "I'm good to see all four. Nothing better to do at night anyway except to roll around in bed, frittering time away from this exciting new city."

After opening another door and finding a soiled seat in the darkest part of the cigarette smoke-filled theatre—thinking this the best way to avoid detection and subsequent, unwarranted ejection—I accepted a playbook given to me by a man with white hair and crooked front teeth. He didn't ask to see my ticket. Maybe he knew, by the look of me.

A young woman arrived onstage amid coughing and spirals of cigarette smoke billowing up toward the ceiling. She had the transfixing beauty of a screen siren, and her appearance was made unique by her eyes: one chocolate, the other azure. A duality, a rooting to the earth combined with a sky bound gaze, a sort of pragmatic idealism which, had she been in monochrome moving pictures, would have gone virtually unnoticed. She was extraordinary, exquisite. I immediately wanted to come back here again, to see those eyes.

Onstage, a man in a pressed uniform, Lieutenant Dick Campbell, confessed his affection for her in the setting of a luxurious London home. The skunk was home on leave while his best friend Captain Roddy Dunton, engaged to this woman, remained in the trenches of the Great War. Albert, living with Pa now in South Leeds, would surely have done the same.

The lights were extinguished, and several men and women ran onstage, barely visible. The backdrop quickly changed to one of helmeted soldiers, trench warfare, bomb blasts, and barbed wire as the lights came back on again.

Whenever this woman whom I knew only as Violet was on stage, I saw nothing else.

I began attending the theatre as much as I could, an impoverished but dedicated patron of her art.

"I admire you as well," Violet said one evening, addressing me directly as she delivered her lines intended for Lieutenant Dick Campbell. "And with admiration comes respect, and sometimes adoration."

She paused and sauntered to the end of the stage, repositioning to gaze out a window at the painted street outside. Glancing back, she began speaking again, this time of her fondness: not for the Lieutenant onstage, but for me.

I envisioned meeting her unexpectedly backstage. I was a soldier home on leave having come to see her production. She was a woman I had known for a long time, a woman with whom I had maintained a friendship and an unrequited love, who had invited me to stay after emerging from her dressing room and finding me in the empty theatre. We would remain, talking of love and war, moving from the theatre seats and up to the stage. Then after returning from the war and taking the oaths of marriage, we would make love in a corner of the abandoned theatre; finding perfection in the stage props scattered around, the unused scenery, the trays of makeup, and the costumes hanging from racks—this reality behind the illusion. These encounters would express our love, not for each other, but for those moments we shared together beneath the heat of the lights, lying down on paper grass. I would be Petronius, from the dirty poem I passed around one day after school, my mortal part metamorphosed into a vine and enthralling my dainty Violet.

Over time, my imaginings evolved from such encounters to the two of us living in a log cabin between mountains, evergreens and fenced-off, rolling plains like the cowboys of The Lone Ranger. Flipping through Mum's *Grand Tours of Europe* travel guides at night, I pictured the two of us cruising on a new Wolf Motorcycle through Nice and Monte Carlo; or living in a Spanish island hacienda crowded with palm trees and sea turtles atop a cliff jutting out into the sea; or together in a cramped restaurant in the modernized streets and endless crowds of Tokyo; walking among the seemingly infinite skyscrapers of Chicago; touring the immense pyramids near Cairo; climbing the mountains and traversing the high bridges of Soviet Armenia; or floating down canals between multi-coloured buildings and other sailing boats in Denmark. Anywhere but here or South Leeds.

The beauty of these concealed theatre lights kept drawing me back, and my devotion to her grew deeper.

On a wet night in late spring, Betsy clattering to the ground beneath the theatre sign, I fell down exhausted in the alleyway, waiting until after the show started to enter undetected.

Fancying myself out on night patrol between the British and German lines, I would often beat it over to the German's trench. German snipers lurked about two hundred yards apart. I jumped in after one of the snipers, and if he went peaceably, why, all right. But if he didn't, why, then it was all over for him. And while I was in there, I would look around for machine guns or anything else worth pinching.

Out on listening post, a little hiding place by our barbed wire about thirty yards in front of the trench, my duty was to see that no Germans came to cut the wire. In the case of a surprise attack, I would also be able to warn our fellows in time.

I looked at the German trenches through a periscope. Nothing this time. Sometimes, though, I could see a German stick out his head, and then pop down before a fellow could get a shot at him. The Germans often tried to fool me by shoving up a dummy, but I didn't fall for that anymore.

Some time later, I was roused from my nap by voices. The show had likely started, and I could go in now.

There was a conversation here between three dummies, each of whom I recognized from school. They appeared in front of the trench and blocked my path. They wore caps and raggedy clothes and the tallest of them, lean and with a dazed expression, said he knew me from somewhere. He looked like a scarecrow I had seen outside my uncle's house in Northaw.

"What're ya out here for?" the scarecrow asked, his lips barely moving.

"Out for a show," a plump boy suggested, shrugging his shoulders. "But this one ain't no good."

"You never seen it," the last of the dummies said.

The scarecrow turned around, a light emanating from around his cupped hands as he produced a lit cigarette and moved to face me. His dark hair was illuminated by the lights of the theatre, and he stood with a hunched stance and a quizzical expression. My first thought was escape. Second, to fight back. Third, was to fight back harder than they would have anticipated.

"I know you from school," the strawman said, scrutinizing my face. "Your brother's sick, and your pa's a drunk livin' somewhere's else."

"My pa's a war hero, and he sends us coin," I replied. "And aren't you afraid your hands'll go up in smoke with that cigarette? What're you doing in the city, anyway?"

He scoffed. "What you on about? And your pa's a war hero? Says who?"

"He's got three medals, in the British Museum. And you ought'a be back in Northaw, guarding against the crows."

He spat forcefully on the ground. "Only heroes were pilots fought in the war, and chaps who won a Victoria Medal. My pa was in the Royal Flying Corps, was yours? Did your pa win a Victoria Medal?"

"While I ain't seen it, who's to say?"

"Well, then..."

The others stood together, barring the way. The scarecrow drew on his cigarette and let out a long puff of smoke, which reflected eerily in the puddles below. If his straw hands were to unexpectedly ignite, he would have to throw them down into the stagnant water and I could lay some boots to him.

I was facing three German effigies, talking and hovering around with rifles in hand as I stood before them, unarmed, listening as they decided my fate. I would fight back. No escape.

When my father was out on patrol in the Great War, a German sneaked up about thirty feet away before Pa saw him. After slinging a bomb, Pa saw him fall, but he wasn't satisfied with that. He gave the German a couple more and when he went to look, the man looked like a strainer.

Fight back harder than they would have anticipated. That's the lesson I got.

"I tell ya," the boy said. "*My* father was a hero in the war, but I'd clobber him if he ever tried to leave me and my mum alone with a sick kid."

"You'd sock him," I replied. "And he'd give it to you right back, harder'n you'd want. Give you a nice haymaker."

The boys continued talking, and I could barely hear what was being said, as though all the words were being spoken completely in German.

Seeing images of my own bayoneted or bullet-ejected blood splotched on the pavement and trickling into the pools of water below, my rifle—or, rather, my bicycle—only a few steps away, my traitorous legs wanted a getaway, unconcerned with what my mind had to say.

Had my bicycle been a rifle, my arms might have fired successive shots and seen these three German soldiers lying face down in the mud.

My legs flew into motion, betraying me, and this signalled the boys to move in.

They pushed and forced me to the ground, laying boots and punching at my ribs. Lying curled on the ground, I held my hands tight to my head. I was kicked repeatedly.

The boys stopped after a few minutes, and I lay inert for a time, waiting for a shot to be fired.

When none came, I lifted myself onto my hands and knees, coughing up a bit of blood. Looking through blurred eyes, half of my body soaked in mud and water, I saw a cigarette dangling from the boy's lip. He was grinning and staring at me.

I saw in that boy's gaze the last time my father had been home. I had helplessly observed whenever my father simply walked by us and out the door. This German strawman was right, and knew more than what I, until recently, had understood: while not responsible for the family's separation, as the man of the house, I was the cause of its perpetuation. And this haggard boy had even provided a solution that, while not ideal, was right. He had beaten into me that I would have to confront my father to get the family back together again and fight back harder than Pa would have anticipated.

Now standing around mocking and challenging me to try any sort of retaliation, this young man's gaze disallowed any further association with Violet, for in this fight I had no chance of victory. His still, constant stare granted me permission to smother all the stifled laughter on his face.

*You must go with your gut because so many situations you are in are not planned. Your reaction must be instinctual and emotional too. You want to charge a machine gun nest when you see your men being killed, or because you see a section of the army being held up somewhere. It is your reflex, to go and get them. You don't think a lot about anything. Just like when you are bullied as a boy and forced to fight back.*

Lunging at the boy with all the force of my frail body, I thrashed at him like a wild and reckless animal. I was a gazelle, once weak and unstable, suddenly lashing out against its lion tormentor. In that instant, flashes of lightning blinded me. I toppled him onto his back. Both of us splashed into the mud. I struck three successive blows: one quickly, the others decisively, all into the boy's face. Each blow seemed to surprise him, and me, more than the last.

No one moved. For an instant, I startled myself by thinking I had won.

He suddenly revived, his shock turning to anger. Not apparently hurt, he struck out. My face became his focus, then my stomach. I was sent to the ground, breathless.

I lay there, enraged but immobile.

Watching the lines of their boots, I awaited further punishment.

Their boots did not move, perhaps waiting momentarily to see whether I would regain the fury that had overwhelmed them.

But before anyone could strike more blows, before I could rise, the boots scampered away.

And with their departure came a hint of the strange and surprising sensation that somehow, in some small way, I had accomplished something.

# 4

The evening's offering was a reddish-brown lentil stew that smelled horrid. Some nausea to add to my wretchedness, considering I had been trampled by three horses a few nights ago. A dessert of canned fruit sat in a bowl in the middle of the table, out of my reach. Pa sat at the head of the table, all of us together for dinner in our London home for the first time in what must have been years.

Why did he come back, and why now, with my face all banged up?

Full bowls of steaming stew sat unconsumed on the table, our visages flickering in the hazy light and wavering shadows of a sputtering tallow candle. Pa resembled a grey ghost, some quivering manifestation that was not conceivably human, and that could not possibly be here.

Pa ate more greedily than ever before, a relapse, I was sure, from army-turned-mining days when justifiably presuming that someone might snatch up his meal at any time; or when extended periods of hunger were followed by wretched food options such as sour jam and maggot-filled cheese, or other fare such as the meal we had before us tonight, disgusting and only tempting when the sole alternative was famine.

Pa appeared to have aged decades since I had seen him last. The creases on his face seemed more pronounced now, his cratered countenance sunken into his skull and resembling sand charred from the heat of the sun. Maybe it was the lighting in this room, or the soot on his face that Mum once scrubbed and cleaned for him after his shift, in the brief time we lived in South Leeds together. Mum would crouch down over the bathtub in our tenement as she rubbed his skin, me and Ian observing and saying nothing. To us, that was all we knew of marital love.

Ian and I sat staring at Pa with uninterrupted intensity.

The ticking of the wall clock was deafening.

No one except Pa was eating, and he didn't seem to take notice or care. I examined the table, my eyes coming upon a picture of Christ our Saviour halfway up the wall, and another painting of a flowered meadow. A series of church bells began ringing faintly in the distance.

Mum, her red-brown hair in a tight bun, sat with her chin in her hand. She turned to examine my injuries, my chin bruised and swollen, and my right cheek on fire. Peering into her green eyes, I imagined that she might have once read from books and poems inspiring her to fight for love. Maybe she had even read the dirty poem about lovemaking by Petronius, although I didn't want to think about that. She certainly must have snuck out of her house at night to meet Pa.

Searching for understanding, knowing now that we had these common experiences, all I saw was her eyebrows curled in wonder; and I questioned, as I focused down on the wood grain on the table, what she suspected of me. She must have recognized my new self confidence. After all, I was in love with a beautiful woman. Pa's war letters were guiding my life. Whatever she presumed about me sneaking around with other boys and starting fights on the streets when I should have been at home sleeping, I had the notion that she did not want her suppositions to be true. She wanted an obedient boy, and not a mutinous and slipshod one.

"Go to your room," she said abruptly.

I began rising out of my seat and was surprised to see her glancing over at Ian.

"Why?" Ian asked as I sat back down again. Ian didn't break his focus on Pa, who had stopped eating to return his son's stare.

Without warning or further provocation, she slapped Ian across the face. He immediately rose from the table, crying, spilling stew, and nearly knocking the candle over. With tears in his eyes, he vanished upstairs. The banging of the bedroom door echoed down the narrow hallway. Her cheeks had reddened.

Good for Mum, but poor Ian. Mum had behaved irrationally and excessively and for no valid reason, but at least she had taken some sort of disciplinary action. Not what I was used to seeing around here, that's for certain.

She glanced over at the wall clock as Pa's eyes remained on her. Turning toward him, she threw her shoulders back and stretched.

I was next.

Pa quickly downed the contents of his water glass before rising out of his chair to stand over me. My attention shifted back to the scratches and crevices of the wooden table. That table had never been so fascinating before.

"Your Ma sent me a telegram," he said, grabbing me by the chin and forcing my face out of the shadows, away from the beloved table and closer to the candlelight. I winced in pain.

"She said something was wrong," he continued. "That our oldest boy, responsible for his brother and mother, the man of the house, was kicking like a steer. That he's sneaking out at night, fighting and talking back to his mother. I saw you wanted to start a scrap last time I was home, so not a big surprise I suppose."

That was why he was here. Mum knew I was leaving at night, and maybe how often I missed school, too. She must have told him that I was refusing to do my evening Bible studies before dinner as I had since I was a boy, maybe surmising my motivation being to hurt her without threat of reprisal, except to miss dinners occasionally. As I refused to nurture my spirit, she said, she wouldn't be nourishing my body. But with dinners like this filthy concoction, that didn't concern me much.

Pa had my head contorted toward her now, and, peering into her sea-green eyes, I got the sympathy I had been searching for only minutes before; her expression reflected my own.

"Stop it, let him go," Mum said. Pa glanced at her and released his hand.

"Where you been off to at night?" he asked.

The clicking clock and the fabric of the table lampshade gave me no idea what to say, except: I didn't ever sneak out unless on patrol or listening post between the trench lines. When you went out on patrol at night between the trenches, in no man's land, with a Sergeant and an officer, you came across three Germans who beat it. You went after them, but they slipped away. You had revolvers but dare not fire or you would have bombs and everything else coming your way. My three Germans slithered away too, and I had no way to stop them.

I verbalized the only words that came to mind.

"I went to the theatre," I said.

Pa said nothing, and I could feel his stare.

"Don't try to hoodwink me," he replied, shifting as if poising to strike me with the back of his blackened hand. "And look at me when I'm talking to you."

Pa's eyes were red, apparently dry and stinging. My gaze was still important to him when he accused me of deceit, as though he could discern insincerity visually.

"So, who were these boys you fought?" he asked.

"I fell," I said. Pa's face was askew, his dark, narrow eyes and pallid complexion expressing frustrated disappointment. I peered over at the wall, Christ's picture staring back at me, hands outstretched, knowing that my fabrication would soon be discovered. My father's stare I could handle, but not my Lord's. So, I added: "After some boys pushed me."

"Really? Who?"

I glanced back down at the marks on the lovely table made through years of plates and cutlery falling at erratic angles and with varying force. I should not have said anything about the theatre. I had met an exquisite woman and had fought with some boys from school who wouldn't let me see her. That's what I should have said, instead of aggravating Pa with my silence. He would understand battling for the opportunity to see a woman again.

"He didn't know them," Mum said.

"Really?" Pa asked.

Without moving or attempting a reply, I simply sat there with my shoulders slumped. The candle sputtered, and Mum wiped her forehead with her hand. I could not tell him who they were. I wouldn't. I had to withhold this information, the same as I would keep confidential any secret that, if revealed, might cause me further beatings and accusations.

I wanted to tell Pa how I had taken on three older boys in a fight and, at least for a moment, believed I had won. That I didn't think of bravery or courage and what that meant, but my cowardly legs had simply acted only to escape. Much like a rat or a pig. But if I said anything about fighting back against boys who knew where I was going at night, and who might possibly return with knives, bats and other more aggressive accomplices to finish the fight the way they wanted it finished, then Mum would bar my window and lock the doors. Or worse, she would take away my bicycle. I couldn't have that. Let them believe that this was a simple, random act of violence.

Pa's gaze was hovering over me, and I mustered the words which formed on my lips:

"Some boys from school pushed me, but I don't know their names. The fight was over a girl." I shifted my weight in the seat. The stew was no longer steaming, and the smell of the bowl's brown, lukewarm contents nauseated me.

As the candle spilled wax, I began to spew out nonsense, starting what would've been a capricious and blatantly fabricated explanation about how I met the boys that night. I was grateful when Pa interrupted.

"Your brother sure thinks a lot of you," he said, turning toward me. He leaned over the candle to illuminate an unshaven and emaciated face, and rancid breath. "Ian can hardly breathe sometimes, and he does nothing but sleep now."

I did not respond immediately, which only annoyed him. What I said next irritated him more.

"I know, ya," I replied. "I know better than you."

I stirred my grimy stew. Pa forced my chin up again and into the candlelight, contorting my head. I protested with a shout as his hands pushed hard against my cheek.

"Stop," Mum said. "Don't fuss. You're hurting him."

"How old are you now?" he asked, his grip firm.

"Fourteen," I replied. "Fourteen and a half."

"Stop," Mum repeated. "He's hurt. Let him be."

Pa's expression turned from anger to tempered astonishment, perhaps from having become aware of my age this way; maybe thinking me much younger. He may have wanted his son to stay a boy when, in the only time we spent together, we had fished at Uncle Devon's house during those wonderful summers in medieval Northaw. When my endless questions had led me to ask why fish couldn't breathe in air, then having inquired as to whether Ian was like a fish in that way, Pa had replied that Ian was especially sensitive to the smog.

"What's smog?" I had asked.

"Smoke from factories. Chimneys."

"Why can we breathe, and he has troubles, then?"

"Some fish stay alive out of water longer than others," had been his final reply before we sat, for the next hour, staring out at the river's undulations and contemplating what this meant. Pa had told me about Ian's diminished lung capacity, which was brought on by pollutants that filled the streets and the interior of our Whitechapel home. When I pulled a lengthy fish out of the river, a sturgeon, I watched as he removed the hook and threw the flopping, shiny mass on the ground. I envisioned my brother with a scaled chest and full tail, his silvery body intermittently writhing with spasms in the dirt.

"I was seventeen when I enlisted," Pa said now, bringing me back to the table in our home. "What do you think of enlisting? You're young, but almost a man."

I didn't have a reply. I hadn't contemplated my own death before reading Pa's journal. Notions of losing one's life had once seemed inconsequential next to friends, girls, books and magazines, radio shows, and after-school games. But early, youthful death in my father's writings had made the idea so easy, so palpable, that the notion of dying in my confrontation with the boys struck me now as a possibility. One wrong blow to the head, or a knife drawn and sunk into my abdomen would have done the job.

"The army's not for me," I said. "Especially, not during wartime."

Pa coughed and stared at me with a dazed expression. Beneath my words was a concern more for a girl and the company of disreputable boys than for responsibilities, including those my father had thrust upon me.

As I lay in my bed upstairs staring at the cracks in the ceiling, my parents began shouting about mortgage payments that were apparently weeks behind. There were letters I noticed at the post office, addressed from the bank, as I had been surveying for others from Albert in South Leeds. More had been arriving recently.

"The bank's going to repossess the house," Mum yelled.

"Apparently," I told Ian, who was lying down and whimpering beside me. "We might not be able to live here anymore. Bankers might be moving in."

From my father's calm reply, he seemed to *want* people from the bank to live here instead of us.

As the front door creaked open and then slammed closed, Pa probably on his way back to South Leeds, I realized what I had done.

The fight I had engaged in, which had led to Pa's concern for me, had caused him to return to his London home.

And I had the power to do more of the same.

# 5

A few weeks later, a game of Pitch and Toss started up in the yard after school one day, the lads playing for Hershey bars, and Black Cat and Navy Cut cigarettes. The job of teacher lookout was relegated to a kid who had no money or valuables, and who was lectured on the importance of his job by those who did.

Having nothing to bet, that was me.

I whistled a few times when I saw Ebenezer Rattray, the principal of the school with round glasses and hair parted straight down the middle, as he came out of the school on his way home.

Seeing the gathering, the Scrooge scoffed, rubbed at his thick brown moustache, and stopped before us. He squinted at me.

"Nicholas Dixon?" he asked.

"That's me, Mr. Scrooge," I replied with a smile. Some of the boys laughed.

"What's that you say?"

"I am Nicholas, sir."

"Are you not a Prefect?"

"Certainly," I said, patting the back of a redheaded boy with freckles. "And I am looking out for these boys."

"Good, then," he said. "I need to know someone is."

Seemingly no longer interested in disciplining anyone outside of school hours, he scrutinized us closely as everyone carefully stuffed their pockets. He was likely identifying which boys were at school that day, and who had only showed up for this mysterious gathering of pocket-stuffers.

Having therefore earned some trust from the lads, as the Scrooge walked off into the distance, I was handed two pennies and told to stand in an area marked on the concrete with chalk. A group of boys gathered around me.

Then I saw the three dummies from the alleyway outside the Duke and Duchess Theatre.

They stood here in the same caps and raggedy clothes. The tallest, lean one, apparent leader of this gang of three, stood with the same stupefied expression between his plump friend and the bony boy.

"Last I saw you," I said to the leader, "you were gettin' a swell look at the end of my fist."

"Big words, little boy," he retorted.

"Ya, I was thinkin' the same."

After readying to unleash another volley of successive blows to his face, if only to restore his recollection, I was surprised when he smiled. Introducing himself as Glen, and his chums as Boris and Charles, he patted me on the back.

"No hard feelings, son?" he asked.

I struck him in the face without warning, and blood rushed from his nose.

"Not from me," I said, flipping the coppers still in my hand. "So long as you take back what you said about my pa not being a war hero. A missing father, a drunken gambler, riskin' his life for nothin' now, all that might be true, but he's still a war hero."

"Whatever you say," Glen said, cradling his nose with his hands.

There was laughter as some of the other boys moved in.

"Let's start," someone said. "You're up."

"What's in it for me?" I asked.

"If two pennies come up heads," Charles said. "Then everybody who bets on you wins. Then you'll get some coins, or smokes, coming your way."

"Ya," Boris explained while rubbing his fists, "then if two pennies come up tails, everybody who bet again' you wins. Then you'll get it good by everybody who bet on you."

"Then," Charles said. "If there's one of each, nobody gets nothing. Then, still, you'll get it good, but this time by all of us."

"Lovely," I replied.

I made one toss. Two heads. Some chocolate and a cigarette were thrown at me. Sustained shouting. Then another. Head and a tail. I was pushed. The boys from the Duke and Duchess Theatre won once, and then again. More shouting, then the boys began pushing me through the school yard. A punch came my way, and then another. Another toss, head and a tail again. Then two heads. Some more chocolate, and then a couple more punches to the face.

Before I knew it, as if I was responsible for the results of my throws, I was herded by the group along to the fence, next to a wide willow tree.

I climbed up the tree, still throwing and taking bets as I did, eventually jumping over the fence to the other side and throwing the coins back. By the time I made it home, I had some scrapes and bruises, some on my face, enough to get Mum worried again.

My job was done and a few days later, I would see the results.

We sat around the kitchen table, leaning forward over crumbs and consuming a breakfast of black tea, stale bread and crabapple jam, with the lingering flavour of rotten apples. Sunlight filtered in through dirty curtains. The quiet was conspicuous, unpleasant, and only interrupted by the clattering of knives over plates, and smacking lips.

As I ate, recalling the peach and gooseberry jams, the fresh bread and honey that I had enjoyed so frequently at my uncle's farm, my eyes wandered from the clothes dryer, an inverted rowboat with its skin off, draped with clothes and hanging from the ceiling over top of the kitchen fireplace, then to Pa whose eyes were fixed to his plate, home now because of my bruises, again. I understood that my triumph was only temporary but still, I had succeeded. So, what now?

"We need to talk, Nicholas," Pa said with a hoarse voice, scrutinizing my bruises in this light. "In the scullery. You and me."

Mum dropped her bread into her teacup, and hot liquid overflowed onto the wooden tabletop. The tea ran down the surface indentations, and Ian jumped out of his chair as she moved in with a white towel to clean up the mess. I rose from the table in unison with my father.

"No, we don't," I said, instantly questioning myself. "Do we?" Pa watched as Mum sopped up the brown mess with the towel, before turning back toward me.

"Now," he continued. "I don't want you saying your father didn't know enough to help you. There's lots of talk down at Hyde Park about war, politics, the fate of our nation, all stuff that'll affect our family."

"Won't affect me. Don't see how it'll affect our family either."

"It will. Now get in here. No more arguments from you."

Mum poured herself a new cup of steaming water as we walked into the next room. I sat down, and he closed the door behind us, navigating by the big concrete bin, now empty, in which Mum boiled our clothes clean.

He spoke in a whisper. "The walls in this house are too thin," he said. "We'll have to chat pretty quiet."

After sitting down in an adjacent chair, he pulled up much too close. I could see the deep wrinkles around his eyes and smelled his foul breath and the mustiness of his clothes.

"I talked to some chaps at the mines," he said. "You can work in the offices, after working in the pit for a time. I saw your grades in math. You might have to learn shorthand, but your Ma would look at it as a job with no risk."

"The mines?" I asked. "Why? I can work at the market here instead. Only not with those filthy fishmongers."

He did not explicitly state that he wanted his son in South Leeds with him, away from any dangerous influences here in London that he supposed I had; or that he wanted me to have the promise of an office job in order to obtain Mum's approval; nor did he indicate that I could help earn money for the family that we now sorely needed; or that he wanted to have more autonomy, less moral responsibility, and increased funds for his own drinking and gambling. But I figured that all of these might be true. What he said next only partially confirmed my suspicions.

"You're old enough to help make coin for the family now," he said.

Concurring with my father's wishes in the past, without having disagreed or confronted him, I immediately perceived that I would be departing the only city I had ever called home; and I was repulsed at the thought of returning to the infernal South Leeds with its buildings slowly sinking into the earth, the dust and the dirt that seemed to cover every surface, and the miners whose lungs were slowly being deprived of breath by coal dust hanging heavy in the air as they worked by the stifled light of Davy Lamps.

One day, I knew I would have to help provide for the family. But my mother certainly didn't want me in the mines, and I didn't want to be there either.

"There's no work in London?" I asked.

"Your Ma and I chin-wag about that a lot," he said. "The Depression and the Great War left us with no jobs, not here."

"You can work at the market with me. I know an empty stall far away from the fishmongers, next to the old vegetable woman with chubby hands and squinty eyes."

"The market doesn't pay."

"We can sell cucumbers or cabbage. Grow it in our garden."

"And live in poverty, somewhere else? We couldn't afford this house."

"I won't be off to the mines," I said. I wasn't prepared for any of this. "Mum needs me. You don't."

Instead of such open defiance to my father's wishes, though, there had to be another way. I asked how Mum felt about all this. His answer was not what I might have expected.

"Another scrap," he replied. "You're a fighting man once more. But you'll be off to South Leeds soon. And you can't tell her. If you say nothing, that's not a fib, is it? I'll tell her you're going to the country for a while. Helping your Uncle Devon. You'll be there to help support the family. She'll understand that. She knows if we're not careful, we might lose this house. I haven't the coin to keep paying out for this place, for my flat there, and for everything we need year after year. But I'll tell her that again, too. And don't fret. I'll tell her where you really are. Some time, but not straight away. We won't have to continue this for long. She was fine taking care of the two of you; she'll be fine with one. Ian will be head of the house now. Your Ma wants to keep her house? This is how she will."

I envisioned myself in South Leeds wearing a pressed shirt and tie and meeting my father after each of our shifts, drinking beers, and then going home to eat. His hands would be blackened with coal dust and calloused with overuse. Someone would have to bathe him. Perhaps the landlady, or Albert, or now, me. My hands would become stained with ink as the conveyors rattled the earth beneath, the same earth Pa crawled through on his hands and knees for an hour, each way, to get to his work site. I the bureaucrat would be recording numbers and generating paperwork as my subterranean cave-dwelling father generated the product, without which all the numbers and paperwork would be meaningless.

"We're going to Speaker's Corner in Hyde Park next week," he said, rising from his chair. "You and me. Then, I'll let you know what's what with the mines."

"Have you seen Speaker's Corner lately?" I asked. "It's far too crowded. Like being inside a tin can with a bunch of kippers, that is. I stay away from there."

"We're going, you and me. So you can know what is happening here, and in other countries. Millions out of work here in England with no help in sight. You'll see how important it is to get paid however you can, how desperate people are now, and how fortunate people are to have jobs. My own Pa told me how proud he was when I joined the army, and that I could make a good living as a soldier. But neither of us knew what hell I was in for... but anyway, I've been to a few rallies and lots of political talks in South Leeds. There are more and more chaps at each one. They remind me of the crowds in the Great War that took to the streets. They swamped city halls to enlist. In Germany right now, Fritz isn't happy with the way the Great War turned out for them. They don't like to be beat, and they don't like the terms of their surrender."

"That's Germany. Has nothing to do with me."

He paused and rubbed his nose, sniffling before he continued. "You know loads for a boy your age. But I thought about what you said, the army and war not being for you. There's something doing in Germany. And let me tell you, fighting for your life day after day, year after year, well... that Wilfred Owen poem, though gruesome, says it all. If there's another war coming, you don't need to be sent there. They can't draft a man who's supporting his family."

"Where'd you hear that?"

"From one of the fellows at the mines."

"Would they have enough men to send to war, then?"

"You don't want to go through what I did. They can't draft you if you're there. And pulling coal would be important for the war effort. But stay here, unemployed, and they can do whatever they want."

"Did that happen in the Great War?"

"No, but who's to say what'll happen if there's another one? And anyway, if what that fellow told me is wrong, if you're gonna fight, you need to come with me to the Speaker's Corner, so you'll know what's doing. You'll see what you'd be fighting for, or rather, what you'd be fighting against."

A few minutes passed by in silence. Pa rose and began fumbling with the window, pushing the lace curtains aside. As he worked the frame back and forth, I contemplated how he had volunteered for active service in the Great War. He hadn't been drafted.

Ever since reading his wartime journal, I often wondered whether I could have done the same. Now, for the first time in my life, I was also being called to duty. Not to any war, but to the mines of South Leeds. Not to serve my country, but instead a microcosm of my place within it: my family.

Perhaps Pa knew I would go, as this was all he had ever directly asked of me. And this was a great new adventure I should embark upon without trepidation, not knowing what I would face, just as my father presumably was when he was on Salisbury Plains, a few years older than I was now, waiting to go to the front in November, 1914. I read his journal entry later that day.

*E Company, 1st Battalion, 1st Brigade*
*6697 Salisbury Plains, Bustard Camp, England.*

*I haven't heard from Mother in over a month. Maybe she thinks the Germans got me. I haven't heard from my brother Devon either.*

*We are having pretty cold weather here, and rain. It has been raining for over a week, and the mud is up to our shoe tops. Our tent leaks constantly, even though we are always plugging holes. Oh, it certainly is lovely. My feet have been wet and cold for a week. I have two pairs of woollen socks, but they nearly drove me crazy when I put them on. If it gets much colder, I will have to wear them or freeze.*

*Everybody everywhere has a cold. Colds have been pretty common since I joined the Army.*

*Tommy, Carson, and I, all of us Highgate Boys hailing from Highgate, Ontario, are drilling pretty hard. Out on 12-mile route marches with a nice heavy load to carry, our legs are certainly tired when we get back. I am fair at target shooting, and the gun I have is a dandy. It doesn't kick much and shoots straight.*

*We are certainly getting punk grub, a lot worse than the food at Valcartier. And Lord only knows it was bad enough there. Mornings bring tea, bread, and a little bacon which is nearly all fat. Noon brings soup made in a big dish half-full of meat fat, water, a few sliced onions, and potatoes all boiled to pieces with dirty skins. For supper we get jam, bread, tea, and cheese. The jam is made of rotten apples, I guess from the way it tastes, but another chap said it was made of crab apples. The cheese is generally full of maggots and the tea is pretty good, but the milk and sugar are scarce. The officers told us that all the good food is going to the front.*

*The boys are anxious to get to the front, and not only for the food, but for all this waiting.*

*Passes were being issued, and Devon and I had our names in at the beginning, but we didn't get one with the first bunch. I was planning to go to old London for a few days furlough and have a fill up. I wanted to eat all the time I was there. So Devon and I left. We took French leave and went to London for six days, stuffing ourselves like pigs. The English people there seemed to think the Canadians were it. Back at the camp they came out in autos and threw us cigarettes and cigars; and in London, every Canadian soldier got a girl as soon as he got off the train. Devon would talk to the girls, but I didn't bother with them much.*

*The Londoners put out all their lights at night so that if the Germans came over in their airships, they wouldn't be able to see. There were hundreds of searchlights and guns all ready to fetch the Germans down.*

*On a cloudy night, the searchlights were working all the time. They shone all around the sky, and the effect was certainly powerful.*

*In London, we met a British soldier who had been at the front and was wounded there. He said the Germans were starving to death and they had kids there as young as 16. They were apparently using old guns, any kind they could get a hold of.*

*Devon didn't return to the hotel one evening, or for the remainder of the trip. Returning to Bustard Camp alone, I expected to find Devon there and went in front of the Captain for the loss of six days pay and twelve days of Second Class Field Punishment.*

*Devon hasn't been back to the camp. He was labelled as a deserter, and other fellows talk of court martial. I said nothing, tacitly agreeing with this label, and yet hoping that my brother might show up at the camp at any time.*

*Apart from Devon's unexplained absence, I have not felt better, or happier, in my life.*

Later that day, I pulled Mum's rocking chair from the drawing room to the kitchen door, to listen to my parents talking. Mum was making dinner, and the familiar smell of watery, half-cooked spinach soup with grit wafted under the doorway and made my stomach wrench.

"So, what'll Devon have him do on the farm?" she asked.

"Whatever needs doing," he replied.

"How is Devon's health?"

"Fine."

"Then why does he need help? He hasn't asked for any before."

"There's loads to do on a farm. Everything's been arranged."

There was a short period of silence.

"So just a few months then," she said.

"No more."

"And you think that's best for him?"

"I do. And he can help pay for this house, with what Devon pays him. It'll be best for everyone, you'll see."

There was a brief pause before some dishes clattered; the table was being set. After replacing the rocking chair and running up the stairs, I sat on the edge of the bed and stared at Ian, who lay pallid and motionless. My stomach soured as I contemplated where I was going and, instead of seeing a great new adventure before me where I did not feel better, or happier, in my life, I now wished the interval of time until then would be interminable.

# 6

I might have had two or three weeks left in London before leaving for the mines of South Leeds. Mum was becoming ill with wine, and Ian was beginning to breathe like a tuba. These anxieties, along with some of what my father had told me, occupied my mind as I lay awake at night staring at the cracks in the ceiling and following the plaster rivers along their course. There was the potential for another war, which had to do with world affairs of which I knew little.

Mum insisted I start doing my nightly Bible assignments before dinner. One night, she said she wanted me to find what God thought of liars, pointing me to passages in Proverbs and Revelation. So, I found in Proverbs that God hates a lying tongue. Picking up the dictionary to find the meaning of a proverb, I opened the volume to find the word "admonishments." So, I referred to this assignment as my admonishment. In Revelation, I found that liars would be condemned to a "fiery lake of burning sulphur." All I could muster, or tell Mum about, was the stench of burning, rotten eggs for all eternity. As though she knew what my father and I were up to, she told me to remember that stink every time I even thought of telling a lie. So, I resolved to tell her that I would be working in the mines with Pa. She couldn't argue with the mortgage, any more than I could squabble with a rotten stench.

I felt some bile rising from my stomach that night as I lay in bed wondering why my father had wanted us to deceive Mum. And this made me wonder what else he might have been lying to her about, and to me, and what our fate might be.

Over the next week, I divided my time between the British Museum and the Duke and Duchess Theatre. On the streets, I took notice of the hordes of apparently homeless and unemployed men who were sleeping outside, those awake eyeing me as I rode by. Maybe Pa was right about jobs in this city, and in the country.

I went to the museum during the day when I was supposed to be in school, and read a wide array of books in the Great Room. I read about Mary Queen of Scots, some of Dostoyevsky's short stories, Andrew Marvell's poem written to his coy mistress, Goëthe's Young Werther, and a book about the history of London that I read whenever I wanted a quick nap.

The letters and most of Pa's items from the war, confiscated by the skeletal man who had unjustifiably ejected me from the museum despite my generous gift, were now on display. I spent time reading through his letters and examining his enlistment papers and gleaming war medals: the bronze 1914 Mons Star, the silver British War Medal, and the lacquered bronze Victory Medal.

I fell asleep in the theatre at night when I should have been at home sleeping. I met up with the boys who had once beaten me outside the theatre: Glen, Boris and Charles. They weren't great chums, only coming into the theatre with me when they couldn't find any easy targets less prone than I was to retaliatory attacks.

We watched Violet's play from the same area of the smoky theatre, stage left, halfway back, observing with fascination as she declared her secret affection for the Lieutenant onstage. It never grew tiresome. Watching from beneath the dim lights or from the dark corner seats under the proscenium arch of the theatre, Violet expounded her devotion to me through moments where she would arch her head and flip the end of her pale blue sweater in my direction. Her gesticulations conveyed that Violet had a cognizance more of me than of any other man in the theatre. Maybe she found my looks enticing. Of course, the other boys saw this and were convinced that she thought the same of them. Especially Glen.

Then, outside the theatre after the week's second performance, Glen changed his opinion altogether.

"She's only after some coin, some fame maybe," Glen said. "However meagre those are. She's not after any of us."

"Poppycock," I replied. "She's eyeing me. You're jealous."

"In your imagination, maybe."

Performance after performance passed, and I returned home with the memory of her subtle advances, persistent in the knowledge that I would soon return to re-acquire my newfound love, avoiding Glen and the boys. And with each explanation of how Violet had always thought that she and the Lieutenant might find themselves enamoured (sentiments directed more at me than at Glen or the Lieutenant), and how her current fiancé would eventually understand, my affection for her, and my desire to stay with her in London, continued to grow. And I imagined her fondness for me did the same.

But my time in London was short. Returning once or twice a year with my father might mean that Violet would be gone, the playhouse having moved on to a different production with a new troupe of actors. I had to meet her now, to know whether this perceived attraction to me was in fact sincere, or if it was as disingenuous as the props and costumes of the theatre.

I had to discover whether she wanted to be with me, the same as with the Lieutenant onstage. Knowing that I cared for her because of the fantasy, the dreams she elicited within me, didn't help. The ending of the play could be different. She could resolve to be with me instead of the Lieutenant, and we could be blissfully happy near Nice, Monte Carlo, a Spanish island hacienda, Tokyo, or Cairo. Perhaps even, at least initially, in South Leeds. Wherever we were, we would be content together. But first, I had to know if she wanted this too. And talking to her in person, outside the theatre, was the only way.

At the end of that week, on an overcast Friday, I pedalled to the matinee performance. I wore a cap and a light grey suit from Pa's closet. I hit a divot in the road that was unavoidable given that I was trying to adjust my bowtie at the time, and I toppled over, dirtying my suit and my hands with grease and mud.

After the production, Betsy and I waited in the alleyway behind the theatre. As I stood there, the minutes seeming like hours, I continually fiddled with my cap, suit, and asphyxiating tie in anticipation of seeing her. I was now a part of the play, another love interest, hitherto unknown to the audience, who was waiting for Violet outside her workplace. Home from the front unexpectedly and harbouring a suspicion that she was secretly in love with the Lieutenant, I was changing the ending to the production I had seen so many times, anxious to see how this version played out.

Suddenly, while sliding back against the wall, other minor players of "The Barricade" appeared: first soldiers, then London partygoers, then more soldiers. The thin wooden door slammed against the bricks with the emergence of each new group. Surveying the faces, I thought of what I might say to her.

After a while, I wondered why Captain Dunton had not yet appeared and what the Captain, home on leave, had said in the play upon first seeing her. I finally abandoned my plans to say anything at all. Perhaps she would initiate the conversation. After all, I was forcing this meeting, so the next move could be hers.

The old wooden door creaked open once again and crashed firmly against the side of the wall. Violet emerged in a clean white blouse and a yellow hat, alongside one of the other players carrying a blue umbrella, the same Lieutenant Dick Campbell she had affirmed her love for onstage so many times before. I had not expected her to be so scrubbed and polished, that she would have a companion, and that the person accompanying her would be the Lieutenant, or that she would simply walk past without acknowledging or even noticing me.

Leaning over to one side with my hands in my pockets, my cheeks heated with redness now as my hat was certainly as filthy with bicycle grease as my hands and clothes.

But this setback would not dissuade me. I surely still looked sweet. Captain Roddy Dunton, Violet's fiancée and the Lieutenant's best friend, would have been startled had this same sequence of events transpired before him; he would have confronted the Lieutenant. So, watching Violet and the Lieutenant walking with their arms interlocked, I abandoned Betsy and began to follow them just as Roddy certainly would have.

So I wouldn't be noticed, I maintained enough distance, uncertain of what to say once I encountered them. I could improvise, though, and had thought of stuff to say to girls before. Good stuff. But I had never said any of it, and in my haste, I couldn't recall any of these witticisms now.

They turned around, and I jumped behind a clump of bushes. My foot nearly landed on a rat, the size of a loaf of bread from head to tail. The grey monster scurried away.

Walking along behind them again, they turned around, and I ducked into the alcove of a building beside some homeless men resting on a street corner. I bumped into an elderly woman clothed in rags.

"Any coins?" she asked, coughing.

"I don't have any," I said, showing her my empty pockets and then pointing to Violet and the Lieutenant. "But that man, carrying the fancy umbrella, looks like he does."

"You're a nice boy," she said, smiling widely and patting my cheek. "And so fetching."

After a while, I saw that Violet and the Lieutenant were not, in fact, directing their attention back towards me at all. Perhaps they were so accustomed to being watched onstage that they did not notice observers, even while outside the theatre.

Walking now into the familiar Hyde Park, beneath an overcast sky, I watched as they chased away a man sleeping on a bench before occupying that seat together with their backs toward me. The old woman approached them and went away with a coin, smiling in my direction before following others walking through the park.

My eyes wandered from the corner of Knightsbridge and East Carriage Road to the Wellington Arch—reputedly London's smallest police station, with cramped Constables entering and exiting through a small door beneath one side of the brick structure. A portly Bobby, wearing a tall, blue, and badged helmet, directed hordes of traffic through the roundabout. I perused the crowds nearby and those at a distance, the motorcars, the taxicabs, the horse-drawn carriages, and the bushes of Green Park with its conspicuously absent flowers said to be caused by the number of lepers buried there.

I couldn't think of what dead lepers might have done to make the soil poisonous for flowers yet adequate for other types of vegetation, but I couldn't find any answers to that now.

A quarter hour passed. Sitting down on a bench beside the roadway, checking frequently to ensure Violet and the Lieutenant had not moved, my eyes focused on a monument honouring British victims of the Great War.

My father—not the sore, drunken man I rarely saw, but the valiant war hero, the Private turned Corporal Wilfrid L. Dixon, E Company, 1st Battalion, 1st Brigade—might easily, through one stray bullet or by a shell exploding too close, have been one of the casualties of the war engraved on another memorial somewhere thousands of miles away in Canada. This monument was made of dull stone with a forged iron cannon. A tarnished plaque, set atop a stack of cannonballs ready to be loaded, lay underneath the cannon.

*"In Proud Remembrance of the Forty-nine thousand and seventy-six of all ranks of the Royal Regiment of Artillery who gave their lives for King and Country in the Great War 1914-1919"*

The names of key battlefields were etched onto the plaque intended to diminish the effects of weather, time, and fading memory:

*"Mesopotamia, Macedonia, Arabia, Russia, Palestine, Persia, Africa, Egypt, France and Flanders, Italy, India, Central Asia, and Dardanelles."*

I had often visited this place and stared at these inscribed words, thinking of my father fighting his way through the Great War in France. All my life, until I found his journal, the only impression of the war that my father had ever divulged was through an overheard conversation between my parents.

Pa had said that, at one point during the war, he and others had ceased to care which side won. They only cared that it was over. Afterward, of course, they were glad to have won. But in that duration of wartime, he said, all they wished for was an end.

So, I had conceived for much of my life that Pa was a coward who only wanted out. Now I knew that he only went absent without permission on French leave once, when he was at Bustard Camp in England because he had been denied a pass he should have gotten anyway.

By moving to South Leeds now, I might become as nervous and fearful as I had once accused my father of being—wishing only for an end to my existence there, regardless of what the consequences might be to the family.

I stood up and stretched. Violet and the Lieutenant were still seated on the bench nearby, conversing. People in the background were driving in motorcars, or riding in taxicabs or horse-drawn carriages, likely on the way home from work where they had earned money to support their families, or on their way to visit friends or relatives.

The Bobby whistled and motioned for me to go to Violet. He whistled again, and continued waving. I stared but did not move, and for a moment this man's insistent gesture made me question what I was doing there in the park and whether this version of the play I was in would conclude with a delightful blend of inaction, boredom, and apathy.

Glancing back, still standing immobile, I saw the monument with its cannon and cannonballs sitting ready to be fired at the sham Lieutenant. All around were reminders of moral obligations: duty, allegiance, loyalty. Perhaps going away to the mines was my first opportunity to embrace such responsibilities.

The Bobby was still motioning for me to cross, insistent that I confront Violet now. Glancing over at the woman whose real name I didn't even know and who now sat embracing and kissing the Lieutenant, my presence there suddenly seemed absurd. And I was glad Glen and the boys weren't here to see this. But still, I had to make my move.

I walked over to the bench while the two of them were still engaged in an embrace. I envisioned living with Violet in South Leeds and sharing a house together with my father and Albert. We would have to manage with what we had, at first. She could start a theatre there in South Leeds, and all the other wives would help make the costumes and the sets. And I could become a writer of plays, perhaps even taking from my father's writings to dramatize the Great War the way "The Barricade" did.

I would use this exact scene in my first play: the main character approaching a woman he was enamoured with and challenging her other romantic interest. I had never written before, but I could learn. The Reading Room of the British Museum and the Duke and Duchess

Theatre had given me enough time to qualify both as a "reader" and a theatre patron, with the resultant knowledge of plot and character, and such; at least, enough to dupe a theatre full of coal miners.

I approached Violet the same as I would a sick or wounded animal; with as much caution as I could, while maintaining enough distance for a rapid escape. After resolving to ask her how she felt about me, I simply stood there, awaiting a response as though I had already asked.

Smiling, they released each other from their embrace and glimpsed at my stationary figure staring down at them, as though I was in the play now and they were waiting to be entertained.

"Yes?" the Lieutenant asked, appearing strange and unintimidating in civilian clothing, his smile disappearing. He adjusted his position on the bench, producing and lighting a cigarette.

"Your suit," Violet said. "You're covered with grease."

"In this sunlight," I began, "from my view, you're more fetching..." I paused before continuing. "Your chocolate and azure eyes show how unique is your beauty."

I did not add that she also appeared older than I had noticed before. She scrutinized my face.

"You've been to the theatre more times than I can count," she replied. "You always sit in the same spot, stage left, half-way back..."

A smile came to my lips. With her words, speech came quickly, decisively, and as I spoke, my eyes met Violet's with confidence.

"Do you love him?" I asked, indicating the Lieutenant with a nod of my head.

"Excuse me?" the Lieutenant interjected in a puff of smoke, rising from his seat. "Who are you?"

"A young patron of the theatre," Violet said, pulling on his arm. "Now, sit down."

The Lieutenant reluctantly obliged.

Straightening herself on the bench, her chocolate and azure eyes met my gaze. I had never seen these eyes so close, or outside, and they were iridescent in the sunlight; and I had never seen, at such proximity, the curls of her hair that flowed into the nape of her neck.

"You smell of juniper," I said. "Your eyes are kind and sympathetic, empathetic, something like that."

"This is my girl," the Lieutenant said, staring at me.

"You are about seventeen years old?" Violet asked.

"About seventeen, yes," I replied.

"Well," she said, smiling. "I won't tell you my age, but it certainly isn't seventeen."

The Lieutenant, his arms crossed, the cigarette perched at the corner of his lips, suddenly appeared the same as any other statue in the park. For a moment, I contemplated lunging at him, knocking him onto the grass, and striking his bronzed face.

"Do you love the Lieutenant, or Roddy?" I asked her.

She paused, staring at me. After a moment, she replied: "That's just a play. It's not real. You understand that, of course."

"Of course," I said. "But I'm talkin' about the real people, not the characters."

Thinking again of a quick blow to the Lieutenant's face, now staring into mine, provided me with a sense of relief. If I attacked him, though, she wouldn't be interested in talking anymore. Perhaps not now, or ever. But I had started on a course of action that was just as irreversible.

Pausing for a moment and with both watching me intently as though to discern my intentions, I decided on a conclusion to this situation. I would come back to London occasionally and become acquainted with her. Then, my thoughts were interrupted.

"Thank you for attending the play," the Lieutenant said, rising from the bench and turning toward Violet. "We're off."

Her eyes and demeanour indicated that she was not being entirely truthful in her apparent aloofness. Had the Lieutenant not been there, she might have openly declared her secret affection for the man who she had noticed sitting stage left, half-way back so often and with such unwavering devotion.

"I'm off to the coal mines in South Leeds," I said quickly, looking into her eyes, "and I want to come back here and see you. To know you. To while away the days with you."

The Lieutenant was still gazing back at me.

"I ain't thinkin' to while away any days with you," I added, indicating Violet. "Only her."

"How are you spelling that?" the Lieutenant asked. "Do you mean to wile, deceive, trick, ensnare?"

"I'll be at the theatre," she said. "I won't be going anywhere. You seem a sweet young man, and quite handsome besides. You can come and see me at any time."

"Outside of the play?"

"If you wish," she said, smiling. "We'll take a turn in the park. While away the day, as you put it."

The Lieutenant pulled on her arm and a bird coasted over us, the sunlight receding behind the clouds.

"Go home to your mother," the Lieutenant said. "Our play is fiction, like what's playing in your head."

They walked away, turning back occasionally, presumably so the Lieutenant could ensure that I was not following them.

I stood there, watching them disappear into the distance and thinking that they could end up together.

Except now, I had the contentment associated with a newfound expectation that the conclusion to the play might be changed.

# 7

W e didn't gab about our fathers at school these days.
          If we did, though, I would have explained that Wilfrid Dixon
was living in a hole. A hole full of coal dust, groaning conveyors, and
sweaty solitude that kept him isolated from some of the business of the
country, its political uprisings, and the self-proclaimed leaders of
tomorrow. A confinement that must have kept him unaware of the
Oxford Meeting in 1933, a meeting I had read about in the local paper
where fascist Blackshirts were accused of throwing hecklers down stairs
and beating their heads on stone floors. It likely did not echo word of the
weapons the Gloucestershire Echo alleged were at the Blackshirts'
headquarters: the chair and table legs covered in barbed wire and six-inch
nail spikes, the potatoes entrenched with razor blades, the knives, the
"knuckle dusters," the "coshes," and the stockings stuffed with broken
glass. The limited news probably did not deliver Lord Rothermere's Daily
Mail headline proclaiming, "Hurrah for the Blackshirts!" or the series of
articles that followed under that same title. It was a restriction that
confined him during the meetings, and the subsequent Albert Hall
speech delivered near Knightsbridge to an estimated eight thousand
people on a March evening in 1934:

> *In the long story of the human race, races have struggled up to*
> *nations, and nations up to mighty empires, and scaled the heights of*
> *history...alit by the flame of such insurrection, that moment rises from*
> *the very soul of England, that give all, that dare all, that England may*
> *live in greatness, and in glory.*[2]

          But he had to eventually depart from his quarantine, and on the night
of the Olympia rally on June 7th of that same year, he took me to the streets
of London and Hyde Park where, at Speaker's Corner, we first saw a

Blackshirt: an elderly man dressed from head to toe in the colour of midnight with a lightning emblem on his sleeve. Standing on a brown soap box on the sidewalk by a low, grey metal fence as other Blackshirts distributed pamphlets to the crowd around him, he addressed a question about the violent demonstrations reported in the papers.

"We hafta defend ourselves," the man said, slurring his speech, probably drunk. "They don't want us to speak, 'cause they know we're right. Those rabble-rousers'll do anything to prevent us talking."

He explained to the alternating cheering and derision of the crowd that they had the right to be there, that they had earned the freedom to convene and discuss the issues of the day through the riots of '66, and that they should all follow him to the Olympia rally where thousands more were gathered.

Britain's glorious and great head held high, a nation with cheerful, untroubled people: now, that sounded like something worth fighting for.

We were anxious to follow this man anywhere, and the crowd began to push along the road with the current of a river. Past Marble Arch, a light rain began to fall. We were on a boat in a rainstorm, being carried away with the weight of the water.

Men standing nearby shouted insults and hissed at us as we shuffled through a stadium entrance. We covered ourselves against the onlookers and the rain, drifting in to the shelter of the shore, and I yelled the same insults back without knowing what half of them were.

I had read of the opposition and did not know whether those in the blur of people shouting were communists, Independent Labour Party members, or Jewish radicals. The Bobbies intervened though, keeping the men back. The law was on our side.

But my indifference to the protestors only seemed to make them angrier, as did Pa's expression: his eyes cast forward, intent and defiant as he covered his head and led me to a standing position among an enormous crowd.

"I've never seen so many people all in one building, all at one time," Pa said.

"Why're all these men here?" I asked.

"Same as us I suppose, whatever our reason is."

He smiled and looked over at me.

"If you forgot, and I don't know," I said, smiling, "then we're off."

There were rows of men in bowlers and wide-brimmed hats and cloth caps. Many had moustaches, but few were old enough to have beards. There was the dull roar of a multitude of subdued voices, a few of the men shouting here and there. No women were in the crowd. The men had dull, cheerless faces, all of them somehow eager to be inspired, to have something to believe in. They occupied almost all the floor space, and some had scaled the rafters and were holding on to pipes wherever they could. Men overflowed from a second-floor balcony, draping over and leaning against iron railings. There was a sense of loneliness about the crowd despite its numbers, and an overwhelming sense of desperation for a cause.

"I don't know how they keep things in order," Pa said. "Not with all these protestors and supporters. I saw crowds like this, I told you before, when chaps took to the streets in droves to enlist at city hall back in Canada, in Highgate, at the beginning of the war. That was organized chaos."

"This is a confused mess."

After a short time, a moustachioed man, dressed entirely in black, walked out and began pacing on the stage. A spotlight turned on, the light finding him as he limped across the floor dragging his black boots and kicking up dust. The crowd's roar dwindled, and then hushed.

The man began speaking; each of his words uttered slowly and with weight as if each was of great consequence. He chopped at the air while he spoke:

*"In the lives of great nations, comes a moment of decision, comes a moment of destiny…we go forward to action!"*[3]

Standing there for a moment, he awaited an applause that did not come. The near-silence turned to shouting: first from near the exits, and then from a scattered caterwauling that came from various locations throughout the room. The speaker continued, apparently not oblivious to the fact that he was being heckled, but covertly aware of it.

A rain shower of papers suddenly fell from the girders of the ceiling. The audience expressed approval through more shouting and sporadic applause.

The spotlight moved to two protestors clutching onto the steel structure and dropping the leaflets. A group of Blackshirts gathered and began pointing at the men in the rafters, apparently discussing who would climb up and force them down.

"Let's go," Pa said, nudging me toward an unoccupied section of the floor situated between two folding tables.

I thought we were finally leaving until Pa sat down in an area between the tables, turned on their sides to form a barricade from the crowd. There were several chairs and ashtrays, a break area for Blackshirts who were now otherwise occupied. I sat down as the speaker started up again, this time accompanied by a renewed onset of taunts from the crowd.

The spotlights alternated focus between the two men clinging to the girders, the two Blackshirt stewards climbing up after them, and the speaker who continued his speech.

"This is a circus," Pa yelled.

"Ya," I shouted back. "A bunch of animals all in one place. A regular Barnum and Bailey, this is."

We focused on the speaker as he discussed millions of unemployed men and other repercussions of the Depression and the Great War—all of which had led more than a thousand people to flock here. He described an uncertain future that could lead to another war, one in which England and Germany could potentially become allies.

The speech echoed throughout the foyer along with the thrashing of hecklers. The spotlights probed the audience, flashing on those shouting comments, and then over to someone I recognized from our neighbourhood—Mr. Milne—who was being hauled away by three Blackshirts. He kicked and shouted profanity as he was dragged through the crowd, a lit cigarette dangling from his lips.

Without a word, Pa rose from his seat and walked over to the men assembled around Mr. Milne. Pulling them back by the shoulders with his slender arms, he caused two of them to lose their balance and fall to the ground. Years of fighting had hardened him and made him dangerous.

At seeing such impressive behaviour, I wanted to show him that I was once nearly victorious in a confrontation with three boys outside the Duke and Duchess Theatre, to demonstrate what I had learned in that fight, and others, by joining in this one.

As I rushed over, two Blackshirts ran in to assist the others by sweeping up my father's thin body. Both he and Mr. Milne were escorted down a narrow hallway, and I followed close behind.

The two men were thrown onto the floor in an area where others were receiving blows from sticks, feet, and wooden clubs.

Stepping into the room, I saw Bobbies standing with their backs against the wall, their clubs drawn and ready. These officers were not interfering in any of the fights, though, only observing when they should have been breaking things up and jailing our oppressors.

After kicking Mr. Milne's knees, the Blackshirts began hitting his head, his chest, and his back. Blood discharged from his nose and soaked his clothes. He lay curled with his hands over his head.

Huddled along one edge of the hallway with their arms crossed, three Blackshirts began moving toward us.

"You fellows want to get a scrap started, do you?" Pa asked as he rose from the floor. "Well, I'll try not to hurt you too bad."

This was the night outside the Duke and Duchess Theatre all over again, only with more people joining in on the fun. Fight back harder than they would have anticipated. Go with your gut.

I lunged at one of the scrawniest men as if he was Glen outside the Duke and Duchess.

Pa also sprang to action, aiming at a larger man with a dark moustache.

We toppled to the ground, all of us together. The sound of my adrenalized heartbeat thumped in my ears.

My man's head hit against the pavement and he was suddenly immobile.

Then, there was an abrupt blow to the back of my neck.

What a lovely day this was turning out to be.

I toppled onto the floor. There was the flash of a police badge. Finally, one of them had gained enough courage to step in. Only they were on the wrong side. Apart from a sharp pain in my head I could hear, and feel, almost nothing; only blurred and indistinct shapes.

I awoke sometime later to the wet street outside. Pa and Mr. Milne were standing there, hacking, spitting blood, and cursing. They removed clumps of mud from their clothes.

Rising and stretching my back, I felt a lump on the back of my neck. I had a serious headache.

Mr. Milne started back toward the entrance of the Olympia as shouts from the rally permeated the air.

Instinctively, I followed him.

"Where are you off to?" Pa asked, waving his hand in the air dismissively. "You want more of that? Because I don't. He works at a factory making crude tar, explosives and sulfuric acid, but that's not enough punishment for him? He can have it. Let him go."

We walked home together, darting in and out of festering alleyways. In the alternating shadows and dim lighting, my father appeared as though he had been trampled by a horse.

"I had a problem with your job in the mines," Pa said, turning toward me.

"So, I won't be going then," I said. "Good."

"Albert told the foreman your mother wouldn't want you there."

"All good stuff. Never liked that Albert before, but—"

"Don't go off the rails," he interrupted. "I talked to the foreman and set things right. You'll start in two weeks. Before you work in the office, I'll teach you how to get through those tunnels. You'll have to work in the pit for a time, maybe a few months."

"Mum knows something's doing."

"She suspects, maybe. But I told her you're going to your Uncle Devon's farm."

"When're we to tell her?"

He sighed. "Now's not the right time."

"When will be?"

"You'll know, and then you can tell her yourself."

Staring out at a sparsely populated, starlit sky as we discussed the country's uncertain future exemplified in the circus of the Olympia rally, I contemplated leaving the only home I had ever known. Mum's worst fears would be realized. Between then and now, I would have to avoid her and the knowing looks she would certainly dole out for free.

Pa stopped, wiped his bloody lip and produced a package of damaged Navy Cuts from his pocket. He straightened a bent cigarette, and then stooped over to light it with one of the matchbooks Ian and I had assembled in the kitchen. I asked for a cigarette as well and was surprised when he straightened and lit one for me.

"I want fellows to get work," he said, the cigarette dangling from his bleeding lip, "But if you could see the amount of dead Germans in the trenches in the Great War, you would wonder how they had the heart to keep on… and for Fritz to try again now by starting the whole thing over… well, that speaker for sure was never in the trenches, and this malarkey of England united with Germany… he doesn't know what he's saying."

There was pain in his eyes and even a tear, although it was difficult to tell. Brave men weren't supposed to cry. In one of the letters home to Pa's mother, though, Pa had said that men cried in the trenches all the time.

We walked for a while in silence before he began speaking again.

"I saw what you did back there, going after that man," he said. "You did good. Although I don't know how I'll explain this to your Ma, both of us coming home all beat up. I didn't know you could fight like that."

"I knew," I said, to which we both smiled.

"You see now, if we have another war, what we'd be fighting against. Men like that speaker and those Blackshirts. If you can call them men, that is. But another week and we'll be in the mines together."

"You'll be there, I won't."

"Still on about that? You want another fight? Cause you'll get one. If you're not there in a week, I'll come back here and drag you off by your ear."

The rain began to come down hard.

We ran home, Pa slowing and then limping along after a time on his bum leg with rainwater drenching us. After we arrived, I sat at the foot of the stairs until long after he had changed from his wet and tattered clothes and slipped into bed.

I went upstairs listening to the rain's tempo fluttering on the roof, thinking that nothing would ever be the same again, a realization that made me silently sob as I fell asleep.

# 8

Mum was chopping vegetables, and the pot smelled good as I opened the kitchen door in our London home.

"Lamb stew'll be ready soon," she said, releasing a handful of chopped carrots into the boiling pot. "Now we finally got some money from your father. Are you feeling better?"

"Not so much. But only a couple of bruises is all."

"And have you got anything you want to tell me about where you're gonna work?"

Putting the knife down, she raised her eyebrows at me expectantly. I hesitated before answering.

"No," I said. "Anything you want to say?"

"Well," she replied, retrieving the knife and slicing some celery stalks. "I know that concealing the truth is deceit, and a sin against God."

She glared up suspiciously before adding some celery to the stew.

If Pa was right, a lie wasn't a lie if we didn't say anything. Mum's interpretation might be different, but she'd been wrong before.

"How is it your father's story seems not quite right?" she asked sternly, stirring the pot with a wooden spoon. The sweet aroma, with a hint of parsley, drifted toward me. Maybe getting some of that stew was contingent on my response. I was hungry, but this wasn't going well.

Obligated by her stare to say something, I simply replied: "It doesn't?"

"No."

"Well... do you think I could talk Pa into coming home to live?"

"Your father is endlessly stubborn. I've been after him for years with no results. And besides, you say you're off to the farm. That doesn't ring true, as your uncle's farm couldn't bring us much money. It isn't much of a farm. Your uncle bought the land after the war because it was cheap, and he's never been a farmer. I don't think he'd be chomping at the bit to get a boy from the city to work for him. And I could write a letter to him, we've always gotten on well together, and that's all it would take to find out if you were there. *He* would be honest with me. But I'm sad to say that my own son and my husband are not. I am very disappointed with your father, and more so with you. So much so, I'm not going to allow it."

So, I wasn't going anywhere. And I wasn't getting any stew now, either. A crust of bread, if I was lucky.

"I'm going," I said. "It's all set. He's waiting for me."

"Who is: your father, or your uncle?" she asked.

I did not reply.

"Now, go tidy up for supper," she said.

So, I would be eating after all. And I would be going away. There was no debating either.

My father and all the other soldiers of the 1st Contingent hadn't wanted to move overseas to risk their lives in a war they had only read about in the papers, at least, not if they knew what horrors they would face. But they adapted, and before they had truly experienced war, they were eager to get to the front. If they could deal with four years of what must have been constant, varying degrees of dread, I could certainly live with the harshness of a few months in South Leeds. Mum would learn to forget about her eldest son just as she had learned, over time, to do with her husband.

That week at the post office, I snatched a letter Albert had sent to Doreen. The letter described the deplorable condition of the mines, and the number of fatalities and diseases that had occurred in the past year in the mining town of South Leeds. Worse, he said that I was expected there any day. The skunk.

Now that I would no longer be in London to catch such letters, I told Ian that the bicycle was his. I instructed him about the mail delivery time, the short window he had to intercept any letters before Mum showed up at the post office, and how to crimp and adjust Betsy's gears to coax her into going faster when her pedals only wanted to seize up.

Still, Ian spent loads of time in bed and I expected he would be unreliable, so I would also have to work from South Leeds by taking mail to the post office for Albert as often as I could. I would discard any letters addressed to Mum before they were sent.

I taught Ian how to use the blowtorch to unclog frozen lines leading down from the water tank on the roof, and I drew a map to the market so he could shop for meat and vegetables whenever Mum needed him to go.

Ian protested constantly during all these discussions.

"I won't be well enough to take Betsy to the market, the post office, or anywhere else," he said. "I'm too sick."

"Part ways with your bed, it'll make you better," I replied. "You'll see. You two are needin' some time apart."

"Where're you off to, anyway? When'll you be back?"

His questions were only met with silence.

Mum asked repeatedly about South Leeds, Uncle Devon, and Pa; I said nothing. She bought a block of paper, a pencil, and some pens for me to start another year of school that was not compulsory, in September.

I could entice Pa back to London, not as Mum had tried to do by arguing about his life decisions, but by making this my full-time occupation. There was work to be found in London: shops, stores, and perhaps some factory jobs that may not pay as well as the mines. But still, there was work. There had to be.

I was tired of this delay before my departure, like Pa had been eager to get to the front in the Great War and put an end to the anticipation.

I visited the Duke and Duchess Theatre for the last time, eager to meet Violet after the production, alone this time, finally changing the ending to the play. She had called me sweet, and quite handsome besides, and invited me to see her any time. To take a turn in the park after the show. All delightful candy to my ears.

I recalled her shimmering eyes up close and the stark impression they left upon me as I approached the theatre. I saw there were no lights on, inside or out. The doors were locked, and a sign indicated that the basement had flooded. The date of the next showing was yet to be determined.

For several hours Betsy and I wandered the streets, hunting for Violet in different theatres as though she might be there, hoping that the performance had been relocated, or she was playing another part somewhere else. Entering various theatres through back alleys, past unattended booths, I discovered only angry men trying to sleep. Violet was nowhere to be found. But I resolved to continue searching.

The next day, I cleaned the house and the fireplace, made the beds, and folded the laundry. I went to the market for Mum, where I bought stinking fish and assorted fruits and vegetables with some of the money Pa had sent. Yanking out some parsley from the back garden, I cooked soup for Ian, and made tapioca pudding for dessert.

Insisting Ian come with me, we took a long walk together. I propped the bedroom window open for additional air to help him breathe, the scent of ripe flowers from the back garden wafting in along with the smell of local coal fires.

Once a layer of dust had accumulated on the windowsill, I pulled the window closed again.

And after all this, I could certainly take a bit of time for myself.

Afraid now that I might never see Violet again, envisioning myself as her fiancée Captain Roddy Dunton, I took Betsy through the streets. Searching with as much determination and intensified interest as a man with a once great love that had been abruptly lost, I combed the streets along the Thames endlessly and, seemingly unnoticed by those I passed by, I imagined myself at once transient and ethereal; as though I had already left the city and was only traversing these streets in my mind, reiterating this fruitless pursuit as if in a recurring dream that I might have in the upcoming days, weeks and months. I sought her out until the final hours before I had to leave, when I still expected that I might find her alone, walking over a bridge and sobbing as if in the pages of Dostoyevsky's White Nights or Goëthe's Young Werther—hoping for an opportunity to first ask the source of her pain, and then to console her.

A woman walked by with a hood covering her head. Violet. Cycling close to this person, I descended from the seat of my bicycle and began walking alongside her.

"Have you read Andrew Marvell?" I said. "Our vegetable love can grow."

She turned toward me. It was not Violet. I continued walking my bike without altering my pace, not recognizing her, smiling at this young woman's strange stare as I passed her by.

Walking my bicycle past the old Bell foundry and turning toward Cable Street, I continued through lit areas alternating with patches of darkness. Seeing the old Bell foundry made me recall a nursery rhyme with disputed origins that Mum had recited to me when I was very young: Oranges and Lemons. We would sing the nursery rhyme along with the bells that tolled at night. The song mimicked the same rhythmic clanging of the chimes at St. Clements, a church twice destroyed; St. Martins, destroyed but the bell preserved; the twelve bells of Old Bailey, housed in the city's largest church and ringing for executions and condemned prisoners; Shoreditch in an impoverished area; and the great bell at Bow, still signalling to the fourteenth-century Cockneys that the time had come for them to go home. Mum taught me that "Oranges and Lemons" was about poverty. I discovered from my schoolmates that the song was about sex, for reasons I could not discern or ask anyone about, and did not involve bells or poverty at all.

I stopped at the intersection of Fulborne and Whitechapel Street. I kept walking and turned onto Vallance Road to see the Hughes Mansions, a long three-block semi-Victorian tenement. Bells rang again in the distance and I turned the corner toward home, defeated.

Mum and Ian were already in bed when I stepped through the front door of our house. I would have to leave within an hour to catch the train to South Leeds, and I still didn't have my books, comics, and clothes together. The time had slipped through my fingers.

After packing, I sat in the scullery alone beside the concrete bin, now half full of dirty laundry. The light from the gas lamp above flickered with a sudden draft of air through the gaps around the closed window. I didn't have to go. I could stay and elude my father upon his promised return. Reading through my father's wartime journal, I came across the last entry he wrote on Salisbury Plains, and re-read the ending several times.

*It is up to me to do my duty and I am certainly glad I have the chance to do so. I will write to Mother and tell her not to worry about me, that I will be all right.*

*I will write to her as often as circumstances allow.*

With or without leaving Mum a letter, perhaps a modified version of this, she would have to understand. This was my war.

I sat there and stared at the words on the page.

Maybe Pa's lie was part of an assortment of greater, more hurtful lies, and as such was easily overlooked. Maybe this duplicity was perpetuated because Pa had his own reasons for *wanting* this situation. Maybe he would never return to live in London, and I was being duped by his cunning and my own flawed judgement.

A foul odour, that of stinking vegetables from the garbage can outside, wafted into the back of the house through the drafty window and combined with the scent of the dirty clothes. It sure was lovely.

*It is up to me to do my duty and I am certainly glad I have the chance to do so.*

Without writing a word, and rising with a creak from the chair, I extinguished the gas lamp, took the journal, and opened the door. I entered my bedroom with a candle in hand. The room was cold with the scent of the night air, and I closed the window and set the curtains back in place, so its blue and yellow flowers were visible again.

Minnaloushe slept coiled like a sailor's rope on top of Ian, who lay motionless on his bed. Ian's pallor in this light made him resemble a ghost. The feline raised her dark head and yawned as the door creaked fully open. Ian's snores were interrupted momentarily, and then resumed.

There was a lingering smell of stale urine from the chamber pot. On the dresser beside the water jug and basin for morning washes, were six jacks and a tiny ball. Ian had always favoured games of manual dexterity, his slender fingers making it easy for him to win; one bounce picking up four, or sometimes even five jacks before catching the ball again. He would repeat it, endlessly practicing, seemingly ad infinitum.

In the same sort of methodical motion, I reached down, placed my hand on the bedpost, and leaned over to kiss my brother's forehead. Through my work at the mines over the next few months—whether it was money for medical care, or for travel where we could all meet in the countryside at Uncle Devon's cottage, and where Ian always seemed to get better in the clean farmland air—I could help to improve my brother's health.

Minnaloushe's eyes gleamed back like green saucers, as though my mother's gaze was upon me.

My decision to leave would mean running away, repeating what my father had done, to pay the mortgage for a house he didn't inhabit and provide for a family from whom he lived apart.

But, I told those eyes, that didn't matter much now when one contemplated what had to be done.

# 9

I stepped on a train in London and emerged in South Leeds, hours later, carrying all my belongings in a canvas rucksack slung over my right shoulder. I walked down a muddy street lined with attached row housing. Women holding babies stared at me beside children with filthy faces and grubby clothes. Traversing through the muck, down a familiar narrow, brick-lined back alleyway that separated two rows of houses, past some children standing beneath hanging laundry, I knocked on the soiled wooden door of the tenement Pa shared with Albert.

I hadn't been to this place since we had all lived here together. A reminder that our family would be living collectively again soon, only not in this forsaken place.

The door opened slowly. Harriet, our landlady, the stocky woman with brown hair tied haphazardly in a bun, stood in the opening. With an oversized body seeming too large to fit through the doorway, she lived on the first floor and never parted with her apron. She reminded me of Mum—with the same shade of green eyes and tone of voice—but Harriet's wide girth, sloping greasy forehead, and nasty disposition was nothing like my mother's thin, rakish appearance or meek temperament. This woman, who had sometimes fought bitterly with Mum over the high rent and sub-standard food, mumbled incoherently and reluctantly invited me inside.

"A joy to see you, Harriet," I said. "I thought for a moment you'd shut me out."

Upon seeing me, Pa smiled and hugged me for the first time in as long as I could remember. Albert stood nearby with the left sleeve of his shirt empty, tucked into his belt, and I recalled that his arm had been crushed by rubble following the underground explosion my father had caused. Another reason for Albert to despise Pa. Why Pa continued living here, I didn't know.

My father was smiling too much—at times, for no reason at all—and he embraced me over and again as he hadn't before. Albert stood by unflinching for the next hour, staring at us, saying little and, I suspected, concocting details for a letter he would try sending to Mum in the coming days.

Later that afternoon, I went out for a walk with Pa. We passed between two rows of houses on the street, arriving at an area with children at play.

"Albert didn't want you here," he said, neatly avoiding a boy who ran at him. The boy slipped in the mud and dropped his hat, recuperating, then continuing.

"Wasn't so keen to come myself," I replied. "Well, you know."

We stopped at an enormous pile of coal, glimmering blue-black in the sun. Pa bent over, picked up a chunk as big as his fist, and tossed the mass at an erect shovel. He threw another, and then another.

"We had a row," Pa said. "Albert and I. He saw the foreman, and he wrote some letters to your Ma about my plan to bring you here. I ensured the letters went in the fire, where they belonged."

He continued throwing the dark rocks, one landing with a clink at the base of the shovel. I recalled the letter from Albert that I saw, which said the same.

"I didn't draw a shilling this pay," he continued. "Your Ma needed all of it. With your pay, though, we could live in our own tenement."

"No need to worry," I said. "We'll get as far from this place, and from Albert, as we can."

The meal that evening was stale bread, watery chicken broth, and black tea served by Harriet's meaty hands. My father said I would have to get used to this, even after we moved to live on our own.

"Constant hunger," I said. "No change for me."

Sharing a bed with my father that night, I saw that his back was rough and uneven. In the dim illumination, its surface was more akin to a piece

73

of darkened rock streaked with blue veins. This must have been from the burns in the underground explosion that had taken Albert's arm.

On that first night, I lay there staring up at the broken plaster ceiling. Outside on the street below, children threw rocks at screeching rats. My father, who lay beside me, didn't seem to care about the circumstances under which I had left London, only that I had. And my penance for deceiving Mum was to live in this place that seemed not quite suitable for human habitation.

The next morning, we entered a small metal elevator with a group of men, the cage snapping shut as we began our descent.

"We're off, a hundred and six feet into the earth," one of the men said.

"How'd they measure like that?" I asked. "I mean, did they use a wire and some long string and a ruler maybe? What else?"

"I dunno," he said, glaring at me. "They just know, that's all. What's the matter?"

"Makes me wonder what else the workers don't think about around here."

There was silence for the remainder of our descent.

After the elevator clattered to a stop, we all moved toward tunnels leading in different directions. I knelt by my father's side at the mouth of his tunnel leading off into darkness.

Removing my shirt as my father did, I crawled after him carrying an unwieldy Davy Lamp through narrow tunnels of rock almost too constricted to fit through. The rocks scraped along the length of my bare back.

Rumblings of mechanization echoed through my ears, at times, to a deafening level. I shouted back at the machines with equal ferocity, until I was nearly hoarse.

A couple of hours, and I was ready to go home.

An incredibly long time passed as we navigated through the tight passageway until, finally, we arrived at an opening. There were small tools, pickaxes, and shovels spread out over the floor, and rats scurried away at our light as we entered the space. There was insufficient head room to stand. A groaning conveyor dropped into darkness and out of sight.

"Our worksite," he yelled.

"Swell," I shouted, to which he gave no response. "This day has been nothing but a delight."

He leaned over, gave me a shovel and, grabbing a pickaxe for himself, he began plucking away at the blue-black walls while still on his knees. I took hold of the shovel and plunged it into the earth. As I lifted the shimmering rocks onto the conveyor, the space quickly filling with dust and the light gradually fading, I contemplated how much easier this would be if we were able to stand. After years of having endured such torment, my father would certainly be amenable to departing this place.

Less than one day on the job, and I was certainly ready to scurry away.

He explained that evening, after scrubbing the blackness from my skin in the washtub, that Mum would receive nearly all his paycheques now. My cheques would pay for the tenement and any food, drink or other expenses in South Leeds; which would include any drinking and gambling debts incurred.

We drank beers after dinner, for which I would soon be paying. Our cycle of dust ingestion, intense manual labour and cleaning ourselves up enough for supper was finished for the day.

He showed me a letter, written in Mum's cirrus script and addressed to Uncle Devon, in which she asked if I was at the farm. Uncle Devon had not responded, but had forwarded the letter, asking Pa how he should reply.

"He'll say you're working like the Dickens," Pa said. "Write to your Ma about the farm. I'll send your letter back to Devon, and he'll post the letter from Northaw. She'll be glad to get it."

He held a pen out over a piece of paper. This habitually passive and now more intentional dishonesty seemed far too easy to Pa.

"We're going to loads of trouble to dupe Mum," I said.

"One day, she'll understand," he replied. "You know, she's nothing like my Ma was. My mum would have a fit and yell and throw lamps and plates on the floor till she knew the truth. Then it would be over. Your mother's anger, if she knew what we're up to, would turn inside and only get worse with time. You see, we're doing what's best for her."

"Or maybe what's best for you."

He slapped the pen on the table and took a long drink of beer, finishing the contents of his glass.

"What are you on about?" he asked, wiping his mouth with his sleeve.

Harriet came in, pouring him another beer. As she walked away, mumbling, he raised his glass in her direction.

"Thanks," he said, shouting after her. "You're a good woman, Harriet. Some people say you're gruff, but we know better."

"I forgot those hands of hers," I said quietly. "Oversized crabs, red and gnarled and meaty."

He smiled. "Yes, I suppose they are. But don't get in such a knot about telling Mum. We'll go to London and you can tell her...for now, though, write that note..."

I could write that I was working in the mines and not the fields, explaining that I would bring Pa home to live in London even if I had to carry him like a sack of potatoes on my back. What she had said was not likely to happen, could occur. What she had suspected, I would admit to.

While in London, I would seek employment there. Mum could help by starting now. Maybe she knew the wives of men who worked in the factories, in shops, or on the docks. Then Pa's new job would force him to stay there.

As my father declared in his war journal, the objective of winning at any cost, while contemptible, had to become palatable. I would seal the envelope and send the letter to Uncle Devon, to be forwarded to Mum, myself. The duper could become the duped.

"Sounds like a splendid idea," I said, retrieving the pen and beginning to write.

# <u>10</u>

I began accompanying Pa to the South Leeds pub after every shift, paying for pints of sour ale and throwing darts, or playing cards. Early one evening, with the place packed with patrons thirsty for conversation and drink, our discussion was focused on the dismal and rainy weather. Brazen from the effects of the alcohol, I resolved to initiate my plan, the details of which were on their way to Mum.

"We need to go to London," I said.

"We'll get there," he said, smacking his lips as he took a drink. "Why all the fuss now?"

I stuck to my scheme.

"There's factories opening up in London," I said, taking a long drink of ale and wondering if this was true.

"Claptrap. That's your mother talking. Here, it's not the best, I know. But there's no one out of work here. Can't say that about London, or anywhere else in England. It certainly would be alright to be in London, but it isn't my fault I can't get a decent job there."

"What about Beckton Gas Works?"

"You know about that place? Our neighbour, Mr. Milne, he works there. He told me they boil crude tar and make raw materials for explosives. I read they're opening a plant to make thousands of tons of sulfuric acid next. That stuff eats your skin down to the bones, and then keeps on eating. Anything toxic or poisonous, they'll manufacture it. If you're not a boffin, one of those dim-witted scientists mixing chemicals, you're in the thick of it working alongside tanks of the stuff. Not for me, no thanks."

I had a sudden notion, a scheme that I hadn't considered before.

"What if you stopped sending your pay home?" I asked.

"Then your Ma couldn't pay the mortgage," he said. "I wouldn't do that, though."

"Why not?"

"She'd lose the house."

"And then she'd have to come here. You can force her hand."

He paused, looking around as he sipped his ale.

"I wouldn't do that," he said quietly. "It's underhanded."

"And what we're doing now isn't? You want her here, don't you?"

"Seems you don't know what you want. Do you want to be in London, or here?"

"I want us all together. Ian can't breathe in London, and there's less smog here, but more dust. Maybe he'd be better off. Who's to say? We could keep the windows shut. He was fine when we moved here before."

"But that was only for a short time."

"Too short."

Wilfrid paused for a while, taking one drink, then another, staring out at the crowd.

"It could work," he said. "Only your Ma doesn't want me working in the mines. She's afraid of you boys working there, too."

"You could work in the offices," I continued, flushed now. "We both could."

Pa's gaze was intent and defiant.

"You'll eventually be in the offices, but not me," he said. "I'm no good with numbers."

"Mum's afraid of death. Not her own, but yours. And mine. She's probably not sleeping well. I used to rub her feet to get her to sleep...didn't you ever think of your own death here?"

"Not really."

"What about during the war?"

"I volunteered for war back when I was young, fit and active. I didn't consider consequences. When I was in the trenches I remember wondering when the next meal would be, whether I had enough ammo, if I had water, when I could have a cigarette—the Germans used to see smoke coming up over the trenches and then throw bombs in that direction. Then, when I was promoted, I remember constantly contemplating if my men were okay... as an officer I had to do double duty, thinking about my own survival and that of my men... I'd think, *I have this guy here, and should he be here, and have I got a sentry out there,* and *where are the Germans now, where are the Germans now,* you know. I wrote a journal and looked at it a few times since the war. I didn't mull over what was going on back home much and didn't think about my own death, only what the next day would bring."

"I saw the journal."

"You did? How?"

"I found it in the attic. I know you were nearly killed, lots of times."

He stopped, emptying his glass before continuing.

"Ya, I was wounded in the war. A bunch of times. Sometimes after being unconscious, I didn't know what was going on around me when I woke up. I had nightmares about being wounded. Some of my brother officers, five of them, were killed all at once. We were crouched down together in the middle of a battle in the trenches. Artillery was coming in, and then it suddenly stopped. All the officers couldn't bring our heads up at once as the sharpshooters might get us. So, I poked my head up slowly, the others still crouched down, and a shell exploded at that same moment. Shrapnel was everywhere, and the metal that hit my belly hit them on the head. They were killed instantly. I never wrote about that in my journal. I never even talked about it till now... I fell to the ground unconscious and must've got hauled out on a stretcher some time later... If that bomb fell a second or two earlier, I wouldn't be here today. And neither would you... But you don't think of that at the time. I thought then that I was lucky to wake up, when the others didn't, and now I know it was the hand of God... But to see those under my command being killed, when praying was only something we did before going into battle, the same as we checked our ammo pouch to make sure we had enough... well, let me tell you, it was... and still is, since I had a promotion here at the mines that was taken away because of a fatal accident... it's awful... when you're in command of men in action, you always think about your people. Even in overwhelming odds, they still depend on you to get them through. Anyway, I'm rambling."

"But they wouldn't obey an order. Not if they thought it put them in too much danger."

"In the British Army, there was strict obedience. You didn't dare disobey an order. That was what got on your nerves, knowing that the men would obey. They wouldn't question their orders, so you had better consider them carefully. And there could be no mistakes. No errors like the one—" He stopped.

"You're talking the accident with the Davy Lamp?" I asked.

He glared at me, ordering another ale. The bartender, with a weighty tray of drinks, stopped to nod quickly before walking over to a crowded table.

"How'd you know about that?" he asked.

"Your back. Albert's arm. Albert sent a letter to Mum telling her. I didn't let her see it, though."

"Really? I'm glad your mother doesn't know."

A beer was delivered in a dirty glass, and I placed a coin on the bartender's tray before Pa took a drink.

"I don't know why Albert would send a letter like that," he said, wiping his mouth with his sleeve and slouching down in his chair. "He's too interested in your mother. Ever since she was here with you boys, I knew. When we were in our own flat together, he spent so much time there... but how did you get the letter, without your Mum seeing it?"

"I hoofed it to the post office before her. I read the letters he sent and tossed them in the trash, where they belonged."

"That's swell," he said, smiling. "There were other letters, then. And you read them all?"

"Not all, but most. They said what was happening in the mines. Mostly accident reporting and some gossip about people who worked here. Maybe he wanted to be a newspaper man, I couldn't say, but his reports left more questions than answers."

His smile disappeared.

"He never said he loved her?" he continued, imbibing some ale, "nothing like that?"

Albert's letters had contained ridiculous statements about him wanting to be married to Mum. Some declarations of love. Nothing Pa would want to hear.

"Not from what I saw," I replied. "But there were lots of letters. He wrote about me coming here too, and I got it from the post office before Mum did."

"Did she ever write back?"

"I saw a few letters over the years. I read one, where she asked about some of the miner's wives. The rest I tossed in the trash unopened."

He smiled again and touched my shoulder. "That was good, what you did. Very good."

The bartender returned with another drink. Reaching into my pocket, producing a coin, I set it on the tray before the man left. After draining the contents of his first glass, setting it aside and taking a drink from the other, Pa lit a cigarette before continuing.

"Albert," he said, shaking his head. "The snake."

"The skunk. The weasel."

I drank more slowly now, continuing my previous course: "We can force Mum's hand," I said.

He sighed. "Ya, and then she'll be here. But she won't be happy for a long time; that much I know. She loves that house, and that city. I don't feel good about this. I'll find a way to use up the coin we're not sending home till then, though. At least that part won't be hard. Maybe you can help."

He raised his glass and then placed the cloudy vessel back on the table, pausing to inhale from his cigarette while glancing around at groups of filthy men around us.

"Do you know how your mother and I met?" he asked.

"You met during the war," I responded.

"Christmas 1916," he said, exhaling a white cloud. "At a place like this. Only with women. Loads of them. Lovely ones, too. Your Ma was the loveliest. Her father was a retired Lieutenant whose wife had died. Your Ma went with him to hotel lobbies and bars where his friends and other soldiers were. Loads of girls took up with one soldier, and when he was out fighting, they would take up with someone else. I wasn't sure if your mother was like that or not at the time, but I had to trust her. And her father was always there to keep other men away. That was what kept me going during the last years of the war."

His voice trailed off as a group of men departed, several of them patting my father's shoulder and greeting him, and acknowledging me as they walked by.

"But anyway," he concluded, stubbing out his cigarette, "you don't need to hear such things about your mother, or what I thought of her. And now I know that none of what I thought was true."

The bartender, listening in, began stacking glasses behind the bar.

"Mum told me and Ian about how brave you were going to war," I said. "Some expression she said, that bravery does not plan ahead. She told us you were a hero."

"Hardly... we'll go now. No more to drink for tonight."

Finishing my ale, emboldened again by the booze and invigorated by what I had learned so far, I asked what had caused the accident underground with the Davy Lamp. I had to know.

Maybe we should both be afraid of death.

He scoffed. "You're still on about that?"

"I want to know."

He produced a cigarette from his pocket, struck a match and lit the end before continuing.

"I don't know why it happened. Just nerves I guess. I dropped the Davy Lamp when I heard the conveyor start. My carelessness and George is dead. I haven't seen a man killed in front of me in fifteen years. If I had caused one of my own men to die as a Corporal in the 1st Battalion, 1st Canadian Regiment, 7 Section, 4 Company, on active service with the British Expeditionary Force, there might have been a Field General Court Martial hearing... they tried others for murder on the battlefield and carried out executions. I never saw that myself, but I knew about them. It was rare, but still, it happened... your uncle Devon thought he might be put in front of a firing squad for a different reason, for French Leave, desertion, but that's a different story... and seeing George's wife after the accident, watching her move away, the guilt, the sleepless nights, it's enough to kill a man... all because of my nerves... some hero..."

He paused for a moment, glancing around at the unoccupied tables, before adding: "I dunno. Maybe it's time to go back to Canada. Your Uncle Devon talks about that too. He's still not married, and he lives in that farmhouse alone."

I shifted in my chair, and he continued:

"We drank rum in the war, when we had any. We had to calm our nerves. Those days in the war are when I thought I did my best. Something I can never beat for the rest of my life, whatever I do. Now, I'm only filled with regret. I should have dragged George like I pulled Albert out, or like the wounded Sergeant I put on my shoulder and carried for a mile and a half to a dressing station when I was one of the Bomb Throwers in the war, when I too was wounded..."

"You're lucky you weren't killed," I said. "In the war or in that accident."

"Ya, lucky." He inhaled from his cigarette, and then stomped it out with his foot. "We'll go now; I've had enough of this."

I read through part of my father's experience as a Bomb Thrower that night. There were statements such as "I was so wet and tired," sentences written without an apparent sense of worry, fear, or apprehension. This was a focus on the physical, and not on the emotional toil of war. And while in London on a pass that he had been eagerly anticipating, all he could write about was what was happening on the battlefields of France.

There was a blunt and factual, almost journalistic quality to the entry, the same as he had exhibited in our conversation about the accident in the mines. He had documented their three-day march that ended with a long walk through communication trenches in the rain with the objectivity of a reporter.

*We left the billets one night at 7 o'clock, with orders to take Hill 63, a few days away. We marched all night, checking maps and compasses along the way, before landing in a line of reserve trenches at about 5 o'clock in the morning. After two days rest, we marched out through a town all in ruins, Festuburg. Then we went up to an old German trench the English had taken a few weeks before, where we were called upon* to attack some German trenches on a nearby hill. Our trench was 20 yards away from the German trenches.

The Germans shelled the Canadian trench all night. The next morning, the Canadians attacked, capturing the German trenches and bombing them all out. Talk about helmets, they had all kinds. The Germans made three counter attacks. During the first one, they meant business, but still, they were easily repulsed. The second, at noon, was pushed back easily too. On the third attack, they were all drunk. Some had no guns, some had no coats on, and they were all mowed down like grass.

Then, we moved a mile to the left. In one place there were no fire line trenches for a couple hundred yards, so we went to work digging. Just where I was going to dig there was a dead man lying there, so I had to bury him. Believe me, it was some ticklish job. Then, I had to hurry and catch up with the rest.

We dug till daylight and then lay low all day. That night we had to send a patrol out in front, so the Germans could not take us by surprise while digging. The patrol came across three fellows who had been wounded, and who had been lying out there for somewhere between eight and ten days. One fellow's leg was as green as grass. He died, and the other two lived.

The next night, we finished our trench, and then Fritz got wise to it. The Germans started a bombardment and their attack sure was heavy. I hadn't slept very much for two days, and so I had fallen asleep without thinking. Just as I began to sleep, after what might have been an hour, there was a loud bang, and a shell burst right over top of me. It was a no good way to wake up, I'll tell you that. The shell wounded both me and the Sergeant. So, I put the Sergeant on my shoulder and started with him to the dressing station, about a mile and a half away.

I got him out on the road all right, but they were shelling so heavily that we took to the fields. But how we managed to escape without getting a few more wounds, you couldn't say.

We passed near a farmhouse, where we stopped for a rest. There was a little girl about two or three years old lying there, dead. When the

Sergeant saw her, he started to cry and said, "Take me away." He was a man about 48 years old and was pretty peevish and childish.

At last, we got to the dressing station. The Sergeant was taken to England right away, to be sent back to Canada. I was soon back with my Company.

On the day I returned, we started on a three-day march. The first night I fell out of line and had to get a ride. For the next two nights, I stuck into the line all right. We had a few days rest before starting for the high ground of Hill 63 near the catacombs, about five miles away. It started to rain at about the same time as we left our billets, and it didn't let up. We landed at Battalion headquarters at about 10 o'clock at night.

There was about two miles to go before the trench. The Bombers were last, as we had to take up bombs. We had to cross a bridge leading off the road and go to a field heading toward the trenches. As it was night time, we had to wait for a star shell to go up, so we could see.

At last, all the Bomb Throwers crossed over the bridge.

I was in front. I saw the other fellows go straight, so I led the others behind me for quite a way. After a while, I couldn't see anybody in front of me, so I stopped and looked around. At last, we found a communication trench. So, we got in that and walked through the trench for about an hour. It was still raining all the time. We had never been there before, and not one of us knew the way.

We stopped and chewed the fat for a while before starting off again, walking another two more. It seemed to me that we had come to the end of the trench, so we had to turn around and come back down another communication trench. We walked for about an hour, stopped and had another chewing match. Then, we went on again. I was so wet and tired that I felt like lying right down in the mud. The star shells were going up on each side of us and in front; the line was just like a horseshoe.

After another half hour walk, we landed up in the front trench. We got right out as the Germans had it mined. We had to be on the job all the time.

We never made it to Hill 63. Fritz still had it. But eventually, we would take it.

Flipping through the journal, I found a purveying sense of optimism: anticipating future victories in battle; looking forward to furlough, instead of focusing on the horrors he saw by day. His constant sense of fear was an unspoken element of daily life, one not to be reflected upon; as such thoughts might invariably lead to his own death. There was limited retrospection as to what might happen. These entries were focused only on the present situation.

And this is what intrigued me most as I skimmed the journal. The sense of propinquity that lent an authenticity and a gritty realism to the courageous fight not only for God, King, and country, and for victory, but most immediately, for survival.

# 11

In the months following my arrival at the Middleton Colliery, we moved out of the tenement we shared with Albert. His letters and his share of the rent were no longer important.

Living with Pa now in our own upstairs tenement deprived me of any dreams of faraway lands. Distant and exotic locales from Mum's travel magazines no longer unravelled in the nighttime ramblings of my subconscious.

In my sleeping mind, I crawled through tunnels on my hands and knees with Pa ahead of me. We crept through the darkness, both of us holding Davy Lamps. I was compelled to peer upward but couldn't. Still, my head did not strike the top of the tunnel, and I was able to glance skyward and see an array of stars.

This star field was interrupted by bursts of light illuminating a battlefield that had materialized around us. There were bursts of mortar fire and shots ringing out in the darkness. We had emerged from the trenches and were fighting our way past barbed wire to the German front lines. Then, suddenly, Pa was gone.

That was the moment when I awoke.

I opened my eyes and quickly turned over on the bed to see Pa's waiflike physique. Seeing his outline lying concealed beneath the sheets, I returned to sleep.

When I had experienced this dream before and we were on different shifts, I had turned over to find that the sheets were deflated. No longer able to fall asleep again until he came home, I lay awake, feigning slumber when I finally heard him.

On day shift, after inspection of our shared safety lamp, Pa and I descended in the cage down the shaft to our destination that someone had somehow determined was one hundred and six feet below the surface of the earth. The same as my first day, I removed my shirt as Pa did and crawled after him, carrying my Davy Lamp through narrow tunnels of rock almost too constricted to fit through. Unlike my initiation here though, I knew what to expect. Talking was impossible, the conveyors and ventilation equipment too loud. The days were spent thinking about Pa's wartime experiences; never seeing Violet again; me and Pa no longer moving back to London, but living here together with Mum and Ian; reliving our times spent together as a family at Uncle Devon's farm; and humming hymns and band tunes to pass the hours, which grew increasingly black as the place filled with coal dust.

The rocks scraped along the length of my bare back as we navigated through the tight passageway to our worksite opening, what we called our cabin or station, at the start of our workday. Our tools, pickaxes, and shovels were spread out over the floor, our pet rats Punch and Judy scurrying away as our light entered the space.

After a couple of hours, sweaty and bone-breaking work, the sound of our conveyor suddenly ceased.

This had not happened before.

My ears were ringing in the silence, and there was blackness all around.

"What do we do?" I asked.

"Nothing," Pa's voice came back. "We wait. For now, I'll have my snap before Punch and Judy get it."

I sat down, extracting a hard biscuit from the wrapping and pouring some cold tea into my tin cup.

"I was reading about your war experiences last night," I said.

His voice came back after a moment: "I really don't want to talk about that, not here, not now."

"You woke up one time to a shell burst on top of you, and you dragged your sergeant a mile and a half."

There was some shouting through the tunnels in the distance.

"They were shelling along the road the whole way too," he said. "My sergeant was sent home, and then I was ordered to go through some trenches and over a bridge, in the pouring rain at night, to take a place called Hill 63 near the catacombs. We never reached that hill, and some men died along the way."

"Did you ever think some of those men in the war died for nothing?" I asked.

"Not once. But I will say that my time in the trenches changed me for good."

"How?"

"I became afraid, nervous. Sometimes I still wake in the middle of the night, the same way I did back then, and feel shrapnel raining down on me. Or I hear shells exploding in the distance, or bullets whizzing by at close range. Or hear men screaming. That's something that never leaves you."

"I suppose not."

There was more shouting through the tunnels, the words too distant to be heard.

"I'm not waiting," he said. "We're off."

And then, as Pa began crawling by, I could see his ghostly form with the Davy Lamp high above his head, his attention cast forward and his figure outlined against the backdrop of the blue-black walls. For an instant, I extended my arm out to stop him, but my hand did not reach.

"Let's wait," I said. "It's only been minutes."

"I need some air. I'll give up the coin for this shift."

"I'm staying here. And you should, too. We'll chat about something else."

And then, an instant later, as his silhouetted form began crouching through the tunnel opening, our conveyor suddenly came to life.

The initial rattling might have resembled that of a field gun.

Glass shattered. Darkness. Then, all at once: a flash of intense sunlight; a loud thunderclap; the air was hot; a shower of stones came from above; a shockwave hammered my ears; I was thrown back by an intense wind.

I landed near the conveyor. My back was pinched. My back and leg were ablaze with needles of agony. I would have been forced into the gears of the conveyor if I had been wearing a shirt. There was blood on my side, and the sickening scents of singed hair and burnt flesh filled the air. I was falling into unconsciousness.

The conveyor shut down again, and there was an excruciating silence. Blackness.

Pa was not answering when I called. I repeated his name. Quiet.

I crawled over to find that Pa was not conscious, and the smell of burnt flesh around him was overwhelming.

Unable to revive him, I tried over and over to force air into his lungs. Each time, after pushing on his chest and forcing air through his mouth, he remained stagnant, unmoving.

I shouted through the tunnels, in each direction, without answer.

For what seemed like hours, I shouted, pushed, forced air, and slapped his face to revive him. No response. I needed to get him to the surface. First, I would have to drag him through the tunnel.

Tying our shirts together formed a makeshift stretcher beneath him. The only way to put him in tow. Avoiding the broken glass and the remains of the Davy Lamp, I pulled the shirts along, but they caught on the bottom of the tunnel as we moved. I had to lift him, and then pull, lift and pull seemingly ad infinitum. His bloody legs dragged behind.

After countless hours, we were able to get back to the cage. The men helped me lift him in and we rose up the shaft, back to the sunlight where I saw the extent of the burns over his entire body. His hair was gone. A stretcher was brought out, and he was taken to the doctor.

There was scorched flesh that, I realized later, would permanently scar the left half of my face. Half of my hair was singed off nearly to the scalp. I did not yet realize the extent of my back injury. Yet none of this mattered as, minutes later, the doctor pronounced that while I would survive the accident, my father had not.

Late that evening, as I lay staring at the crooked windowsill, there was a knock on the door downstairs. A shuffling up the stairs was followed by a rap on my door, which echoed through my room.

"What?" I asked, clearing my throat. The door screeched open, and with light from behind, I recognized Albert. The armless half of his body was consumed by shadow, his one arm visible in the faded light trickling in from downstairs.

He set an envelope on the dresser beside the bed and left the room.

I sat up at the side of the bed and took the letter, shaking, opening it slowly. This letter was all that made the nightmare tangible, the only reality to this illusion.

Reading through the contents revealed that the accident had occurred because of a Davy Safety Lamp dropped in the tunnels near a worksite conveyor. An investigation was underway. I would need to submit a written statement. A check for forty pounds was enclosed.

Holding this in my hand, I contemplated what the true monetary worth of a man's life might be; knowing that forty pounds certainly wouldn't cut it.

With the loss of my father, the vision I had of an intact family had vanished. If not for the letter I had sent to Uncle Devon, to be forwarded to Mum, I would not have been able to go home to say her dream had also been destroyed by this new reality.

Albert sat beside me on the train to London, the October afternoon bleak and rainy. We were now financially obligated to share a row house together, until I could find someone else with whom to live. He had insisted on accompanying me to see Mum in London. I had taken a job in the office, informing the pit boss that I would never crawl into those mineshafts again.

Time passed with Albert coughing and repeatedly adjusting his position while he slept upright in his seat, a manila envelope with a letter and the check from the colliery tucked under his arm. I glanced past him out the window, into the bleakness, where I saw only raindrops pounding against the window of the train, endless trees, and a single, solitary orange light in the distance.

Examining the light and then my reflection in the glass, I saw a tired, haggard man with dark eyes, a blackened face, and a scalp resembling blue-black coal veins. Now, more than ever, this man resembled his father in the lines on his face, his dismissive gaze, the scars marring his skin, and his darkened pores. This was a man defeated, beaten by the underground, who ruminated, the same as his father likely had, about how he might be received at his London home. And such thoughts transformed this darkness and these ghostly images into hours of sleep intermixed with periods of tired semi-consciousness.

Avoiding the mud puddles and potholes, I approached the front door of our London home. I disregarded my reflection cast back in the glass of the front door, but not before I became cognisant that I was wearing similar clothes as my father had on his last visit here, and that my hat hung over my face casting a shadow that might cause me to be mistaken for him. My hands were blackened with soot, and Mum's suspicions—if she had, for some reason, not received my letter sent by Devon from Northaw—would soon be confirmed.

And just as Pa had, we appeared without any forewarning at all.

Albert knocked once, then twice, waiting, and then tapping again. I pulled my cap down and turned the left side of my face away from the door, so my facial scars might blend in with the shadows. There was the shuffling of feet before the door slowly creaked open. Mum appeared in the opening, closing the top of her nightgown upon seeing Albert. Ian peered out from the hallway behind her. The place was cold, empty, and devoid of furniture except for a single chair. There was an odd silence: no cuckoo clock, no wireless.

"Who's there?" our neighbour Mrs. Milne asked, speaking loudly. "Maybe I should be getting home."

"Greetings, Doreen," Albert said quietly, putting his hand on her shoulder. The empty flap of his coat fluttered in the cold breeze. The envelope he had been holding under his arm dropped to the floor and I quickly retrieved the package, keeping the right side of my face toward her.

Mum cleared a couple of pairs of raggedy shoes scattered on the floor in the entranceway. But Ian, sickly and pale, still stood in our path and stared at the empty flap where Albert's arm once was.

"Mum, what happened to his arm?" Ian asked. Then, receiving no response, he turned to Albert. "Uncle Albert, what happened to your arm?"

"He's not your uncle," I said. "And it was crushed in an accident underground."

Albert handed Mum a bag of coal and a newspaper he had brought. Ian grabbed this copy of the Gloucestershire Echo, placing the pages under his arm as Mum took the bag.

Mrs. Milne pushed her way through, sauntering leisurely over to close the door.

We entered the room and removed our coats and shoes. I kept my hat on.

"What happened to you?" Ian asked, observing the left side of my face. "Your face is scratched up. Looks awful."

"I'll share with you later," I said quietly. "Now hush up."

Albert stood before the iron-hooded fireplace, which was now full of soot, the blue and white decorative tiles covered in a thin layer of the same dust. I remained standing between Mum and Mrs. Milne, pulling my hat down to show them my right profile.

"I've yet to start this evening's fire," Mum explained as we stared at the bricks. There were no indications that a fire had been started recently.

"Well," Albert said, "I can take care of that."

He retrieved the coal from Mum, and returned to sweep the fireplace.

Mum began sewing some black curtains, sitting at the edge of her wooden chair in the drawing room. There were no curtains on the windows, the light of the setting sun filtering into the dusty room, and the drapes she was sewing would not fit the opening. She was sewing these for mortgage funds, I found out later.

Ian's gaze was transfixed on my face until I raised my eyebrows at him. He crouched down, cross-legged, onto the cool linoleum floor, and began leafing through the Gloucestershire Echo. I sat down beside him. Mrs. Milne's voice chattered to an uneven rhythm. She stopped, coughed, and continued:

"All 'cause of my cold and drafty house," she said, "and my husband's smoking which never ceases—both are giving me whooping cough and both will be the death of me."

In the morphing light from the windows, penetrating the shadows, Mum stopped sewing, and Ian surveyed the room from behind his newspaper. Mum continued again, the curtains suddenly alive, then limp, then animate again as Mrs. Milne continued expounding criticisms of her husband.

"If you're not keen on him," I said, "you should toss him to the street."

She glared at me as I continued: "But then you could only grumble about his absence."

"Some mouth you have," Mrs. Milne said. "My husband's a louse, yet he's there. Where's your father now?"

"Nicholas," Albert said, "you and your brother can go in the scullery. And I need that envelope."

I stood there for a moment, unmoving, until Albert finally grabbed the envelope and pushed me into the kitchen with my brother, who was fiercely clutching his newspaper.

As we went out, Ian pulled me back.

"Who's that?" he asked, pointing at the newspaper. There was a photograph of a man being led away by two Bobbies on the beat in tall hats, their gloves matching the dark coat of their prisoner.

I shrugged. "I dunno."

Using a match from one of the unassembled matchbooks piled high on the kitchen table, I briefly illuminated a gas lamp to cast an eerie glow on the clothes dryer. The lamp extinguished, and we were in shadows again.

"Can't use those matches," he said. "Not allowed. And there's not much oil left."

I looked through the cupboards. No food except for a can of ham and some dried beans.

Glancing at the newspaper, I moved with Ian over to the window. Quickly skipping through the caption and the title of the article, I read through the news item while Ian stared at my face.

"That man dropped a loaded pistol at the King's feet," I said. "Says he's innocent."

Ian was silent for a moment before responding.

"Innocent?" he asked. "How's that?"

"That's what he says. But he should be punished like he shot the King."

"But somebody else might'a dropped the pistol," he replied, pointing to the group of male onlookers in the background wearing suits and dark hats, as women in long dresses glanced with intense interest at the man being led away.

"The world's full of liars. And liars are sometimes people who don't challenge a lie, like those in the background who may've seen something. Those people have the makings of cowards... But sometimes, I suppose, cowards do things with good intentions... anyway, somebody's got to be punished."

"I'm not sure what you're on about."

"I'm not either. Maybe, one day, we'll both understand."

Ian crouched down a moment later to listen at the keyhole. "Mum's crying in there," he said. "What's wrong?"

As I walked out through the door, Ian was close behind. Mum sat in the chair rubbing her eyes while Albert, stooped over the fireplace, was busy cleaning with a broom again. I stopped, and Ian bumped into me. Mrs. Milne was no longer here.

"What happened to her?" Ian asked, turning toward me. "What about your face?"

I didn't answer right away as Albert swept grey dust into a pile.

"Pa's never coming home," I said quietly. "There was an explosion. For me, it wasn't fatal. For him, it was."

"Explosion? What's *fatal?*"

"Means he's not coming home."

After escorting my brother upstairs to sleep, I resolved to tell Mum that I was sorry for having misled her. I didn't know if she had received my letter, and I was eager to explain how I had tried to get Pa back to London. There was so much I hadn't told her.

Descending the stairs, I saw Albert placing some sticks and coal in the fireplace as Mum watched from her chair.

"I wish we didn't lie to you," I said, approaching her. "I tried to get Pa home. Not as I should have, but I tried."

Her face was red, her eyes tired.

"Let me look at you. Albert said you were in the mines when it happened? Your face…and you're walking with a limp."

"My back's a mess. The Doc said it may never heal."

"Thank God you were spared."

She ran her hands along my scars, lifted my hat, and then set it back in place.

"Why not say where you were?" she asked.

"I should've," I replied.

She shook her head and continued. "Ian said you sent him to the post office to get letters, once a week? I suppose you intended us to take separate trips, without me knowing that Ian was doing so?"

"Yes," I said. "But I only wanted to help you with your errands. I forgot to tell you. Handing my bicycle, old Betsy, over to Ian, having him go, it could've made him healthy again."

"But remember," she continued, her voice stern. "You're being truthful now."

Albert, piling kindling on the newly-cleaned fireplace, seemed oblivious to our conversation.

"Albert was sending you awful letters, all the time," I said quietly. "Telling about the mines, the fatalities, the conditions of—"

Albert interrupted on his way to the basement, stopping in the doorway with a shovel. He turned to address me.

"That's cause your Ma told me to," he said.

"But there was only a few letters over the years," she replied.

He continued into the darkness, shaking his head.

"Every month I wrote," he said loudly. "Sometimes more. Now I know why I got nothin' in return."

He emerged with a shovel of coal, depositing the contents into the fireplace and heading back toward the crawlspace in the basement again.

"Every month," Albert repeated as he descended the stairs, adding: "At least. Not much coal down here. You need some more, with this cold weather."

A moment later, I continued: "Uncle Devon, did he send you a letter, from me, posted from Northaw? I wrote I was working the coal mines, and not at Devon's farm like we said. I was there to convince Pa to come home to London. I thought you could help us find work here. Then, I got the idea to no longer send money home, to get you and Ian to move there."

"So, this is your scheming too," Mum said, looking around at the empty room. "I had to sell all our stuff. I took on extra jobs to pay the mortgage. I got your letter, sure. I was not the only one you were hoodwinking."

"I only wanted us all together," I replied.

She gazed at the fireplace as Albert deposited another shovel of black rocks onto the pile.

"I don't see why you kept Albert's letters from me," she said. "I don't need such protection."

She peered into my eyes and continued.

"Don't abandon your brother and me like your father did," she said. "Please."

She glanced away as Albert dropped the shovel. I took her hand in mine.

"We'll all be together soon," I said. "For now, I'm starting in the offices. No more work in the mines."

Albert struck a match and set the kindling alight. Mum had always been overtly sore at Pa for living away from us. But as Albert watched the fire he had built, the flames quickly consuming the sticks and licking at the coal, I stood beside him to recall Pa's final visit home and produce some memory we could all retain. Nothing immediately came to mind.

I walked upstairs and crawled into bed beside Ian. For a long time afterward, there was silence and muffled conversation downstairs. I fell into sleep thinking more about Pa's final visit home, realizing that in taking me to the Olympia rally, he had come home to try to make his eldest son a man.

Mum was shouting. Running to see who was downstairs, anticipating in my drowsed state that I might see my father, I instead saw Albert standing too close to Mum, his arm wrapped tightly around her. Despite her protests, and the writhing and shouting that should have kept him away, he would not let go. She pushed him away, slapping him across the face. He advanced toward her again. As I reached the base of the stairs, he moved in to kiss her, and she whacked him again.

Albert, startled, pushed me away, stumbling backwards in the process. He smelled rank, boozy.

"What's your game?" he asked, recovering his balance.

"I should'a done this quite a while ago," I said.

I grasped tightly onto Albert's arm, led him toward the front door, and forced him outside as he protested wildly.

Returning by myself a moment later, I secured and locked the door.

Now that Albert and I were living together again, I wondered what might happen because of this confrontation—whether my clothes and books would be out in the street upon my return to South Leeds. They certainly would be, and I wanted to beat it back there with my key, on the next train, to toss his belongings outside before he had the chance to touch mine.

Mum sobbed as I stood embracing her. She wasn't crying because of her husband's death. She had grieved for him over the years in continual, recurrent anguish reiterated with each visit that might have been his last.

She was instead crying to mourn the loss of her eldest son, who would have to return to the mines again to support the family.

Another soldier returned to the front.

# <u>12</u>

In the early morning, I removed Ian's blanket to flood his face with white light, the sunlight casting shadows on his shape. The smell of sweat, and urine from the bedpan, was strong.

"Tomorrow, I'm off to South Leeds," I said. "But today we're headed out."

He rolled over, squinted, and shielded his face from the sun.

"Where? Why you shouting?" he asked. "Where's Mum?"

"I'm not shouting. And get up. We're off."

Forcing the window open, I emptied the contents of the bedpan onto the side of the house.

"I can't go," he said. "I'm not well. Where's Mum?"

I set the pan back in place and closed the window.

"Mum!" he shouted down the stairs. "Mum!"

There was no reply. Ian repeated his plea a minute later. The house was quiet. No ticking clock in the hallway, as though I had finally tossed the infernal contraption through the window with a smile, to watch as the device that kept me up so many nights with incessant clicking and constant eruptions of song smashed apart on the ground.

"Where's Mum?" he asked.

"At the market. I gave her coin for some grub."

I tossed Ian's stinking blanket to the floor. His pallor was accentuated by the stark sunlight. For a moment, his foot seemed to be tinged with green, the same as the man my father had watched die in the war. But this hue was only a trick of the light from a reflection off the emerald-coloured dresser.

"We're off," I repeated, lifting him up slightly by the arm and tightening my grip.

He began to rise slowly, sitting up for a moment before flopping back down onto the bed like a sturgeon. Holding on to his arm again, helping him up, I took him by his scaly fins and led him out. The stairs squealed and squeaked with our weight as I descended with my giant catch.

"Where to?" he asked.

"You'll see."

As I limped alongside Ian down Great Russell Street, he motioned me toward an area at the edge of the sidewalk, where we sat down on a wooden bench.

"I'm tired," he said, squinting. "This sun's too bright. I want my bed."

"I know, separation's tough," I said. "You'll be together soon. Now, come on."

We rose after a time and walked through the heavy iron gates, past the elderly guard hidden by his newspaper, to the main entrance of the British Museum. I bought two tickets, and we walked in.

People inside the museum stared at Ian, this sickly ghost walking with his escort through the portico, down the hall to the left past the library, and over to the section on trench warfare. We immediately walked past the artefacts and weaponry to the area with the newspaper articles, war journals and letters from the Great War encased in glass.

"Why you stringing me along?" he asked, slumping down as if ready to fall to the floor.

"I left stuff here, a while ago, for safekeeping."

"In a museum?"

After pointing to one of the letters Pa wrote during the war, I directed Ian to a picture of our father in his army uniform that was hanging on the wall.

"Who's that?" Ian asked.

"Corporal W.L. Dixon," I replied. "Wilfrid Lionel Dixon. Back when he was a Private."

"Da."

Ian moved in to scrutinize the monochrome image more closely now.

"What's this doing here?" he asked. "You sure it's him?"

"Of course. Look at the hair, and his eyes. Look at his chin. It's him."

We examined the photograph closely. Our father's cheerless expression in front of this unknown house seemed quixotic now, and in his still gaze there was the realization that he did not yet know anything of life. He seemed somehow peaceful in his naiveté, the cigarette dangling from his right hand resembling a tiny Davy Lamp.

I walked over to the glass case where the letters and war journals were stored, directing Ian over.

"What's this?" he asked, pointing into the case.

"A short letter about the Battle of Givenchy."

*We had the German trench mined, and at 6 o'clock it was blown up. A lot of dirt came back and hurt our fellows, but over into the German trench we went. There were Saxons holding them. They slung down their arms and said, "you Canadians, we Saxons, we no fight." Our Captain gave the order to take them prisoner, but when he and a few men went to take a support trench, they fought back, and our boys had to bayonet nearly all of them. We should have had between three and four hundred prisoners, but we only took three prisoners for information.*

*The 12th Division made an attack on our left, but they failed, and the Germans started to close in on each side of us. The 3rd Battalion wouldn't help us, so we had to retire. Well, I guess that's all I can recall about it for now.*

"And this one," I said, turning to Ian and pointing the way, "is about a pass that Pa was waiting for. An attempt to take a much needed vacation from the fighting."

*I am trying to get some souvenirs to send home when I go to England on a pass. The last pass I got was no good.*

*My last pass was supposed to start the 23rd of the month. I walked about three miles to one station to get the train. When I got there, the police told me the line was broken. So, I walked to another station. Another six miles. Fritz was shelling it, so I had to move on to the next one four miles away. Waiting there a few hours, Fritz started to shell it with long range guns, so I walked to the next one four miles away. I was just in time to catch the train. Then, I went to the place where I was supposed to catch the boat.*

*We had to stay there overnight, and Fritz came over in aeroplanes and bombed us. We were turned back as Fritz started to make his drive coming back. As we were going along, our train was bombed, and I happened to be in one of the cars that was smashed. But I made a jump and got away with a couple of scratches.*

*That night, Fritz came over in aeroplanes and started bombing the train. The bombing continued for four hours. The train was never hit, but the bombs came so close that there was no fun in it at all. It sure was some trip. We all took it pretty good, but I couldn't help being a little sore about not getting my pass. I hope to get another before long.*

Ian appeared confused.

"I didn't know about any of this," he said.

"I'll give you some of his letters to read," I replied. "We have to remember our pa this way. As a man who fought four years in the trenches and got three war medals. A man who did the best for his country, same as he did for us."

We perused his enlistment papers, signed at age 19 years and one month at Valcartier, Quebec at around the same time the picture was taken. We next examined Pa's three war medals and the souvenirs he had mailed home.

"The letters here," I explained, "they're Pa's written passage into quick maturity. A boy's growth into hardship and manhood."

We scrutinized the picture of our smiling father in his uniform for a long time before starting home. There was a perplexed and rejuvenated grin on Ian's face.

# 13

I moved in with another office worker, Robert, who spent loads of time reading in his room. Shuffling paperwork every day in the offices at South Leeds, my fellow workers treated me with both trepidation and respect, perhaps honouring Pa's memory by showing consideration for his son. I awaited any miners who might accuse Pa of wilful suicide or blatant clumsiness, ready to teach them a lesson with the blunt edge of my fist; none came.

News of a threatened coal strike arrived during a shift of seasons. Mum began to rearrange the bedroom for me after I arrived home, moving some of Ian's comic books and games out. She used the money I gave her for a new wireless, curtains, coal for the fireplace, a new couch, and a stocked pantry. The strike was subsequently averted. Big business had prevented the labour dispute by agreeing to pay more for their coal, providing part of the increases went to the miners.

Our jobs, and my separation from Mum and Ian, were secured.

I travelled to London whenever finances allowed, and in the summers we all travelled together to Uncle Devon's home in the country. Ian began slowly recovering from his illness, breathing better in the country air.

We began spending more time than ever as a family, picnicking and eating cherries from the orchard, fishing at the lake, going to movies at the cinema in town, and taking the local train from Cuffley Station to shop at the market. The time I had spent there with Pa was always on my mind as part of the pleasure in being there. He was there with us all the time, his presence now only a simple, quiet solace.

We left the movie house in Northaw one rainy afternoon, my back aching.

"This is the joy we long for, what's yet to come?" I asked. "Not that *English Harvest* movie we just saw—that was dreadful. I meant all of us together. Even you, Uncle Devon."

"Even me?" Devon said.

"Even you," I replied. "All of us."

"I thought *English Harvest* was well done," Devon said. "And you need to get away from South Leeds, if what they say about another war is true."

"I agree," Mum said. "On both counts."

"But you can't make lives of country folk interesting enough for a movie," Ian interjected.

"Especially not if they're showing long scenes of men drinking water, horse-drawn wagons ploughing fields, and women in gardens working to music," I added. "I thought none of it would end."

Mum smiled.

"I heard if there's another war," I continued, straightening my back, "I won't be conscripted if I'm working the mines. If I'm supporting the family, they can't force me to go."

"Even if that were true, which I suspect it isn't," Devon said, "they may even conscript men to work in the mines. Not in the offices where you are now, but in the pit. Coal is a valuable commodity in wartime."

"I hadn't thought of that," I said. "So, I could be forced down in the pit again?"

"You may not have thought of moving to Northaw either," Devon said as we entered the train station. "The lot of you. There's not much to be made in farming here, but my house could be made suitable. Nicholas, you can take some time to save money before you leave your job. We'll need funds for livestock and a new tractor. In wartime or times of peace, the best plan is to live in the countryside."

"I hadn't thought of that, either," I said.

At Cuffley Station, we overheard a man and woman talking. They were dishevelled, ragged farm workers, and their accents and expressions revealed they were from this area.

"Those rallies in London are same as what's happenin' in Germany and Italy," the man said. "In Spain, Germany is fighting for the fascists, Russia for the communists."

"Another great war won't happen," the woman said, adding: "I will bet our farm, and all its livestock and crops."

"I'll take you up on that," Devon said. The woman glared at him.

"How do you know about another war?" I asked, turning toward Devon.

"Have you seen the rallies?" he asked.

"I've been to them. So, yes."

"Well, you should know then. That tells the story. Soon, we'll all be involved."

The couple stared at us, the woman simply grimacing as they walked away.

In October of 1936, when I was back in London, I forced Ian to take a long walk with me. We stumbled upon a rally in Hyde Park where, it was announced, one hundred thousand people had gathered to hear of their "destiny of greatness." They professed this destiny had also brought the leaders of the newly re-named "British Union of Fascists and National Socialists" to the East End, proclaiming through loudspeakers about worthless elected officials, and the power of finance to govern given cheap labour abroad:

*"...the British, who for one-thousand years have never been conquered by the foe without, have been subdued by the foe within. To our brother Britains we say: unite. Britain united is invincible and irresistible. And together we will build the mightiest civilization mankind has known. A new world awaits: the united will of Britain reborn. Britain's advance in British Union."*[4]

We watched as a troupe of men, Blackshirts dressed in the colour of midnight with lightning emblems on their sleeves, marched into the crowd and stopped to make a speech. One of the men stepped up on a soap box and read from a pamphlet we were handed:

"*Not so long ago East London was the home of British stock. The cabinet maker, polisher and tailor were Englishmen. Today the Englishman in East London is the slave of the Jewish master.*"5

As we made our way home, a crowd turned out against the Blackshirts, barring their path and ours with furniture and using stones as weapons. We were blocked by a lorry filled with bricks and turned on its side on Cable Street. We wouldn't make it out of here without being hurt.

Bobbies in uniform and Blackshirts littered the streets along with the enormous opposition. The Bobbies had clubs and knives, and the opposition hurled rocks at a group of us, as though we were part of the gang of ragtag Blackshirts responsible for this mess.

"Here," I said, taking Ian's arm and ducking down a familiar alleyway as we were pelted from all directions. "This way."

Ian and I read in the Gloucestershire Echo, the next day, after we had cleansed each other's wounds in the scullery, that the resistance had prevailed. The leaders of the Blackshirt movement, including the man Pa and I had seen speak at the Olympia rally, were imprisoned.

A short time later in our row house in South Leeds, over a breakfast of black tea, marmalade and toast with my new chum Robert, I read in the Gloucestershire Echo about changes on the throne that had seen King Edward abdicate in favour of the Duke of York, within three days.

"King Edward loves that divorced American woman more than he loves his country," I said as I buttered my toast.

"Quite so," Robert said, hovering over the table. "The Coronation of his brother, King George VI, will be the beginning of a new era of peace in this country. War has been averted, you'll see."

"I read that the rallies in London have ended. I'll need to see for myself when I go. Like my Pa said, I'll go to London and look that burg over. Mum will know that our new future will mean living in Northaw with Uncle Devon."

"She'll be amenable to that, I'm sure," Robert said, pouring hot water into the teapot.

"Then you'll have to enjoy working through the payroll cheques and electrical bills at the mines without me."

"There's certainly no enjoyment in that."

So, I wrote from South Leeds to say that I would come to London to attend the Coronation Procession due to take place May 12, 1937, starting and ending at Buckingham Palace.

Mum, Ian, and I watched from Hyde Park Corner on a drizzly day with a slight wind blowing periodically at erected British flags. The procession was to go from The Mall, to Whitehall and to Westminster Abbey; north paralleling the River Thames, to Northumberland, past Trafalgar Square, to St. James, and to Piccadilly; north on Regent street, west on Oxford, south on East Carriage. The exquisite carriage that was pictured in the newspaper recently, along with the collection of horses and guards, all in full regalia, was heading towards Hyde Park Corner when I saw her: a woman I recognized in the crowd across the street. A woman I could not forget.

Wearing a gold dress and a sparkling hat that resembled a large bow sitting on her head, she held the hand of a tiny girl in a faded dress. A man with a beard and a pushed-in bowler hat stood close beside them. The woman, who had played Violet at the Duke and Duchess Theatre so many years before, perused the crowd eagerly.

Boyhood reminiscences began returning to my mind. She had never been more beautiful. The man beside her was Lieutenant Dick Campbell. Violet had forsaken both Captain Roddy Dunton to whom she was engaged, and me who was once enamoured with her, in favour of the fake Lieutenant now standing at her side. The play had ended as these two main players had wanted. And I had never been able to change that outcome, until now.

The imitation Lieutenant seemed to be staring back in my direction, but my attention was focused on her as she glanced at the cheering crowds. I could see no one else apart from her. The Lieutenant at her side, the little girl, the crowd, and the advancing procession all seemed to evaporate into some distant and faded reality.

Our last encounter, years ago, suddenly came to my mind. She had been kind, stating that I was sweet and quite handsome, and that I could see her at any time; even outside the play. If given the chance, I could have expounded my devotion to her. Life with Violet in the mines would have been wrong; being together in Northaw could be a dream.

I had seen more of marital love now, having observed the other miners blackened with soot, and their wives constantly scrubbing and bathing and feeding them every night, the same as Mum had done to Pa in the brief time we were all living together in South Leeds. Watching the miner's wives raising their children in an unsuitable habitat and remaining loyal to this cause year after year brought me to the realization that this sort of sacrificial love was a rare phenomenon, to be cherished if found, and a marvel. This, I would explain to Violet. We could have this sort of love, only in an ideal place. Details of my plans to move to Devon's farm, and for her to accompany me, would follow.

Mum grabbed hold of my arm as I started to leave. Violet remained in place as the noise of the marching band approached, and I broke free. I would have to navigate through the crowd on this side of the street, then cross over the wooden barrier, and traverse the busy street to get to her.

As I began meandering through the crowd, the procession close by now, I contemplated how this encounter would be different than the last. I would begin by telling her of all the silly dreams I had had about her when I was a boy. The play she was in wasn't real, and I had now put aside such foolish and childish notions as I had been taught to do through the verse in First Corinthians that Mum had made me memorize in contemplating God's love.

*At present*, I would add, *childish fantasies have given way to more of an acknowledgement of the harshness of life and death than I have ever known, and an appreciation of passionate devotion leading to love; my time in the mines had had that effect upon me.*

I ran over, knocking the wooden barricade down and plunging myself into the crowd at the other end of the street before the barrier was erected again and the soldiers marched seamlessly past.

I had been shoved around, this way and that, and surveying the crowd revealed that Violet was gone. The crowd had moved in to fill the void as though she had never existed; as if the colourful streamers and British flags, the cheering and the throngs of people had absorbed her.

After an array of Royal Guards mounted atop white horses passed by, followed by marching army and navy personnel, I disappeared into the horde of spectators and searched for her in vain. There was rapturous applause as an elaborate carriage appeared, propelled forward by a team of black horses. Three conductors with triangular hats were on board, one seated at the front and two standing at the rear. The carriage was adorned with life-sized, golden angels and ornate gold ivy leaf that formed the sides and the roof. Shortly after the vehicle had passed, the last of the soldiers marched by and the crowd began to disperse. I resumed my search, but to no avail.

Violet was gone.

When I arrived home after hours of wandering the streets aimlessly, I explained to Mum that I had seen Violet at the procession, a woman I knew from productions at the Duke and Duchess Theatre. I described how I had snuck out at nights to see her. I told Mum of my vision for a new future in Northaw with Uncle Devon after I saved some coin, one in which she and Ian would move out to be with us. Along with the money from selling our London home, we would be able to start again, together, as a family; perhaps with our own farmhouse near Devon's.

Mum smiled for the first time in recent memory, before kissing me on the head.

"An unreciprocated love," she said, her smile persistent, "and this woman now a wife and mother perhaps, but still, your first love."

"I can't think of her with anyone else," I said. "And what of Northaw?"

Her smile turned sombre.

"I'm not interested in your Uncle Devon's hobby farm," she said. "I believe he's not so keen about it, either. Your uncle fancied that we should move there, not me."

"That farm'll bring us together."

"Nothing doing."

The following day I pedalled my old Betsy, left out to rust in the rain and almost dead, over to the Duke and Duchess Theatre. The lights were out. A series of long planks were stretched across the entryway, secured on each side by nails set haphazardly in place to fasten them against the brick wall. The same sign I had seen so long ago was still here, indicating that the basement had flooded, and the date of the next showing was yet to be determined.

As I ate boiled potatoes and charred beef later that day with Mum and Ian, a sputtering candle between us, a news report on the radio questioned German military might, considering the German airship called the Hindenburg that had burst into flames over Lakehurst, New Jersey in America the previous week.

"A terrible shame," Mum said, "but a sign of the peace to come."

I relived the Coronation Procession of the Duke-turned-King George VI in exacting detail including the girl and the bearded man with the pushed-in hat, Violet's downcast eyes and the apparent sadness I now perceived in her, all reproduced multiple times in my dreams.

# <u>14</u>

Prime Minister Neville Chamberlain's September 3, 1939 declaration by radio was replayed, over and over, in and around the mines:

*"This morning the British Ambassador in Berlin handed the German Government a final note stating that, unless we hear from them by 11 o'clock that they were prepared at once to withdraw their troops from Poland, a state of war would exist between us. I have to tell you now that no such undertaking has been received, and that consequently this country is at war with Germany."*[6]

I immediately left a note on my boss's desk, departed the office, packed my belongings, and left South Leeds. If what Devon said was true, if I would be forced to descend into the pit every day for the war effort, and if Pa was wrong and I could still be conscripted regardless, better to depart that infernal place in favour of the beauty of Northaw.

Moving in with my Uncle Devon, I did little to help on his farm. The crops had dwindled down to a measly patch in the yard, and there were only a handful of chickens and pigs to feed. My time was spent working on other farms, for more industrious farmers.

I sent a wire for Mum and Ian to join us, Mum replying with the simple phrase: *"Nothing doing. Come home."*

Months turned into a year and London city officials began warning of impending German bombings and gas raids. There were anti-air raid exercises in daylight and darkness. "Black out" tests were held so people of the city could grow accustomed to extinguishing lamps at night to highlight nothing for enemy planes above. Provisions for firefighting were accumulated and stocked, and the main streets were lined with hoses and masks. Air raid wardens, those who would assist citizens in the event of bombings, were recruited and trained. Trenches, lined with sandbags, were dug around Hyde Park. The production of twenty-six million gas masks was underway.

We listened to such news over the wireless as we sat down to yet another dinner of chicken scraps and half-rotted potatoes, a regular staple, but preferable to the memory of South Leeds dinners of watery soup and stale bread with black tea.

"I'm leaving on the train tomorrow to fetch Mum and Ian," I said, separating the thin chicken meat from the bones. "I'll have to sell our home there."

"No one's buying houses in London, not now," Devon replied, stabbing at pieces of potato to collect them with his fork. "I can send them another wire to come here."

"The wires do no good. I want to fetch them myself."

"Why? This farm is being overrun by children evacuated from London on the train, every day."

"You want me to stay here and help shoo them away?" I said, taking a drink of water. "Don't think of them."

He pulled back the curtains. There were four boys outside, trampling through the garden. Another group of boys resembling Glen, Boris, and Charles lingered in the distance, smoking.

"Hard to ignore that," Devon said.

"Keep the curtains closed and you'll be fine."

As the curtains fell back into place, the wireless provided warnings to all those living in London. *Stay indoors. Always know where the nearest shelters are. Bomb shelter inspections are underway, and procedural reviews to evacuate the city centre have begun. The German Luftwaffe might fall on the city any day, don't let it fall on you…*

I left the following afternoon on the first train from Cuffley Station to London, carrying the empty, bulky, green suitcase. My city had been transformed. As reported, the main streets were filled with hoses, masks, and working men. The men dug trenches and piled sandbags. Underground shelters were being reinforced. Black curtains lined the windows.

"I'm here to take you and Ian to Northaw, Mum," I said as she opened the door.

"We've already begun collecting our things," she said, taking my hat and the suitcase and inviting me in. "You can help."

We listened to the wireless as I folded Mum's dresses and stacked them in the open suitcase on the floor. German destruction of civilian targets in London had led to the British bombing of non-military targets in Berlin. A bombing retaliation against London was not only possible, but probable. City officials had begun evacuating children to the countryside as Devon and I knew well, while parents remained behind to work for the war effort.

Hundreds of German and Italian bombers, dotting the air like a swarm of flies, cast an eerie shadow over the dusk of the city and specked the darkening landscape of the sky. Tons of incendiary bombs, high explosives, and parachute mines fell like rain. The deafening noise of plane engines, explosions, anti-aircraft guns, and alarms engulfed the air; 'moaning minnies', sirens that would become commonplace, wailed in the background.

The city was in a blackout, and we ran down the street, crowded now, Ian clutching the family cat Minnaloushe tightly to his chest as Mum pulled him along. I scurried alongside with the green suitcase, and we ran through the busy, darkened streets toward the underground, our safe haven, while searchlights feverishly probed the skies for movement. There would be no trains for us tonight.

In my father's war journal, he described Zeppelins over the city, and how the people were as nervous as kids. Now, fears had shifted to a sky littered with aeroplanes. A row of grey barrage balloons above was forcing German planes higher, amidst ricocheting machine gun and anti-aircraft fire. There was overwhelming panic in the streets.

A wireless radio report echoed from a nearby house, the reporter stating that because of the blackout, German bombers would be forced to rely on the moonlight covering the Thames, the fires blazing below, and the light of the incendiaries to show them where to drop explosives.

We ran through flocks of people gathered around the entrance to the Tilbury stop of the underground subway system. Air raid wardens stood outside the entrance, directing us down to an area just beneath Commercial Road and Cable Street.

A putrid array of human smells greeted us, accompanied by an assemblage of shadowy figures standing, sitting, sleeping, or squatting and choking the place. A pleasant welcome indeed. Hundreds had taken refuge here, a comfortable solace amidst friends, family, and strangers of common circumstance.

We huddled together into a space near the wall and found ourselves listening to the rumblings above as we soon fell nervously into exhausted sleep, Minnaloushe pacing around our collective feet before finally settling down on top of Ian.

The next morning, we emerged into the daylight to wander through smoking streets. This was a city we no longer recognized because of buildings that had disappeared. Broken glass crunched underfoot. The scent of dirt and burnt wood, dust, and brick powder permeated the air. There was the occasional odour of raw explosives accompanied by the sight of fragmented bomb casings, as well as unexploded bombs and debris; there was the overpowering stink of sewage; the noxious scent of domestic gas; and the only pleasing aroma, one of sap from trees that had been cut in half by the shelling. Some houses also seemed to have been sliced in half, the rooms still intact as though a doll's house was on display.

Dozens of dwellings had crumpled to the ground.

When we arrived back at the doorstep of our house at 21 Grove Street, we stood there for a long time, staring into the pile of bricks, dust, and rubble, knowing what was once there but attempting to contemplate what was now here before us.

The home for which my father and I had worked for so long had been suddenly and violently obliterated.

Even though I had read of such destruction in my father's war journal, it never seemed real—just words on a page—until now. With this mess before me, I wondered why my father's writings always seemed so calm and free of dread. And why the terror and anger that certainly must have taken hold of him never came through in the text.

All I knew now was that we had to get away from here.

We went to the local train station to discover that the northbound train to Cuffley Station was no longer running. A conductor said that several locations along the main line had been bombed, and no service would be offered until repairs were made. We sent a telegram to Uncle Devon letting him know about the house, that we were staying in the Tilbury station underground, and that we would be in Northaw as soon as we could. We returned every day to check the progress of the increasing number of railway line repairs, surveying the disintegrating city as we did. Our nights passed immersed in the delightfully potent stench of faeces, surrounded by the faces of strangers trying to sleep despite the rumbling of bomb blasts on the streets above.

As I lay awoke one evening listening to the explosions, I was preoccupied with thoughts of my father's meaningless death. The managers and owners of the mine had determined that 40 pounds constituted the worth of a man. I had escaped with a disfigured face and a hobble in my step. I envisioned Mum holding the check in her hands, and Albert attempting to hug her, wondering how long we would be here in this place ruminating about such repugnant reminiscences.

Families huddled together all around me, sleeping or chatting to protect possessions and food from pickpockets and the eyes of rats that glinted back from the darkness.

Once we could get away, our family would finally be together in Northaw, with Uncle Devon as a surrogate father, and for reasons that no one would have wanted to contemplate. Glaring back at those tiny eyes, I fell asleep.

# 15

*I hadn't slept very much for two days, and so I had fallen asleep without thinking. Just as I began to sleep, after what might have been an hour, there was a loud bang and a shell burst right over top of me. It was no good way to wake up; I'll tell you that...*

A thunderclap came, shaking the ground above, arousing me from slumber. Along with the blast came a gaunt man approaching me who stared back with a face reminiscent of my father's. He was calling Mum's name. Unshaven and dirty, his clothes were dishevelled.

Uncle Devon greeted me, smiling briefly before suggesting that I not awaken Mum and Ian who were still somehow sleeping on the floor.

"I got your Ma's telegram saying where you were," he said. "Cable Street's out. Hit tonight. Stepney's been hit, too." His voice echoed throughout the cavern, and, when he stopped, someone coughed. Others could be heard faintly whispering.

"There's pamphlets going around," I said quietly. "Talk about what's been bombed and it causes nothing but panic, and everybody's terrified enough...if you start telling people that they have nowhere to live but here in the underground, well—"

"You know my old lorry that was in the barn? It's dead now, but it got me five miles north of here, to a crater where the road was. I walked by the train station. Northbound trains are running."

"We've been waiting for a train to Cuffley Station."

"You'll be waiting quite some time, by my guess."

Devon beckoned me to follow him. Walking away from Mum and Ian, we shuffled over to a lit area near the edge of the platform. The smell of faeces and urine wafted up from below.

"France, Norway and Denmark have surrendered," he said, coughing. "German troops are moving in on our Channel Islands."

"We have to get back to Northaw."

"To blazes with Northaw. You're all coming to Canada with me."

"Canada? What about your farm?"

"Your great-grandmother, she lives in a small town in Ontario. Your father grew up there, you know."

"I know, but we're not going, not now."

I moved away from the platform's edge.

"Look at this place," he said, following me. "You want to stay here? The trains heading south are running, probably not for long. A ship is leaving out of Portsmouth tomorrow."

"We can get back to Northaw easier than hopping across the sea."

"There are a dozen children living on our farm. And you've seen the streets. The Germans are coming. Soon they'll be in our Channel Islands, then on to the coast, then inland. Then, they'll chase us out of sap. You heard what they did in France, Norway, and Denmark. Blitzkrieg, they call it. Lightning war. Attacking by ground, and from the air, at the same time."

"You're going all to pieces."

"It's already started, and I'm not waiting around to see it finished. The same as your Mum kept you and your brother away from the mines for so long to protect you, she'll want to keep you away from England for the same reason."

Another blast shook the ceiling above. Devon led us back to Mum and Ian, who were still curled up on the floor. Mum looked up, and then rose to stand beside us.

"Devon," she said, smiling as she embraced him.

"I'm going away to my Gram's home," he said. "I want you, Nicholas, and Ian to come."

"To Canada?"

"Yes. She's alone, now that Grampa's gone. She's not faring well. It's a good time to leave. Good for everyone. I brought some money for our passage."

"It's a fine idea," she said, as though trying to convince herself. "We'll leave as soon as we can. But what of your farm?"

"It's not safe there, or anywhere here."

"And yet children are being evacuated there," I said. "Some kids are looking after the place now."

We huddled together on the floor to sleep, the family cat frantically poking along the edge of the platform for mice. Our only possession, the small pile of bills for passage to Canada, which Devon failed to mention was gathered through my years of work at the mines, was guarded by everyone squeezing in together.

Early the next morning, I went alone to the British Museum before anyone was awake. On the way, atop one of the masses of debris, I found a screwdriver and a hammer in amongst other tools, promptly placing them into my jacket pocket.

The trees lining Great Russell Street were mostly gone, along with several portions of the street, and the heavy iron gates were lying on the curbside. Walking between the colossal Roman columns and up the twelve wide Portland steps, I found that the main doors to the museum were closed. No one was about. A chain and padlock were tied tightly around the door handles.

Placing the screwdriver through the eye of the padlock and leveraging against the door, I hammered down hard. After a few attempts the lock fell apart, and the chain came rattling to the ground. The main doors creaked opened, and I was inside.

There were crates strewn everywhere, some still in the process of being assembled. Only a few paintings remained on the walls. The exhibits had all been partially dismantled. Sunlight filtered in through a part of the museum beside the Reading Room, where the outline of an unexploded bomb sat ominously silent among the rubble.

Walking carefully past a grey tailfin and over to the exhibit on trench warfare, I found the exhibit was not yet packaged for shipment. Producing the hammer, I smashed the glass and retrieved my father's letters, medals, a photograph of him in uniform, and some of Pa's other memorabilia from the war. Large sheets of brown paper were in a nearby crate along with some lengths of string. Carefully wrapping my father's former possessions, as I had watched the butcher do at the market innumerable times, I tied the package tightly with string. No one saw me as I walked out of the main entrance, replaced the chain and broken padlock, and continued down Great Russell Street, smiling at the parcel under my arm.

As the train to Portsmouth swayed and groaned back and forth along the tracks, the arid landscape made me recall my only memory of Great Granny. She had come over from Canada on a boat when I was very young, staying for a month while my brother and I recovered from the measles. She tried to teach us shorthand and played cribbage with us, and read us books. I still remembered seeing her off at the docks in Portsmouth, wondering, as the boat departed, how she was apparently immune to catching the disease Mum had said was so contagious.

"Why's Great Granny living in Canada if she was born in Ireland?" Ian asked.

"The Canadian government gave free land to attract immigrants, decades ago," Devon explained, "the only condition was to build a house there and farm the land."

"I would've taken the whole country," I said, to which Ian agreed.

Mum, who had her arm around Ian, stroked the gleaming black cat on her lap and peered out at the blurring landscape.

"We're running away, though." I said. "We should be staying here to fight."

"You can't fight bombs," Devon said. "And these Germans are taking over. Our family is together. Now there's something to fight for. A new start for all of us. No turning back."

The dock at Portsmouth was overcrowded with families: men, women, and wailing children departing together, others bidding farewell, all beneath seagulls probing for food.

We ascended the platform, and an hour later, thick ropes attaching the British cargo ship *Luffworf* to the dock were untied and thrown aboard. As we began walking around the deck, the vessel slowly pulled away from shore.

An assemblage of people lingered on the docks, continuing to wave until they were too small to be seen. Waves crashed and pounded against the doddering vessel's sides, the wind and cries of the family cat howling in my ears.

After two weeks at sea, up on deck for some air to alleviate my queasy stomach, I overheard one of the passengers talking about a U-boat that had torpedoed and sunk a British civilian liner, also headed to Canada, only three days ahead of us.

Eighty-three children were killed, along with two hundred and eleven passengers and crew who had been evacuated from England.

"You feeling any better?" Mum asked as I arrived back in the cabin.

I didn't respond.

"What's troubling you?" she asked.

"Our house in London, flattened," I said. "Seasickness. Wondering why we're off to Canada. Word up on deck is a German U-boat sank a British civilian ship three days ahead of us."

"Oh, is that all?" she replied.

I spent the remainder of the trip with an unsettled stomach, not only from the effects of the rolling sea, but from trying to forget my terror that the ship might go down.

After our arrival in Canada, while clutching on to my father's wartime journal on the train from Halifax, I grasped that I had run away from my own country during a time of war when I was nearly of the age to enlist. My country was in danger of being invaded, and the capital was being bombed. Pa had never seen such aggression toward English territory in the Great War, and he would have been ashamed of my actions now.

*Our family is together. Now there's something to fight for*, Devon had said. *A new start for all of us. No turning back.*

Meanwhile, my country was on the other side of the ocean, waiting in expectation for the courageous to defend her.

# <u>16</u>

The town of Khartum in Ontario, Canada, was named in honour of Ottawa Valley *voyageurs* in the 1860's who navigated from Alexandria, Egypt up the Nile in a failed attempt to rescue Charles Gordon, a British war hero in Khartoum, Sudan. Here in Khartum in Canada, news of the fighting was everywhere. I found some books in the house, which I didn't have the stomach to read: one called *Men of Iron*, with a cover depicting a painting of a proud knight perusing the landscape, mounted on a strong horse, as peasants cowered beneath him; and a book about deserters executed in the field during the Great War. My mother had a collection of romance novels as well as some travel and gardening books. Great Granny had a collection of Tennyson's poems, and she chastised me for cracking the spines, explaining that she had owned these books since childhood, and they were the only remembrances she had from her mother who died young. Great Granny did not express what I had perceived, that she had maintained the books over the decades in impeccable condition as a memento to what she might have considered an implacable, though inadvertent abandonment, that which her husband was also so recently guilty of.

My father's journal was more enticing than any of these, although I refused to crack that spine. I tucked his army photographs and war journal away in my drawer.

As she had done in London so long ago, my mother tuned in to the wireless newscasts every night, only these broadcasts were grainy and barely audible.

"Countries such as England continue to fight," Mum said one night after the newscast as I stood over the sink, handing her a washed plate.

Ian was sitting at the table with Great Granny, completing a crossword puzzle that she had made for him, while Devon was outside tending to the animals.

"Other countries are occupied," Mum continued, placing the plate in the drying rack. "Or waiting for—"

"War!" Ian interrupted, shouting excitedly before filling in the puzzle.

"Waiting to see what's happening next," she concluded, as though insinuating that men such as my father had the courage to fight, while others such as Devon and I were idle spectators simply awaiting its conclusion.

I read a portion of Pa's diary that night before tucking it away in my drawer again, recollecting the life story of a man who, at the instigation of the last war, had decided of his own accord to sign up as one of the first Canadians over to the battlefields and one of the last to return, marching all the way to the Rhine at the end of the entire mess.

Devon would listen to none of my complaints or wishes, and he disregarded any news of the war, or Mum's impressions of them. He had seemed content to run away from England, just as he was pleased to stay away from any news of the war in this isolated place, and as such, he must have wished that the ears of other members of the household, and the community, were similarly closed.

In mid-December of 1940, a family I did not recognize walked down the main street of Khartum.

We all peered out the window at the three daughters and their parents, a raggedy, unkempt bunch with tattered clothes, walking down the white, snow-lined street. The parents had their heads down and their hands clasped tightly together, as if humiliated at having to return. The three daughters darted their heads around nervously, cognizant that everyone in the town was staring at them.

"The Frances family," Great Granny said, looking at me. "They left Khartum years ago. Their oldest daughter, Jane, she is about your age. When they moved away, she was a girl with dark pigtails and a dirty face."

The townspeople seemed somehow pleased in their animated conversations, almost proud of this family's apparent disgrace; watching what might be construed as their rationale to remain in Khartum, while a failed escape attempt now paraded down the street before them.

"Some families try, but cannot flee this place," Great Granny said, removing a jar of pickles from the cupboard.

"One day soon, this town will be abandoned," Mum replied as she set plates on the table. "Gone to the mice and the weeds."

"They're already building a town of their own," I said. Mum smiled. "They'll really spruce the place up."

"Some of us, though," Great Granny replied, "like the Frances family, have nowhere else to go."

The oldest daughter in the family seemed familiar, as though I had seen her before. But that couldn't be. As she walked by, I scrutinized her face. Carrying a basket of dried flowers, she had iridescent azure eyes, the eyes of an angel, which seemed to heighten the image of whom I thought she was.

This woman partially hidden beneath a thick jacket and fur-lined hood had the elegance of a screen siren without the makeup, what they called a natural beauty. She was a younger and more unrefined version of the actress who played Violet at the Duke and Duchess Theatre in London.

Now, this rendering of Violet paraded down the street every day to buy milk from the McIntosh family. She wore dried flowers in her hair and was always smiling. I watched her carrying jugs of milk from inside our front window over the coming days, imagining that she was walking across the stage instead.

I approached her one day the same as I had approached Violet and the sham Lieutenant beside the Wellington Arch in London, as though she was a sick or wounded animal.

Sure, I could come close, but I needed to know where to escape if confronted. And I turned the left side of my face away from her, so she would not see the permanent record of my accident in the mines.

This time, though, I would start by providing some arbitrary observation about her mannerisms: a comment I would make about her appearance, perhaps, or maybe some feminine flaw I had noticed that I could bring attention to, and somehow turn into a compliment about beauty being distinctive and individual; the way my father had coached me in the pub one day after work in South Leeds about how get a girl interested. Before I received this advice, I had utilized this technique to win Violet over at the Wellington Arch. The method did work.

She approached me cautiously too, holding a jug of milk and seemingly unaware of why this young man had interrupted her path.

"Why're you turning away?" she asked, smiling, her voice scratchy and hoarse. "I see your scars, don't be ashamed. My father was injured in the Great War. He has scars on his face, too. Says they didn't pin a medal on his chest but gave him that as a reminder instead. You're too young to have been injured in the war, though. You're a Dixon...Nicholas, right?"

Jane and I began to take long walks in the cold together, despite the snow and heavy winds that sometimes whipped through the open fields, ending with time spent sitting beneath a frosty weeping willow beside Miller's pond where we would kiss and talk.

One particularly cold afternoon beneath the willow, Jane sat in the snow as I stood over her. The icicles were clanging in the breeze as our hands clasped together.

"Tell me about England," she said.

"No thanks," I replied.

"Anything," she said, smiling.

"This place is a barren version of Northaw, where I wanted us all to live. Imagine this place here with more trees, oaks and poplars and some nice willows in the mix, and jasmine in the air. More robins and sparrows. Pastures of sheep. Wild pheasants ripe for the hunt, if we could bag any. That's how it was. Then put loads of raggedy kids trampling over fields and invading houses, and add the threat of the German military doing the same. That's Northaw now. I can't think of England anymore."

She looked around at our frozen surroundings.

"Here, it's peaceful," she said. "Even serene. But much too frigid today."

"This place has avoided effects of the war. No invasions are coming here. That's why we came."

"To escape?"

"My uncle's foolish. He's too easily led by fear. I used to think the same way, but soon got over it. At least, I think I'm over it now."

"Would you want to return?"

"I would. Except, leaving you might knock me to pieces."

We took an excursion into a field of tall grass nearby, at liberty to explore each other's bodies beneath our jackets with cold, freely roaming hands; ashamed at dishonouring God, we repented during church service the following Sunday.

Weeks later as Jane and I walked to Miller's pond together, the snow drifting down over the empty fields, the day overcast, Jane stopped me suddenly by the bank of the pond. The tall grass was nearly buried in white, the pond frozen stiff.

"I don't mean to startle you," she said, "But I'm with child."

"Impossible," I replied instantly.

She stared at me, silent for a moment before speaking again.

"Really?" she asked. "You know how that happens, right?"

"Well... how do you know?"

"A woman knows."

"...and that's all I need?"

"That's all you need."

I was attending church regularly for the first time I could remember, and I began asking God to give me the strength and the means, as an expectant father, to somehow go overseas and fight in the war that was consuming the radio airwaves and my idle thoughts. An honourable man would wait until after we were married, and the child was born.

I began reading Pa's wartime diary again.

*Salisbury Plains, Bustard Camp, England*
*December 6, 1914*
*The weather is getting quite cold. The ground is frozen solid this morning. We got rain instead of snow and the wind is blowing pretty hard. A lot of the tents have blown over. The people of England say they never saw so much rain. On Sundays, church was held in the big YMCA*

*tent. I have been to church more times since I joined the Army, learning of the free gift of salvation through Christ in unruly congregations, than the whole time I was in St Thomas.*

*We have been having sham battles lately under an English General. Last week, all the Canadian Forces got together for big doings. Artillery, cavalry, and infantry all assembled for a big battle.*

*King George, Lord Kitchener, and some other big bugs reviewed us first and said they were greatly pleased with the Canadians. I was second in line from the front when the King arrived, and I had a good look, considering him a pretty impressive fellow. Lord Kitchener, Secretary of State for War, said he wants to finish up this conflict and intends to send a million men to the front.*

*The 1ˢᵗ, 2ⁿᵈ, 3ʳᵈ, and 4ᵗʰ Battalions got out for sham battles. We had blank ammunition and went through the exercise as if we were at the front. The 1ˢᵗ and 2ⁿᵈ Battalions were pitted against the 3ʳᵈ and the 4ᵗʰ. After getting two or three miles apart, we then made for one another. There are so many forests around. One was the attacking party, and they had to find where the enemy was and make an attack. Often, the attacking party found it difficult to know what they were shooting their blank ammunition at, lost in the hills and woods and unable to find the enemy.*

*English instructors trained us to dig trenches, locate the enemy in difficult terrain, and sharpen our bayonets, so we are ready for the Germans.*

*We are expecting to leave before long, and I am certainly wishing to do so.*

Once Devon learned of my impending marriage to Jane, then of our baby, he would be furtively pleased at his triumph of having held me back from any further talk of going away to war.

Our existence in England seemed a lifetime ago, although only a few months had passed.

But I would marry and sign up immediately after for service in the army, to be sent overseas. Whether I would await the birth of our child would depend upon when the notice would come to report for duty. The decision would be in God's hands.

I would serve with my wife and child in mind, the picture of our baby either a photograph or one contrived by my imagination, fighting just as Pa had when he was thinking of Mum and their future together.

# 17

Peering out through the wavering hand-blown window glass of the bedroom I shared with Ian and Mum, I saw Uncle Devon shuffling through the fog. Within an hour, the haze now descending on the countryside would lift and there would be an unfettered view clear to the nearby snow-covered hills. The hills were already apparent as vague outlines of shadows set on the horizon.

Those hills were the reason this site had been chosen by so many Irish men and women, Great Granny said, because it reminded them of their home. There was even a town called Stratford here, a place with Shakespearean productions, swans, a river, and a church like the Stratford-Upon-Avon in England.

Over the past weeks since our arrival in Khartum, Devon had become sore at any mention of the war in Europe. Although Canada declared war on Germany just after England had, I saw no signs of it. It was nothing like what was happening in London. There were no sandbags, no trenches except for irrigation trenches, no blackouts except when the oil lamp ran dry, no evacuations, no drills, no shelters or hiding underground, no gas masks, no barrage balloons, and no clutter of enemy aeroplanes overhead. Just the sky free and clear by night and day.

"Nicholas," Mum said, stirring a pot on the stove.

She smiled as I descended the steps, the smell of oatmeal filling the place. "Twenty years old today. A young man."

"I don't feel much like a man today," I said. "Not yet."

"Sassy all your days," she said.

Outside the window, Doctor Mitchell was talking with one of the families nearby. The Mayor drove by in the town's only car. I sat down, and Mum moved over to stand behind me, stroking my hair as she had when I was a boy.

"Doctor Mitchell once had a hundred patients," she said. "But now the lumber mill is boarded shut, the railway bypassed this place, the land's almost unfarmable, and—what more?"

"The post office is all closed up," I said. "No more mail for us."

"Right. That'll be the death of this town. But Doctor Mitchell will be moving soon, along with everyone else. Still, no matter what I tell your Uncle Devon, he insists we stay. He's not leaving his grandmother, and she says she'll die if she leaves this place. So, for now, we'll not be going off anywhere."

"I should be overseas fighting. I'll certainly be glad to get out of this deserted place."

"You don't need to be part of that," she said as she began massaging my shoulders.

"You're repeating what Devon said."

"He's your *uncle*. Now, since I seem to be repeating your Uncle Devon's words, family is all you have in life. That's all he says when I talk of moving back to England after the war."

"And when I talk of going to fight."

"Still, there is some truth to that...but for now, we made our own family here."

"All his prattle is to make me stay."

"You know he needs your help. We all do. We need our crops here to survive. Not like Devon's hobby farm in Northaw. But don't tell him I called it that."

"I'll tell him nothing, and I won't describe to you the chicken scraps and half-rotten potatoes we ate nearly every night for a year there, with the occasional ham, lettuce and carrots. Here, it's potatoes almost every night, so I suppose that was better."

She removed her hands from my shoulder and turned up the radio to produce the spry sounds of an orchestra.

"Uncle Devon is avoiding military service for me, and himself," I said. "He served in the last war and from what Pa said, his service wasn't very long. I wonder why?"

"He hasn't told me. I would suggest you not ask him, either. He'll become cross with you."

"We're already at odds. Ever since we moved here."

"He only wants things a certain way, that's all," she said, placing a bowl of oatmeal on the table and moving to clean the dishes in the sink.

When I arrived home from the frozen Miller's pond late one afternoon, Ian was sitting at the table for dinner. Devon walked into the house with freshly chopped wood, placed the pile in my arms, and instructed me to stack the wood by the fireplace.

Devon whispered something to Mum, and she laughed, slapping his hand playfully. Her laughter, so infrequently heard, had a peculiar, resonant, and disconcerting timbre.

We sat down to a dinner of potato and leek soup and potato bread, the fire under the cooking pot crackling. For some reason, there was an unlabelled bottle of wine at the table, and Mum and Devon were drinking the murky red fluid.

Everyone waited for Mum to give thanks for the meal. She was silent for a moment, apparently listening to grainy news on the wireless radio; word echoed through the house that the British Army was recruiting Commandos, a group being formed at the order of Winston Churchill to execute raids on German-occupied territories.

"I'll turn that off, Doreen," Devon said, slithering behind Mum and brushing up close as he made his way to the radio.

Mum said a prayer, thanking the Lord that, for now, we were all together.

I experienced the same bilious feeling in my gut as when I left so many years ago for the mines of South Leeds. My imminent departure now for the service overseas would be a proper one, though, and not one which I would leave for unannounced at night without saying goodbye.

Devon tore apart a piece of stale bread with his teeth, making him resemble the biggest of the swineherd tearing at a boiled corncob. I had no qualms about such imaginings, no remorse. But still, I was nauseous at mealtimes now, a vehement repugnance accentuated at the thought that, if he had not taken us away from England to isolate us here, joining the military would have been easier and I would be without excuse.

Dinner passed without conversation, the inaudible rhythm of Irving Berlin followed by the crackly spontaneity of Benny Goodman on the wireless, and my uncle loudly nuzzling soup into his mouth in accompaniment.

After he was finished, Devon rose from the table and added a log to the fire. His wound from a sharp edge of the pig's slop bucket had opened, and he put his hand high in the air to rewrap it tightly in a bloody bandage before sitting back down again.

"You ought to have Doctor Mitchell examine that," Mum said. "While he is still here."

"Where is he off to?" Devon asked.

"Some other place, same as everyone else."

Ian sat on the floor playing jacks as Mum turned the dial on the radio to a different station, reduced the volume, and sat down at the table to stare at the floor as she listened.

At times such as these, when everyone seemed to disregard my presence and there was talk of those who would soon leave the town, I had the notion that I was not here; as though I was the subject of their conversation. I saw myself living for a short time with Jane, until my official notification came to go overseas. Events were beginning to unfold as they would without me. No longer here to argue with my uncle, to assist with the pigs and the fields and stacking logs, Ian would have to help, at least for the next while until I was able to return. Not present to have long discussions with Mum about our lives here and the plans for the family's future with or without Devon and Great Granny (who went to bed early and was often snoring softly in the next room as we talked), or about the people of the town and the circumstances that had led them here and what kept them tied to this place, I could no longer provide the controversy that stimulated their lives and seemed to deepen them and make them whole. Now, at times such as this, we seemed apart, separate, disjointed, and already living disparate lives.

A news bulletin came over the radio. Mum rose from the table and moved to the counter to listen closely.

"Devon, what happened to you in the last war?" I asked.

He glanced over from the fireplace, silent, unresponsive. All eyes were on me.

"I heard you didn't serve for long," I continued. "Something about unauthorized leave in London, and then you not returning to Bustard Camp and being labelled as a deserter?"

"None of your concern," he replied.

"Were you court martialled?" I continued. "Pa said you were worried about being put in front of a firing squad."

Devon was silent.

"Your uncle's right," Mum said. "His business, not ours."

"You wanted no part of that war," I continued, "or this one. That's why you moved us here, to nowhere. So no one, not even the government, can find us."

Devon walked to the door, suddenly sore. "You're hopeless."

As he walked outside, Ian said nothing in response, but we simply stared at Devon through the window. He threw a pile of logs, which impacted heavily against the side of the work shed.

"That's not our business," Mum said to me, frowning.

"Aren't you curious what we're doing here in this deserted town, in the middle of this empty country?" I asked, addressing her.

"Go to your room. Our room."

"I'm twenty, now. A man. You can't tell me—"

She slapped me across the face, interrupting me.

"What's what anymore," I continued, rubbing my cheek.

"I certainly can," she said. "I can take sassy, but smarmy I won't. Not if you want to live here."

She stared at me as Devon walked inside, over to the fireplace, clutching the cloth around his hand. Poking at the fire with a metal rod, the fire crackled, blazed for a moment, and then died down. There was too much moist wood smothering the fire, and the charred cinders had begun to smoke excessively.

Mum rose and began gathering up the dishes as Devon rearranged the logs. I waited for him to pick up a log and toss the smoking mass at my head, an act of which I thought him capable, before walking into the next room where I began reading my book about deserters executed in the field during the Great War.

James Wilson, in the 4th Canadian Infantry, was described as "undesirable" for military service. He was charged eight times with committing crimes while in service, repeatedly going Absent Without Leave after landing in France, and he endured three Field General Court Martial hearings. I peered through this man's record for punishments he received for desertion, to see what penalties Devon might have received. Of this man's record of drunkenness, rowdy behaviour, kicking a Non-Commissioned Officer, and general bad character, there were 28 days in detention, loss of a month's pay, apprehension by military police, seventy days Field Punishment Number 1 (which from a drawing, involved having his hands tied behind his back to a fence), hearings, 90 days detention, then fleeing the scene of the Battle of Mount Sorrel where 2600 Canadian lives were lost, resulting in his own death sentence.

My eyes rose from the book. Mum was staring at me.

"Well, what do you have to say?" she asked. "Your uncle's furious with you. Keeps on about how long he has housed, clothed, and fed you both here and in Northaw, not to mention the summers we spent there together."

Induced guilt. Time for a distraction, one that would turn her mood around.

"Jane and I will marry," I replied.

"Really?"

Her expression changed to a smile. She reached over and hugged me.

"So, when did this happen?" she asked.

"Well, I've yet to ask her," I said. "But I'm certain what she'll say. I just need a ring."

"You can have Great Granny's," she said, clasping my hand. "It has a small diamond. The wedding will be a small affair. Perhaps springtime. We'll invite everyone in town."

"We couldn't have done that in London."

"Definitely not," she said, still smiling as she departed for the kitchen.

I overheard her telling Devon this news, along with his response.

"Finally, he will do something good and decent," Devon said.

Static-filled news of some overseas battles filtered into the room. I put a pillow over my ears to drown out the details as I peered through the window at the Mayor driving with his family in the town's only car. Watching the snow descend gently to earth, I eventually fell asleep in the early evening.

# 18

Our wedding was not spectacular, except for my beautiful bride with her hair pinned up, wearing a lovely, pervasive smile. I overheard some guests commenting on the whole affair as dismal. There were the typical accoutrements as there would be at any wedding: flowers, corsets, buttons, bows, frilly lace, women and men scrubbed with scented soaps. But the flowers were dried and colourless, not fresh, the corsets were not straight, and the buttons, bows, and lace were all tattered and frayed with age. The old wooden church had holes in the ceiling, and light filtered in from above, illuminating an array of weatherworn pews and 30 guests from the few families that comprised the population of Khartum.

Devon gave me some whisky prior to the ceremony, and my head was spinning when I agreed, before God, to stay married to Jane until He decided to part us through death, which I imagined might be closer than anyone knew.

At the ceremony's conclusion, the preacher stepped back behind the pulpit.

The Mayor of Khartum, Theodore McIntyre, walked to the front, introduced himself, and explained that he had been given the title of Mayor five consecutive times with no contenders running against him.

"Not that I'm welcoming any, of course," he said, smiling as people began shaking their heads and frowning.

"His favourite joke," his wife added from the crowd. "I ask forgiveness for how many times you all must have heard these same words, including my apology that I offer you again."

"I'll put my name on the ballot," I said loudly, "just to put an end to all this wry humour."

There was general laughter. Theodore waved his hand dismissively, and his wife smiled.

"There is a certain home in Khartum," Theodore continued. "Abandoned twelve years ago by the Bowen family who, no longer able to farm the land, headed south. This is our gift, from the town to the new couple, Nicholas and Jane."

"Everyone knows this house was damaged by weather and time," he added, raising a finger in the air. "So, there is a provision to this gift. The home will be updated and renovated by the people of the town."

At this pronouncement, I glanced back to see that people were shaking their heads.

And so, the people of the town of Khartum, mobilized through common purpose, came together to scavenge from other abandoned homes to make the gifted home liveable.

The men of the town, led by the Mayor, began by replacing the shingles on the roof of the home. They repaired sections of water-damaged floor inside, tearing out broken windows and swapping them with intact windows from other abandoned homes.

The women of the town, led by my mother, removed old, musty curtains and hung newly stitched curtain fabric that had been re-dyed and cleaned. They stockpiled fresh linens for the home and began making new, hand-stitched carpets. In anticipation of what was yet to come, one of the men made a crib and placed it in a room upstairs, painting pink and blue patterns throughout.

While this was happening, on my way to get some supplies from the general store on a cloudless, warm spring day, I saw a group of farmers chatting in the main street of Khartum. Mr. Frances, Jane's father who was a plump and cheery fellow, perpetually sweating, was talking as I sauntered by.

"Military recruiters are in Wikham," Mr. Frances said, wiping his forehead and then replacing his straw hat. "Gotta be twenty-one years old to enlist."

"Nicholas," Dr. Mitchell called out, a blade of grass protruding from the corner of his mouth. He squinted in the sun, showing the long, deep wrinkles on his face, his ragged white hair glowing.

"Good day, folks," I said, stopping to peruse the elderly faces glaring back at me. "Nice day for a chewing match. But shouldn't you all be digging in the dirt or feeding something?"

"We're in town for supplies," Dr. Mitchell said. "Same as you, I figure. How old are you?"

"He's nineteen," Mr. Frances said. "Is that right?"

"Not old enough to enlist, I'll say that much."

"Like a lady, not giving up her tender age," Dr. Mitchell said, smiling.

I was still staring at Dr. Mitchell when Mr. Frances started talking again.

"I know your father was in the Great War," Mr. Frances said.

"Right, and you were too," I replied, addressing him.

"Have the medals to prove it." He turned his scars toward me.

"My medals are from the mines. Although I could've done without such recognition."

I secretly went alone to Wikham to investigate. Ian would have to till the soil until I got back.

After an hour-long walk through the shade of the forest, along a marked path, I passed by a sign for the town. A long and dusty road lined with homes, many of them shuttered and with broken windows, led me to the recruiters: two men with shaved heads and uniforms, sitting at a stall with flags, military photos, and magazines, with patriotic music playing.

Passing by several times, I vowed each time to approach them and sign up for active military service by falsifying my age slightly. They examined me with suspicion. I stopped to look at some of the canned goods offered for sale nearby, walking up to a store on the street. There were peaches and tomatoes, fish and baked beans. Each depiction on the labels seemed more interesting than the last, and I was beginning to compare the cans when one of the recruiters startled me.

"How old are you, son?" he asked.

"Why's everybody asking me that today?"

"Do you often answer a question with a question?"

"Do you?"

Coming here was a mistake. I needed to make a swift escape.

"I have married my Jane," I mumbled to the recruiter as I walked back toward Khartum, "My family is together and I'm starting to build my own."

"Do you often mumble?" he asked.

"I don't. Do you?"

Later that day, Mum showed me and Jane through our nearly completed home.

"If this is what the townspeople can do," I said as we walked through the rooms, "with such nice workmanship, I'm surprised this town is falling apart."

We descended the stairs to find a group of men who had been working on the house all day, now drinking homemade ginger beer. A gramophone played a static-free Artie Shaw as though he was there, performing in the corner. Ladies sat in the corner at a folding table, drinking tea next to tiered desert trays full of small pieces of assorted cakes and cookies.

The Mayor stood before our oversized fireplace, describing that the mantel had been carefully removed in three separate pieces from an abandoned home in a nearby logging town.

"I thank everyone here for making this the nicest home in town," he said.

"I'll second that motion, Mayor," Devon said loudly, stumbling over an empty chair as he raised a glass of whisky in the air. "A new start for Jane and Nicholas."

The group turned toward him, and Devon raised his glass in the air again.

"To new beginnings," he said.

With Devon's wound infected, unable to use his hand except for dispensing alcoholic painkiller while doing light jobs around this house, I was helping on the farm more than ever. Ian had begun assisting on the farm too, and with this house as well. And he stood here smiling now at Jane, as though she amused him somehow. Ian had been transformed from a sickly child into a healthy young man.

After thanking the Mayor and prompting me to stand beside her, a request which I promptly obliged by walking over with a ginger beer in my hand, Jane began speaking.

"Nicholas and I thank all of you present, who are making this place not only habitable, but beautiful," she said, smiling. "You are preparing a lovely home. For ourselves and our baby."

Everyone took turns congratulating us before returning to their former positions, the chatter livelier now. Devon's smile was persistent, and after a while the commotion settled.

"Everything," Mum said, smiling in the corner and pouring herself another cup of tea, "is according to God's will."

# 19

Rainwater pounded on the roof in July of 1941, several weeks after my beautiful bride and I had moved into our newly refurbished home. I piled wood and old books by the empty fireplace. Jane sat in a rocking chair, reading some romance or other from Jane Austen.

Among the old books, I flipped through the one about deserters executed during the Great War. In addition to executions, there were also details of sentences given to Officers, Non-Commissioned Officers, and other ranks. The sentences went from Life Penal Servitude to reprimands and suspensions. From what I knew of Devon's service, I concluded he was either sentenced to hard labour, six to 24 months of imprisonment, or discharge with ignominy, which I found in Great Granny's dictionary meant disgraceful or dishonourable discharge.

Jane began talking gibberish about contradictions as I tossed the volume on top of the mound to be burned.

"What are you on about, my love?" I asked.

"Stop," she said, contorting her face. "The baby is coming."

I put my hands on the arms of her chair and gazed into her eyes.

"No, it's not," I said.

"Oh, and you know better than I?"

"I know what to do."

Rushing from the house, I headed toward the doctor's home, slipping in the mud along the way. When I arrived, Doctor Mitchell was visible through the lit window, sprawled out on his empty bed, rising at the sound of knocking on the door. He disappeared into the corridor.

There was the sound of footsteps and the doctor appeared as the wooden door creaked open.

"Yes?" he asked, smiling. "You come to tell me your tender age?"

He was asking for it. Squinting accentuated his wrinkles; a harbinger of experience, wisdom and accumulated ill humour. While he was donning his clothes and spectacles, his white hair falling over his face, I wanted to give him a nice haymaker.

"The baby," I said. "Jane's having troubles."

"Too early," he replied, his smile disappearing. "She's only seven months along. Can't be just yet."

"That's what I said. But she has contradictions."

"Contractions."

"Sounds right."

"I don't believe that, but let's go, then."

We left together, traipsing down the rain-soaked roadway as quickly as we could.

Arriving home just minutes later, I opened the darkened door and we ambled up the wooden staircase to find Jane upstairs in her nightgown, rolling back and forth in her bed. The bed was wet, and she was breathing heavily.

"Have you told anyone else?" the doctor asked.

"Just you."

"We need help. And I need my black medical bag. It's at the foot of the stairs in my house. I wasn't expecting I'd need it."

The doctor began to strip the bed of its coverings as I scuttled down the stairs and out the front door.

After running to the doctor's house, I slipped on a small wet patch on the front porch, below where the roof was leaking. Quickly recovering, I stepped inside to find the black medical bag.

When I arrived outside again, I began to run. There were lights nearby.

There was a clanging as some small instruments and examining tools fell out, and I gathered them up from the puddles on the road. Running toward Mum's house, I slipped again.

This time, the headlights of the town's only car suddenly appeared in front of me.

The lights did not stop until after one of them had struck me violently. I flew backward onto the wet mud, and landed on my side. There was the taste of blood in my mouth, and my head was cemented to the ground as though in a dream. I was back in the tunnels of South Leeds after the explosion that had ended Pa's life.

I lay there for a few minutes in the pouring rain, immobile, as Mayor Theodore McIntyre stood over me, liquor on his foul breath, the car's one headlight now beaming off into the distance and illuminating droplets of rain. The contents of the medical bag were on the ground, scattered, and a sticky liquid warmed my side.

Feeling beneath me, I lifted my hand to see red.

Something from the bag had fallen out beneath me and penetrated my side. I tried to move my other arm beneath me but couldn't. Trying to stand, I fell back into the mud.

"I'll go fetch help," Theodore said, running off.

From here, the front door of Mum's house was visible. All the lights were out. If I could only rise, I could knock on the door and my drunken uncle would answer. Mum would see the look in my eyes, and know what had to be done.

The rain was coming down in force.

"Medic, medic," I yelled, as Pa would have heard countless times during the Great War.

Closing my eyes, not knowing if I could get up now, trying again and again to do so, falling back down, dizzy, my heart was thumping wildly.

The darkness and the smell of burning fireplace wood engulfed me. The stars were intermittent with clouds above. Jane needed me. The pain in my head and my side was intense. A metallic taste filled my mouth. My arm was immobile, the thing stinging my side. I might die here right now, and never leave Khartum. Pa's Davy Lamp crashing to the ground in the pit flashed into my mind. Then, lunging at Glen outside the Duke and Duchess Theatre, and toppling a man at the Olympia Rally. With Glen, and the man at the rally, I had accomplished something. Now, I had achieved nothing.

Our family is together. Now there's something to fight for. A new start for all of us. No turning back. That's what the coward Devon said.

This is the man I had listened to far too long, and whose favour and support I had recently gained and even sought. While Devon's military record remained sealed, he was not unlike James Wilson in the 4th Canadian Infantry, "undesirable" for military service, executed after being criminally charged, in Field General Court Martial hearings and repeatedly Absent Without Leave amid the battlefields of France.

Would I be able to show my own child the fortitude required of a man? Given my anxiety at being injured, did I have the strength, the courage, the audacity to risk this again, to go to war?

Mum and Doctor Mitchell were on either side of me, holding my arms.

Theodore was beside us, apologizing profusely.

"When I said I was going to run against you in the next election," I said to the Mayor. "You didn't need to take that to heart. That was a lark."

"Ghastly," Doctor Mitchell said, yanking something from my side.

I yelled out in pain and the doctor, holding the wound, kept me upright. Wanting to punch him and the Mayor in retaliation, I realized I lacked the strength.

Theodore walked away, returning to his car and reversing his previous direction, presumably looking to strike down other Mayoral hopefuls. Now I knew why no one ever ran against him.

"Nicholas may have a concussion," I heard the doctor say. "And he stabbed himself with this scalpel."

He held a shiny, bloody knife that was being washed by the rain. Mum held my arms and he rounded up the contents of his bag. He placed the knife in his pocket and began helping to escort me along, my mother combing my sopping hair with her wet hands, the doctor producing a clean white cloth and telling me to apply the rain-moistened bandage, with pressure, to my side. I did as told, still wanting to strike him as the one responsible for calling me a woman once, and for having forgotten his medical bag and thereby causing me so much pain.

The doctor was first into the patient's room when we got home.

"Nicholas, wait here," Mum said, handing me more bandages. "Keep pressure on your side. Jane needs us."

I went down the narrow staircase, feeling the bitter cold air in the house now, kicking the ashen stump in the fireplace, and tossing in a fresh log from the woodpile. Eventually starting the fire, I took some whisky for the pain, wrapped the bandages, and slept.

I awoke later as Dr. Mitchell was removing and re-wrapping my bandages.

I re-lit the fire and spent the day waiting.

And then that night, I was woken by muted crying from upstairs. The announcement that our child was a boy accompanied the cracking and sputtering fireplace.

As I entered the bedroom upstairs, our child's bawling, a son to whom I had an obligation, who would one day be searching for what was necessary to become a man, filled the space.

I stayed until my boy began to settle. Staring into his brown eyes as I stood over him, I stroked his dark hair. He wrapped his hand around my finger, his head drooping as he fell asleep in his lovely mother's arms.

# 20

My feet took me for a long walk through the shade of a forest, along a marked path back to the recruiter in Wikham. The same man who was there before, an older man in a pressed suit and military hat, with small medals pinned to his chest, sat alone in full sun at his stall with Canadian, British, and French flags flapping in the breeze. Photos of servicemen were strewn about his table. This time, there was no music playing.

Walking over to the grocer's, I carefully inspected a can of stewed tomatoes.

This man was the scavenger, and I was his prey. I had come out of my hole but had not yet committed to running across the field; in fact, I had scurried back to the safety and comfort of my nest before.

But this time, his stare had taken hold and would not let go, of a deserter who had not yet enlisted and whose only punishment came from his conscience.

As he was circling and closing in, I glanced up from the tin can.

"How old are you, son?" his gruff voice asked. "I remember you, so don't ask me another question in return."

"Twenty," I answered. "No, twenty-one, actually."

"Well, which is it?"

"Twenty-one. I used to be twenty. A great year that was, but that's a story for another day."

He invited me to sit on an unoccupied chair at the opposite side of the table. I did not oblige.

"You here for tomatoes?" he asked, observing the can in my hand. "From your accent you're a Limey."

"I am here to sign up," I said emphatically as I sat down in the heat of the sun, my words apparently taking him by surprise. "I'm from Khartum. Originally from Britain."

"Nice to know you. Now speak up, and do not slouch."

He scrutinized my face, observing my scars.

"When you were here before," he said, "you mumbled something about your wife and family."

"That was quite some time ago. Didn't think you heard, or that you'd remember. I was muttering about my wife and our child Daniel who, as the saying goes, was born yesterday. I don't mumble much, so you caught me on a rare day."

I straightened my back and sat up in the chair, as the grocer, glaring back at me with black hair and dark eyes, came over and grabbed the can out of my hand.

"My uncle told me countless times not to volunteer," I said, resolutely now. "My father once told me, too, that he didn't want me to experience what he had. That a man supporting his family cannot be drafted."

"If that were true," he said, "there wouldn't be enough men to fight, now would there?"

"Yes, that's what I said."

"Well, your father and your uncle, they should go overseas and see what's doing."

"My pa died in the mines in England, but he served in the trenches of France in the Great War."

"Ah, a soldier then. And your uncle, what of him?"

"The coward? I don't know much about his military record. He was absent without leave in the last war and was worried about meeting a firing squad. And I've been listening to what he wants for far too long."

"I knew men like your uncle. Spent time staring at prison walls instead of fighting for their country... what now, will he go overseas?"

"Maybe, if he's drafted."

"Well, let's hope that happens then," he continued. "So, you are a soldier's son. You might perchance be drafted if you don't volunteer. The benefit of volunteering is you can decide between the Army and the Navy. For you, I suggest General Infantry."

"General Infantry?"

"Like your father. Army foot soldiers. Or Artillery. 50-millimetre guns, that sort of thing. So, what'll it be?"

"General Infantry for me, then."

"You'll need to pass the doctor's examination. You look fine except for those scars on the left side of your face. And you seem to have a limp."

"I think about the accident that claimed my pa's life, every time I look in the mirror or try to run fast. It was back in the coal mines of South Leeds in England. I was there at the time of the explosion."

The grocer raised the volume on his wireless at the onset of a news report discussing Commando raids on Guernsey, one of the British Isles, now apparently occupied by the Germans.

"What of the Commandos?" I asked.

"What of them?"

"Winston Churchill has ordered they execute raids on German-occupied territories. I can do that, lunge at German throats."

"You have spunk. Those Commandos are British Army, so you would be eligible… but the training is quite difficult. Takes a special sort of person. When did you come here from overseas?"

"Just under a year ago, I suppose."

"Ah, when the going was tough over there many chose to escape. Some ships were sunk on the way over."

"A German U-boat torpedoed and sank a British civilian liner only three days ahead of us. My uncle's idea to traverse those waters. Anything for escape. No one told us to leave the country but him."

"I should have guessed. Cowards die as cowards are. Good for you, son, that you have chosen the better path. When your newborn son grows up, he will know from your example what it is to be a man. He, too, will not listen to deserters. You will be sent immediately to Ottawa, then to Quebec City, then on a transport to Britain for training. You can sign up for the Commandos once you get there. Carve your own way."

With that, the Sergeant licked the end of his pencil, and began by taking down my name and address.

A short time later, with the wireless still broadcasting war news, I started through the forest, the one phrase resounding in my thoughts from all the recruiter had said: *you will be sent immediately.*

# **<u>21</u>**

Mum hosted a dinner at our home to formally thank the town and to celebrate the beginning of Jane, me, and our new baby Daniel as Khartum's newest family. Most of the town's twelve families were represented, a whopping twenty people in all.

Jane and baby Daniel leaned against the wall. Stared at by those around the room, I walked over, putting my arm around her. She smiled as we looked into our child's iridescent, chocolate eyes. I glanced over to the oversized fireplace mantel housing various family photographs, including the picture of my father in uniform retrieved from the British Museum.

The grey-pebbled photograph of Wilfrid pomaded, showered, and shaved glistened with the light of the fire. His army uniform was an inky, nine-buttoned jacket with sagging trousers, his cockeyed, flat-topped hat adorned with a gleaming star. A fine image of a man ready to fight for his country. Shoes were laced with wrapping to the knees and resembled boots. A sombre expression was sculpted onto his face, confounded by what he was about to do in France, a country he had never visited. A cigarette dangled from his right hand and a ring reflected light from his wedding finger which must have made him appear to other enlisted men as married, experienced, older. Nothing doing. To me, despite the uniform and the cigarette and the fake ring and the nonchalance, his picture didn't hoodwink me. He was certainly nothing but apprehensiveness.

Mum announced that dinner was ready, and everyone was seated at the long dining room table in front of the crackling fireplace. After meat pie, asparagus, and mashed potatoes served with a healthy debate on how many children Jane and I would have, wondering as I tried to interject if we had any say in the matter, there was a knock on the door.

Coffee was being served along with rhubarb pie, raspberry pie, and stewed strawberries.

"We aren't expecting any more guests," Mum said, setting one of the pies on the table.

She opened the door to reveal a bulky man with a white moustache, a grey suit, and thinning hair. He introduced himself as the postmaster from the nearby town of Wireton.

Mum invited him in for coffee and dessert, and he sat down at the table and grabbed a fork. As he was handed a slice of raspberry pie, he handed her an envelope in return.

"I'm here to deliver that," he said, the moist pie reddening his lips. "It's for Nicholas Dixon."

"What is this?" Mum asked, passing me the envelope across the table. "From the government?"

I didn't answer but tore the paper open as Mum, accompanied by Devon in his normal rags, and Mr. Frances in a posh suit, moved in to circle around me. They all read over my shoulder.

The letter told me to report for military duty in Ottawa in two weeks. I would then be sent to Hull, Yorkshire, England. Reading through the page again, in awe of the finality of this decision made firm by those words, then looking up, I saw that everyone around the table was staring back at me. I quickly folded the paper. Silence reigned.

"I will report to the army in two weeks," I said. No one could stand in my way now.

"Two weeks?" Mum asked. She grabbed the folded note before I could stuff the page into my pocket.

Jane took Daniel from the room, walking swiftly into the kitchen, pulling me along by my arm.

Jane gazed into my face as we stood together in the kitchen. Her eyes were always extraordinary in this light. I looked down at Daniel, who was also staring back at me.

"You can fight this," she said as I glanced back up at her. "You don't need to go."

"Men are fighting for our freedom over there—"

"And dying. We're at war, but we have freedom here. England's different, I know. You have to think of your commitments to your wife and child. The war's almost over, and you want to risk everything? For what?"

"That I haven't done so earlier is shameful."

"I will never forgive you if you leave."

"It's honourable. Thinking otherwise is shameful."

"You sound as though you want to go."

"I do."

"Think of a time recently when you said that, and what that meant."

"Our wedding?"

She walked quickly into the other room, and I followed close behind.

"I want to sign up, too," Ian said.

There was some stifled conversation before Mum spoke.

"You won't go," she said, shaking her head as she read through the note. "Either of you."

"Your Mum's right, you're not going anywhere," Devon said, addressing me.

"The war will soon be over," Jane said.

Mum looked up.

"They say, on the newscasts, by Christmas this year," Mum said. "The Maginot Line in France should have stopped everything. The perfect defense, they called it. But if that couldn't stop them... anyway, there's no reason for you to go. Not now."

"But the Germans entered through Belgium," Mr. Frances replied, scars casting shadows on his face. "They bypassed the Maginot defenses, which only went along the French-German border... but, I suppose, that's a discussion for another time..."

"Now, there's no choice," I said, turning to face Mum, Devon, and Mr. Frances, all of whom backed away.

"Nicholas, you're right," Mr. Frances said, flipping his pocket watch chain. "There's no argument. Although I didn't know they were drafting, till now. And I also understood you were too young."

Mr. Frances's words and the thought of Jane and Daniel gave me the impetus to speak.

"I'll be off soon," I said. "Although I don't want to leave Jane and Daniel, and all of you. And I'm old enough."

"You won't be off anywhere," Devon said, moving closer, the scent of whisky on his breath.

"Not when your wife and son need you," Jane said.

"But when there's no choice, that's different," I replied.

"News reports say they are not drafting," Mum said, holding the paper high in the air. Turning to me, incredulous, she added: "Did you volunteer?"

Devon moved away and grabbed the page, examining the contents before gazing over at me expectantly.

"You've betrayed us," Jane said. "Me, your son, and everyone around you."

"Why are you doing this?" Devon asked.

"That I haven't done so earlier is shameful," I said to him. "My pa signed up at the beginning of the First World War. I'm resolved to fight as you refused to do in the last war. I'll take bombing courses, not to follow my pa's choice of becoming a Bomb Thrower, but to protect myself as he did. I ran away at the start of this war, but I'm not cowering in this corner of the world anymore, not when the rest of the world is fighting."

"You didn't run away," Mum said, her green eyes gleaming with tears in the light of the fireplace. "We came here together."

In the crowd behind me, I overheard Doctor Mitchell saying that mothers are sad and sore with the system and the government, but for these women, letting their sons go was a duty they had to their country.

"What did you do in the First World War?" I asked Devon. "Why did you fight for such a short time?"

"Who told you that?" Devon asked.

"My father. And I read about it in his journal too. But he never gave me details."

Devon turned, rubbing his forehead, addressing the group now staring at him.

"You may have heard the term before," he said. "French leave, an unauthorized holiday. Nicholas's father Wilfrid and I didn't receive the passes we were expecting, so we went to London for six days. Wilfrid went back without me. That's all."

"My pa had to see the Captain," I said. "Loss of six day's pay, along with twelve days of Second Class Field Punishment—parading around the grounds with all his equipment on his back. That was the first time he had ever been on the carpet in the army, and he got soaked as hard as lots of fellows who have been on the carpet before."

Then, turning back to face me, Devon added: "I met loads of men who were wounded and nearly killed at the front, stories of bullets and shrapnel and explosions, starvation and rats and disease, all of that kept me away. The more gruesome stories I heard, the stronger my resolve became. I told the men I met that I was a city resident of London with no stomach for war. I was pinched by my Sergeant who was at a London pub while on leave, and I went to court and was subsequently sent to prison."

"Your career in the army polished to a fine hue," I said.

Devon paused momentarily, eyeing me before turning toward the crowd again.

"The army," he continued, sweating from drink, "is Hobson's Choice: stay or go, take it or leave it, either option objectionable. Catching a stray bullet, being assaulted by steaming shrapnel, starving to death in the trenches was so meaningless that I chose to leave it."

"I wanted to enlist since before you made us leave England, when the Germans were bombing London," I said. "You were a coward in the last war, still are in this one. Our family's presence here is proof."

"We came here for your Great Granny," Devon said, shaking his head.

"I hear troops now are waiting for the end of the war," Mr. Frances interjected, speaking quickly. "Could be there's not much danger now."

"I relived the wartime story of my pa over and over," I said, addressing Devon, "a man nineteen years old who, at the start of the Great War, decided along with his friends to volunteer. One of the first Canadians over to the battlefields and among the last to return, marching all the way to the Rhine at the conclusion of the entire mess. Then I hear now about you whitewashing your own decision to abandon the army, Hobson's hogwash, which has given me one last thing to remember you by. So, thank you for that. You held me back from enlisting for a long time, refusing to listen to any news of the war, paying too much attention to Mum. She didn't resist you, or your hatred for news about the battles, hardships, and death that enveloped the rest of the world outside our home."

"Hogwash?" Devon said. "Your mother and I are to be married, you know. She has yet to tell you, but I assure you it is so. And you don't want to be here to see that?"

Now the whole tangled disaster had unravelled: Mum and Devon's frequent close proximity; their seemingly inadvertent touches conveyed across the dinner table or while conversing languidly by the fireplace; the subtle laughter; the innocent gesturing; all seemingly innocuous and made without ostensible thought or purpose. That made me ill then and now, as did Mum's shamelessness.

My mother's disappointment was evident in her silent stare; a request for immediate reconciliation with Devon. But I had a better idea.

I lunged at Devon, knocking him to the ground.

Glasses shattered. Women gasped. General commotion ensued. Mum moved away before the whisky glass Devon was holding smashed violently, splintering everywhere.

Pushing me off him with the weight of his lean frame, Devon then rose to face me, rubbing his nose with his sleeve. He was ready to lay a haymaker on me.

Mr. Frances jumped in, separating us with his arms, muttering about peace and amity. Mum was sobbing, pleading with us to stop.

I stumbled backward.

Devon's fist came at me. Contact. My scars were his focal point. Another hit. I regained my balance for a moment before falling backwards onto the table, dishes flying in all directions.

Rising from the table, covered in pie and potatoes and soiled with fluids, I popped Devon in his eye.

His hands covered his face. Mum went to him. His eye would be puffed and blackened by morning, and thankfully, I would soon beat it out of this town.

Mum escorted the guests from our home as I grabbed the photograph of Pa from the mantel, walked into the next room, and opened my suitcase. I placed my father's wartime journal and photograph inside, knowing I would no longer experience shame and disgrace upon reading its pages. I heard mumbling voices outside spreading the word that Devon Dixon, unlike his brother Wilfrid and me, was a coward.

Despite the thought of leaving Jane and baby Daniel and our new home, and Mum's impending marriage, all of which droned powerfully in my head, I knew definitively that I would be leaving Khartum to fight overseas; to do what the bravest souls in the world were doing, and what they all knew had to be done.

Soon, I would show everyone what I was made of.

# 22

O n my open suitcase, beside my father's war journal and a pile of wartime letters written to his mother, lay the photograph of Pa in uniform.

Wilfrid Lionel Dixon's enlistment papers listed his age of nineteen years and one month, a fabrication through the addition of exactly two years of age. His height was more difficult to falsify and listed as five feet four and one-half inches, his girth 35 inches (a tummy tuck before the physician's measurement to be sure, I could see him sucking in his gut) with a two-inch range of expansion noted, medium complexion, brown eyes, brown hair. Nothing extraordinary recorded physically, not even his bum leg, which was hard to see how they missed. Maybe he had waddled into the physician's office on one of his better days.

*I don't think I will pass the doctor's examination because of my leg,* Pa wrote to his mother later, *so I will likely be back home in a month's time, and everyone says the war will be over by Christmas anyway.*

The enlistment papers showed that Pa belonged to the Church of England. The paperwork indicated that Wilfrid Lionel Dixon was somehow fit for the Canadian Overseas Expeditionary Force.

Similar papers were signed for Uncle Devon, and Pa's friends Tommy Leitch and a boy named Carson Thompson; all of whom lived in Highgate, Ontario where they grew up together. The "Highgate Boys," they called themselves. The only other of the Highgate Boys that had no such enlistment papers was Art Maunders, who couldn't pass the physical without the fingers he had lost in his father's carpentry shop.

Pa, Devon, Tommy and Carson were vaccinated at the camp in Valcartier, where they walked three miles to the firing range in their new uniforms and polished shoes, leaving their recently issued grey overcoats behind. The camp stretched for miles through the mountains, and they walked endlessly through the surrounding terrain. There were about 25,000 soldiers there, and an additional 5,000 arrived one evening. Pa went to the tent to change that night, taking everything out of his pockets and putting nearly all he owned in the corner until he changed into his other outfit. He forgot about these items and went up to the store to get a shoelace. When he came back, his money was gone. Someone was apparently walking around pinching what wasn't theirs, and the four of them started looking out for each other's goods after that.

They stuck together as they found accommodation on board the S.S. *Laurentic*, White Star Line's predecessor to the R.M.S. *Titanic* that had sunk and killed 1,500 passengers only two years before as the cowardly and contemptible crew of the S.S. *Californian* sat idle only a few miles away. He wondered why the *Titanic* had sank so quickly, in under three hours; what circumstances might lead any captain to steam ahead full speed into an ice field on a dark, moonless night without binoculars in the crow's nest, with twenty-two hundred souls on board; and how another captain and crew could ignore multiple rockets being fired, wireless telegraphed pleas for help, and a ship disappearing within view. Pa wouldn't have known yet about the *Lusitania* that had sank in 1915, killing nearly 1,200 in only twenty minutes after being struck by a German torpedo, but if he had, he might have inquired how much of that was the fault of the captain. According to his journal, Pa only made inquiries about the *Titanic* to other privates, none of whom gave him any ideas. After meeting the *Laurentic*'s captain, Pa immediately asked about the tragedy of which he had read so much; and although the dark-bearded man with an eye twitch indicated that he knew some of the crew who had died on the *Titanic*, he said nothing more.

The *S.S. Laurentic* left at midnight for Gaspé Bay, five hundred miles distant, near Newfoundland and Labrador. They arrived at a harbour lined by a colossal cliff of sheer, green-crested rock rising triumphantly out of the sea like some great vessel of bygone days.

Over the coming days, while at anchor in Gaspé Bay, Pa's arm began to hurt where he had been inoculated. He sat at the window one day, and he counted four cruisers and thirty-one transport ships that came one by one or in pairs. All waved British Navy flags over innumerable Canadian soldiers, horses, and the heaviness of expectancy.

*On October third, at 4:45 in the afternoon, we pulled out into the big pond.*

*A boat joined us in Newfoundland, along with a couple of big warships. They certainly were some queer looking boats. One had four 110-ton guns and could shoot a shell twelve miles, the shell itself weighing in at 1,250 pounds.*

*We had a pretty good time on the way over. There was a piano in each dining room, and at night there were concerts. Whoever knew how to play was welcome. I had my hand at it. My years of lessons taught me to improvise a tune and keep it going. All the boys stood around me singing along with whatever words came into their heads.*

*At 9:30 we had physical drills up on deck. Tom, Carson and I attended lunch sittings at 11:30. There were parades some days and lectures other days, then suppers at 6 o'clock. We had good grub. Chicken dinners were served three times.*

*I wasn't the least bit seasick on our journey across. We certainly had a nice ride. The ocean wasn't even a bit rough until the last day. I thought I could live on it. Even when it got a little rougher on the last day, our boat was pretty well loaded down so we didn't rock much. Still, Carson and a few others got sick.*

*We passed near the old country where Granny was from, along the coast of Ireland. All you could see were cliffs and green grass that would've brought a smile to Granny's pursed lips.*

*On October 15th we arrived in the Harbour of Davenport. Plymouth certainly was some city from the looks of it, but they wouldn't let us land. Tom said some Canadian soldiers had left their barracks one night to drink and fight the evening away, so ruining the chance for everyone else.*

*We got off the boat Sunday morning at one o'clock and marched two miles to the train station. Then on to Amesbury, about 250 miles from Plymouth, and nine miles of marching to Bustard Camp in Salisbury Plains. After three weeks on the boat with barely a chance to stretch our legs, all that marching with 98 pounds of equipment went pretty hard with us. When we got to the camp, I was nearly all in.*

*We began drilling pretty hard after we set up here in Bustard Camp, and every other day we have been out for a four-mile route march in the wet and cold.*

*I guess we will not be in this camp for long, and that suits me fine. We are all going to get two or three days holiday, so I think I will go to London and look that burg over. A lot of the boys are getting cold feet. I don't feel like that yet, but it is hard to tell how soon I might. We will be leaving for the front in a month. Everyone says we shouldn't expect to be there for long. The Belgians are practically in the hands of the Germans now and the Germans are marching on France again. Still, everyone says that all 32,500 of us Canadians here in England will be home in time for Christmas.*

# 23

"Could be there's not much danger now," Mum said, repeating what Jane's father had said as I boarded the bus to Ottawa in the overcrowded station at Havelock, her statement seemingly both consolation to herself and approbation of me leaving to fight near the end of the war. She handed me a book, some writing paper, and pens.

"You have told me about your father's journal," she continued. "So, use this to write home, and maybe start a journal of your own."

Mum avoided my stare as the bus pulled away, her eyes partly closed as though praying. Ian's tranquil expression darted around before he waved frantically in my direction. Jane and Daniel stood languid among a sea of oscillating handkerchiefs.

As my bus limped along the highway, I opened my father's journal which I could read now without shame, for the first time in recent memory.

I fell into intermittent sleep now with the tremulations of the bus, my mind no longer focused on Mum but on the highway's potholes and the bombing courses I would take for my own personal protection.

The Japanese invaded Pearl Harbour in a surprise attack. All the boys were yelling about how the Americans had entered the war, and that none of us would be home for Christmas.

In Ottawa, we were shown training films in a dim, smoke-filled theatre reminiscent of the Duke and Duchess Theatre in London. I wrote in my journal what we might expect during the war: from medical inspections, kits, equipment and the King's uniforms issued through the quartermaster stores, to marching, and food while in the King's service which, judging by my father's time in the army, would be atrocious. We were to keep fit through ball sports, boxing, and tug of wars. There would be lectures, technical instruction and extreme boredom. Our pay could be sent to loved ones which would make them love us more, and we could keep a sum to ourselves for times of leave. There would be recreation rooms where we could write letters and play billiards and darts. The films told us that military service could be the making of a man. Officers were responsible for their men, as well as leading inspections, marching, and drills. Rifles and guns would be used on firing ranges. We would learn what it took to become a British Soldier. And always, at the end of these films, which I underlined in my book many times, the final, resolute, and splendid words: *Hitler Beware.*

Battle of Britain newsreels showed how Britain was maintaining mastery in the air over Germany, despite massive aerial attacks over London. Propaganda to be sure, but inspiring nonetheless. Nazi bombers, protected by Messerschmitts, were shot down by Hurricanes and Spitfires. There was footage of downed enemy planes, and, thankfully, no pictures of wrecked Hurricanes or Spitfires. Reels asked the audience: *How long can the enemy withstand such losses?*

Royal Air Force fighters were constantly on alert, pilots shown playing ball and relaxing before rushing into action to destroy the enemy. They were efficient, of ruthless spirit, and had a need for victory. Nazis had a clear choice: retreat or be shot down. Successful tactics against enemy planes were discussed, as well as the Spitfire's speed of 387 miles per hour and the German bomber's 220 miles per hour. We all argued vehemently about our air supremacy afterward, as though any one of us squabblers had what it took to go into the Air Force.

We were stabbed with needles, herded like cattle, and squashed onto buses for the brief ride to the impressive stone buildings and narrow cobblestone streets of Quebec City. After a short rest in the city, becoming gaggingly intoxicated in dark, historic stone pubs, we were loaded onto transport ships. The drunkest among them, a fat man with a moustache, sat down beside me and shouted at everyone. To avoid a fight, I opened the novel *Men of Iron* and set the book on my lap, as though I could read anything now.

"He's reading a book!" the fat man said, incredulous, pointing at me.

"I enjoy reading while drunk," I said loudly as the men laughed. "Especially when embarking on an overseas voyage."

"He's a Limey!" the man said, waving his arms frantically. "We got a Limey book nut here who spews out nonsense like a broken typewriter!"

The boat set out into a frozen, angry green sea with a crew of bickering, tan-outfitted privates. If I read anything or looked out at the sea, I might give up my gut full of booze. And I could anyway. Not for me to decide.

A private beside me, not the fat man who was still yelling and wiping spit from his moustache, but a calmer, more tranquil drunk, asked what I was reading.

"I'm not reading anything," I replied.

"What's the book then?" he persisted. "What's it about?"

"Myles Farworth."

"Who?"

We were being drowned out by the clamour of the engine and countless voices. The man of gluttony, laughing beside me, stopped to listen as I spoke louder to answer the question.

"A young 15th-century squire, who works for the great Earl of Mackworth."

"And?"

"He needs to regain his pa's honour. His pa was accused of treason. Says here Myles is seeking to restore the dignity of his family name, to become a man of valour. A knight. Important then, the same as now."

"Oh," he replied loudly. "Sorry I asked."

"Did you hear?" the fat man proclaimed, pointing at me. "The Limey typewriter is spitting out a book review!"

Looking out over the waves and the icy air, I recalled the frigid air back home in Khartum. After walking around frozen Miller's pond at this same time of day, I would pass through the front door to see Great Granny and Ian sitting at the table waiting for dinner. Uncle Devon would walk into the house behind me with freshly chopped wood, and we would all sit down around a circular wooden table to a dinner of potato and leek soup with potato bread, the fire for the cooking pot lingering beside us.

Amid the ship's undulations, we assembled for a similar meal. Everyone was seated at long rows of tables. Mum always gave thanks before dinner. For a few moments I was back in Khartum. The only sounds came from an announcer on the wireless radio and the ticking clock over the mantel. Mum began a prayer as a static-filled Tuxedo Junction began. Uncle Devon sat down as she acknowledged that we were all thankfully together. A bilious sensation began to accumulate in my stomach as I ate, the thought of duping her and everyone else about wanting to enlist swimming through my head. I had hoodwinked her before departing for the mines of South Leeds as well, Pa convincing me that she didn't need to know. Running away didn't matter much when one contemplated what needed to be done.

Devon became the stout private in front of me, tearing at a piece of stale bread with his teeth, the biggest of our swineherd tearing at a boiled corncob. A sickness engulfed me, envisioning the pigs eating as I watched this man, a queasiness accentuated by Jane Frances and baby Daniel whom I had left behind, and by our wedding when I agreed, before God, to stay married to Jane until we parted through death, mine perhaps closer than anyone knew.

*In the afternoon,* I wrote in my journal, *along with several other transport boats and two cruisers from the British Navy, we pull out into the big pond.*

*I am eager to return to England, even if my homecoming is without Mum and Ian.*

*On the way over, there are no pianos, no concerts or singing, no chicken dinners, no joviality—only men in quiet, sombre moods sitting before standard fare three times a day, the conversation sparse and lacklustre.*

*I am assigned to share Third Class metal bunk-beds in a cramped quarter with three other privates who know nothing of what is ahead, as I read through my father's journal in our idle hours.*

*The entire vessel sways day and night, the days passing with drills on deck, specified mealtimes, parades, and lectures, and the nights are filled with transitory fits of sleep. I often awaken in the morning adrenalized, anticipating the warmth of Mum's breakfasts and Jane sewing by the fireplace, even wishing to see Devon outside, toting around his slop bucket for the pigs. Instead, quickly realizing where I am, I can only think of U-boats that might be in the area, my father's journal on the edge of my bed reminding me that I am living out what is written on those pages. The older men, I discover, have lived through all of this before, as I have; knowing and dreading, more than the others, what is yet to come...*

A news bulletin came on the radio one day as we were relaxing in deck chairs between drills. There was rationing in Britain for bacon, sugar, and butter, and the number of pedestrians killed on the streets every week since the mandatory blackouts had increased sevenfold.

On the way overseas, contrary to my father's wartime journey to England twenty-five years before when there seemed to be such gaiety, such anticipation of excitement and youthful adventure, I vomited nearly every day.

# <u>24</u>

W e arrived in the chilly Harbour of Davenport beside Plymouth and marched from the docks to the train station. After travelling for hours by train, with endless trees flashing by outside the windows, we settled near Bustard Camp where Pa was initially stationed. We were given quarters not in the wet tents of his war but in huge, overcrowded, and stinking barracks.

The drilling began with marches in the English countryside, tangling with countless tree roots sprawled over the forest floor at random elevations and in haphazard directions. As I tripped over a knot embedded in the dirt, I thought I heard a growl coming from direction of the trees.

"Are there bears around here?" I asked another private.

"What are you on about?" he asked, sniffling.

"I thought I heard growling. Are there any bears here, in this forest?"

"We have rifles. A shame we don't know how to use 'em, isn't it?"

After that, I practiced at the firing range for hours in the cold, every day, long after the others had gone back to their tents. While I enjoyed hitting the mark on the range, I was still compelled to do whatever needed doing to get out of the place.

Our captain gathered us together one bitterly cold day for an announcement.

"Churchill needs volunteers," he said under a blue sky, his breath forming into clouds. "Storm Troops. Leopards. Special Forces. Army Commandos."

I raised my hand, and he pointed to me.

"Yes?" he asked.

"I think this needs doing," I said. "Churchill, unlike Chamberlain, is a man of valour. I will apply. "

"Good," he said, smiling and waving me over. "Man of valour. I like that. Well now, any other men of valour here, then?"

I sent a letter home to Mum, and immediately afterward, a letter arrived telling me to report to Scotland in a week. I was eager to see the country I had read about in the Reading Room of the British Museum, the country where Mary, Queen of Scots, would tremble with John Knox's prayers, remarking that she feared them more than any army in Europe.

I was pleased with my wartime career thus far, even though I had seen no action, knowing that I didn't want to. Similarities between Pa's journal and my current circumstance became apparent: *a lot of the boys are getting cold feet. I don't feel like that yet, but it is hard to tell how soon I might...*

The fog of Glenfeschie, Scotland greeted me with an eerie glow of sunrise as I arrived by cargo plane. *This set of training began with the basics of parachute jumping,* I wrote in my journal. *How to operate the chutes, where to pull, and what to do if they won't operate: pull again. If that doesn't work, then pray and try again. Now onto the jumps: first from a metal tower soaring high above the seemingly endless expanses of ice and snow, a place from which I never could have imagined throwing myself off before. Then we are instructed to complete three successive jumps from planes flying at an altitude of 20,000 feet. Somehow, most of us step out into the cold open air and plummet toward the ground. We are rewarded with breakfasts of ham and eggs and toast, and dinners of watery soup. Those who choose to remain on the planes slowly vanish from our ranks. Somehow, our cords work to deploy the parachutes, one of the few moments of relaxation, enjoying the green landscape in all directions as we slowly descend to earth before being collected by dirty trucks full of stinking men. Quite a joy.*

Each day started at 5:30 a.m., when we were all woken by the sound of bells and bugle horns and led by officers to run outside. We scampered through ice cold streams of water, before being strapped down with 40-

pound backpacks and running a 20-mile route. Those packs never seemed to part from our backs, even in my dreams. Then, going inside, we were rewarded with a breakfast of toast and tea between 6:00 and 6:30 before returning to the barracks, not to sleep, which I gladly would have traded breakfast for, but to ensure our boots and leather were shined and our beds were made up to be as flat as a board. I was written up once for having dirty boots on my bed while I was outside with a group of privates smoking cigarettes with my boots still on my feet.

I prepared to fight the note, gathering witnesses in my defense and compiling timelines before the case was summarily dismissed with no explanation.

Then, we shuffled outside for additional training; as though we needed more marching, running, and traversing through obstacle courses.

Among the training areas we faced was a scattered assemblage of bushes and foliage set on a patch of grass and situated at the edge of a hill; a region we were told contained ten men hidden in camouflage. We needed to be dodgy to get through the area, and I was somehow first in my group to do so. With the same sort of stealth I used to sneak out of the house at night to ride Betsy through the streets of London, I was proficient at slipping from one bush to another, spotting each of the men in turn and avoiding them by navigating through, undetected, to the next hiding spot. I distracted them with a thrown rock or twig, and plunged an imaginary knife into the sides of these invented and easily-foiled enemies.

One of the other exercises involved live ammunition whizzing by overhead as we were given the task of navigating through trenches covered with barbed wire, which might have been a remnant of the trainer's previous war.

"Such drills are not for this war," I told one of the instructors as I held on to my helmet and crouched down to navigate into a narrow entryway.

"Move! Move! Move!" was his response, his hands waving towards the direction, the men behind urging me forward.

We marched, between exercises, with those confounded 40-pound packs that I would have liked to have sunk to the bottom of the sea, each pound digging into my flesh, and we rested only five minutes every hour.

Becoming accustomed to firing various weapons, dealing in hand-to-hand combat with knives, and practicing how to disarm one's attacker was all good stuff, though.

There were dull and seemingly interminable lectures, and then hands-on demonstrations, where various methods of signalling and communication were discussed. And just when I thought each of these exhibitions would go on indefinitely, they finally ended.

There was a mock beach assault on a Scottish island. Fun and games ensued for a week as we parachuted onto this landmass in groups of ten without food or water, and we were forced to survive while using only knives, a map and compass, some string, matches, and bedding. A radio was made available to the Officer-in-Charge for emergencies only.

"We can carve wooden hooks good for a single catch," I said as we stood over an alcove, showing them a flattened twig with a spike I had fastened to the end in figure eights of string. Running a worm along the spike's length, I tossed the lure out to sea.

"Later," I said, looking back at the group. "I'll show you how to find underground water."

I showed them where to dig up potatoes on a farm we came across, keeping careful lookout for farmers with shotguns or cutting blades, and we found well water and plenty of potatoes.

As we continued moving, we collected rainwater in our helmets and, days later, found a dried stream.

"Keep digging holes everywhere with your hands," I said, perusing the cracked soil.

After a while, I told everyone to stop. I surveyed the holes. Several of them in one area were filling with water from below. We excavated more soil and were all able to drink dirty water from our helmets. Once we all had our fill, we moved on.

Sitting on the ground around a campfire one night, Don, a Canadian boy with red hair and freckles, dimples, and a wide smile turned to face me. His visage wavered with light and shadow. He was a grown version of a boy who once played Pitch and Toss in the schoolyard in London so many years ago.

"Where'd you learn all this stuff?" Don asked.

"Through long summer days at my Uncle Devon's house in Northaw," I said. "My brother and I only had nature and our imaginations to keep us occupied. And potatoes were all we ate in Khartum, a town where there are more mice than people. I won't say that I'd prefer the mice to some of the people there, like my uncle, the Mayor, and the doctor. That's a story for another time."

"We ain't got nothing but time. No time like now, that's what I say."

At the end of our period on the island, our map-reading and compass navigation was tested as we needed to pass around a set of obstacles for the entire day to find a rowboat on a beach. Easy stuff.

Near the wooden rowboat covered with seabirds, only two of the dozens of groups who started met up with us.

After returning from the Scottish island, dehydrated and hungry, but nevertheless reinvigorated, I learned that the famous Lord Baden-Powell, who founded the Boy Scouts, had taught at this camp at the outset of the war. This was, in fact, once his land. An elderly Colonel at the camp, a plump old man with a white moustache and career wrinkles who apparently trained men alongside Baden-Powell, called me into his tent one day.

"Your problem-solving is exceptional," the Colonel said. "I am impressed, knowing that you took a leading role in getting your group to the objective on the island, when nearly all the other groups failed."

"That was nothing," I said to his confused expression. "Try to navigate through the streets of Whitechapel in London on a foggy night by bicycle, a pea-souper we called it, with the smoke of coal fires in the air, and drunks and tramps darting this way and that... now that's something."

"You are aware of the structure of the Army?" he asked, navigating his oversized belly around the dark wood desk cluttered with family pictures, unfolded maps, and thin books open to various pages. He offered me a folding chair.

"Actually, sir," I replied, seating myself while he remained standing. "I'm not certain I am."

"How's that? You know about commissioned and non-commissioned officers, of course."

"Of course," I replied. "From my pa's war journal and training reels in a theatre in Ottawa."

"Then you know that above the rank of Private, such as yourself, there are corporals, sergeants and staff sergeants who are all non-commissioned officers."

I was beginning to recall this, thankful for having been given part of the answer. He paused to light a cigarette, and then continued.

"Yes," I replied, adjusting my position in the chair. "Of course. Certainly."

"And then the commissioned officers are Second Lieutenant, then Lieutenant, then Captain, Major, then—"

"Colonel," I recalled suddenly. He adjusted his belt, the cigarette hanging from his mouth.

"Yes," he replied, taking the cigarette in one hand and waving it in the air as he spoke. "That is correct. However, do not interrupt again. Do you know what one star on your jacket means, son?"

"No, sir," I admitted.

"Well, you will. That is the first level of a commissioned officer."

Pausing to draw from his cigarette and exhaling his next few words in a cloud of smoke, he continued: "You see, I'm recommending you for such a star. A promotion directly to Second Lieutenant. You will need to grow a moustache to look older, because if you pass the interview and the training, you'll be placed in charge—along with two other officers—of a platoon of thirty-five men, some professional soldiers with twenty years in the army. You will need to be a good soldier, and make good soldiers out of your men."

I was unable to formulate a response. Nor could my mind conceive, in such a limited time, whether I was ready for this. Trapped, cornered, my inexperience surfacing in my thoughts as a weakness to anyone of whom I was in command, I needed to fight my way out.

"Sadly," I said, "I must decline."

He stared back, confused. I tried again with whatever came to mind.

"What do you think makes a good soldier?" I asked.

He seemed relieved, pausing for a moment before answering; the only sounds those of shuffling backpacks and shifting rifles outside, along with the more distant echo of those practicing at the rifle range.

"A good question," he replied, sitting down on the edge of his desk. "What makes a good soldier?" There was quiet in the tent again, and I wondered if he was throwing the question back at me.

"A good soldier," he said, "is disciplined. He obeys orders but can still think for himself all the same. He gets on well with others and respects his seniors. He knows that privates and officers can go out for a drink, but never together. Above all, a good soldier must obey orders. And the men know that. So, back to my point, I'm recommending you for a promotion directly to Second Lieutenant. And you mustn't decline."

"Certainly. I won't, sir."

The interview following the recommendation came in the form of a selection committee of three commissioned officers, two days later, all aged Lieutenants seated inside a tent at a table illuminated by the light of a few lamps. The men invited me in and began asking questions, one after another, instantly making me want to flee. One of the officers, speaking rapidly and with Italian-accented English, introduced himself as Lieutenant Carmichael; sounding like *Lieutenant Chemical*.

"You are new to the Army," the Lieutenant said. "Why are you here?"

"Why are any of us here?" I answered, seating myself.

"There's a war on, son."

"You're certain?"

"I'm certain how an Officer needs to be addressed by a Private."

"What I mean to say, sir, is I couldn't tell, from all this training, that there's a war on. The last war was my father's, though, this is ours. The Army is necessary, especially in times such as these. The Army is all that stands between us and the enemy."

"There's the Air Force and Navy, too," the eldest of the men replied, as though I was not aware.

"Why do you want to be selected as an officer?" Carmichael asked.

"I was offered the position," I replied, "and understand, from talking with some of the men, that I am obliged to accept."

"You have no such obligation."

I continued by disregarding this response and providing the words they certainly wished to hear.

"I would become an officer not only because my father was a non-commissioned officer, a Sergeant in the Great War," I said. "But because my father, who died tragically in a mining accident, might have been proud of his son for becoming a commissioned officer, for exhibiting some of the same determination, drive and persistence that allowed them to emerge victorious from the last war."

The men were silent, apparently impressed with this answer and my evident turnaround, jotting notes before continuing with additional questions.

"Did you do anything exceptional at school?" the Chemical Lieutenant sputtered.

"I played tennis, cricket, and football. We did quite a lot of cross-country running and learned about Latin and German. I was chosen as a Prefect in charge of some of the lower grades. I was good at math, but not much interested in it…"

Lieutenant Carmichael asked me to elaborate on my role as a Prefect.

"I was chosen as a Prefect," I said quickly. "In charge of some of the lower grades below me, to watch out for the boys, and to rat on them to the teachers if they got off the straight and narrow. I was to give the boys advice, but mostly make sure none of them got hurt."

I did not add that I should have ended the games of Pitch and Toss instead of participating. I gave no advice, and probably hurt more than helped any of them.

"And you were successful at that?" the Lieutenant asked.

"Not so much," I replied.

"What do you think of commanding men, as opposed to boys?" one of the officers asked.

I felt well prepared to answer this, based on some of the conversations I had engaged in with Pa in the pubs of South Leeds.

"Well," I said, "my father once told me that when he was in command, he oversaw twenty men who depended on him. He thought about them constantly. In the British Army, there was strict obedience. You didn't dare disobey an order. That was part of the burden of command, knowing that the men would obey. So, you had better consider your orders carefully. There could be no mistakes. But he made errors, one of which caused his death."

"Tell us what you know about that," the officer asked.

"My father and I were in the coal mines in South Leeds. We heard one of the conveyors start, with the rat-tat-tat of a field gun. He dropped the safety lamp he was carrying, causing an explosion that brought the ceiling down. That had happened to him before; but this time, instead of killing someone else and destroying another fellow's arm, it killed him, and gave me a limp and these scars on my face."

"Shell shock," the officer said. "Seen it happen to many good men."

A group of privates placed their backpacks down outside. I was not done yet.

"My father had a war journal," I continued. "He wrote in it between battles, I suppose, to pass the time. He didn't worry, or spend time writing of fear or emotion. He wrote like a reporter in a courageous fight not only for honour, for King and country, and for victory, but most pressingly, for survival."

"In the Great War," Lieutenant Carmichael said, "there were diaries issued to all of the privates. Many of the men kept notes in them. I did so myself. But keeping a journal now is strictly forbidden. However, that stated, what else did your father say about overseeing the men?"

"He knew that being in charge meant double duty: looking out for yourself and making certain your men survived. You must be instinctive, react without planning ahead, the same as when you're bullied as a boy and forced to fight back... but he said his time in the war, the worst hell of his life, were when he did his best. Something he could never beat for the rest of his days, whatever he did..."

"Well spoken," the Chemical Lieutenant said, his dark eyes peering into mine. "Presuming you pass the training in Wales, I'm assured you will make a fine officer, son."

# <u>25</u>

I was transferred to Wales, going through Officer Training with more written tests, interviews, and constant drilling than I cared to admit. We were given two lengths of rope and boards and told to fashion a way across a flowing river. Tying the ropes to trees on each side, and stretching the boards across the taut lengths, I created a wobbly but traversable bridge. We learned how to look after people under our command, and we were taught to fire Bren machine guns and revolvers. Having grown accustomed to the rifles we were issued as Privates, as officers we were told we would have to get used to .38 calibre Webley revolvers for close quarter fighting and for guarding prisoners. Sure, anything to wrap up this somewhat interesting but endless training.

After several weeks, I was told that I had passed the Officer Training. I was given an armband with one pip. Sewing the insignia on, I learned how to quickly cut the markings off while in action so the enemy would not know who was leading and who was not. A good precaution to not draw fire to oneself, if I would see any fire at all. I was instructed one day by letter to report, not for active duty, but back to Scotland for even more instruction and preparation.

Back in the bitter cold of the Scottish Highlands, this time at the special training centre at Lochailort, amidst crab apple, silver birch, scotch elm and pine trees, for further Commando exercises, I began intensive mountain training. We had a great time climbing sheer embankments and learning to slide down patches of loose rock for surprising the enemy on cliff sides; reluctantly practicing various methods of signalling, without recognizing if such skills might be useful; and discovering with enthusiasm how best to defend oneself and then take out an attacker when fighting in close quarters without weapons. We were taught to demolish bridges and trigger landslides using explosives. All good stuff.

Then, after weeks of such exercises, I found myself smiling for the first time in a long while when I wrote in my carefully concealed journal that we were being sent out on our first assignment.

Launching in the morning with a group of destroyers from the east coast of Scotland, our clothing, helmets, boots, and rifles all painted white, we were told that we would be invading Norway.

An assault on an entire country, by the lot of us squabblers. We were keen, organized, and equipped to fight in the snow of the mountains; but still, we were young and without any experience in battle, or in taking over and running a country.

"There are U-boats in these waters," the Captain announced. "So, we'll need to stay vigilant."

"A British civilian liner was torpedoed and sunk as I was en route from England to Canada," I replied. "Now, the memory of those children, passengers and crew only anger me toward the action to come."

"Certainly good to keep them in your thoughts," the Captain said. "Loads of civilian casualties in this war."

I spent the hours contemplating what we might come across in those mountains. Over lunch, I talked with Hector, another Second Lieutenant who was in the fifth decade of his life. Between the two of us, we had command over this mission.

"My men and I will look for any signs of enemy positions hidden in the snow," I said. "Outlines of entrances, any sudden shifts in the size or quantity of mounds in the snow. What will you and your men be looking for?"

Hector seemed more interested in his soggy potatoes and hardened bread than anything I had to say.

"Germans," he said, eating without looking up.

We were halfway across the Baltic when the Captain smacked us across the face with his news.

"There is good and bad in everything," the Captain said. "The good in this is we have not encountered any U-boats. The bad is that we are turning around. The invasion plans have been terminated, and we are being recalled to Scotland awaiting further orders."

There were murmurings that this entire deployment was a fake to keep German troops concentrated in Norway, and that Britain never intended to invade that country at all. As nothing was confirmed or denied when I pestered my superior officers for answers later, no one could be sure.

All I was certain of was that my first chance for action had been thwarted, and we were headed back for more training.

I was granted leave to go into London, eager to return, with the additional incentive of getting away from the endless war games for a week. But when I arrived in a city covered in rubble, sand bags and broken glass, dirt and burnt wood, dust and brick powder, explosives and bomb casings, the stink of sewage, domestic gas intermingled with sap from trees that had been cut in half, and the rooms of houses on exhibit from the effects of the bombing, I only wanted to depart as quickly as possible.

This was much the same as when I had walked the streets with Mum, Uncle Devon, and Ian after the bombing began, only the damage now was extensive and beyond the boundaries of our small neighbourhood. And now that I had enlisted for "active" service, I could peer into the faces of those who had been bandaged and crippled, to see the same fright that once overwhelmed me with a need to escape to Canada, or anywhere else that this war had not touched. These sentiments were replaced now with a desire not only for vengeance, but a paternalistic need, the requirement to protect this place and these people that I would soon be away from, perhaps fighting on the battlefields of France as my father had.

After sleeping for a few days at the Cecil Hotel, I recalled a man named Oliver who once introduced my parents to each other at the bar of this same hotel 25 years ago. There were plenty of girls here, as I understood there were then, and lots of soldiers for them. Half of the girls here, who stared at me as I walked in, might be married and not faithful to their soldier husbands; which made me disregard them, despite their obvious beauty, as an unsightly sort.

1916

*Tommy, Carson, and I got to London for a week of Christmas holidays. Getting away from the trenches was a great relief as bad winter weather set in. Rain was falling nearly all the time. Our trenches had three feet of water in the bottom, and they were nearly all caved in. We waded in water up to our hips.*

*We got rooms at the Strand Palace hotel and went out strolling. I looked everywhere for Devon, half expecting to see him, half hoping not to. We got lost but came back all right, and I am certainly enjoying myself. It was great to be in a place where I can get a good square meal. Four of us had dinner together, and it cost $9.25 but it was certainly the best, and well worth the expense. My room alone cost 13 shillings a night, but I intended to have a good time, for it might have been my last. And when I got into a nice feather bed the first night, I thought I was in heaven. We went out to the London Tower the next day, the castle the old Kings used to live in. We saw the Crown Jewels and the gold dishes, gold swords and gold sabres, all decorated with diamonds. There was a big diamond there, the size of your fist. The valuables were all in a big glass case with iron bars all around, and everything inside was charged with enough electricity to keep the thieves away. All kinds of old guns and armour were there, some that Charles the First and Charles the Second wore. A block that was used for beheadings was on display. It bothered Tommy, but not me and Carson. We counted the chips; around fifty victims.*

*None of the tours cost a cent. All the soldiers get a free ticket for any place in England.*

*Tommy went to Glasgow, and Carson and I drank our nights away in the London pubs. As I went through the British Museum during the day, Carson slept away. I passed hours in the enormous library, called the Reading Room, wishing I could spend days or weeks there. I heard the British Museum tube station was being used as an air raid shelter for the Zeppelins, but I saw the tunnel was dusty and vacant.*

*I had a bunch of meat coupons, and gave them away. They were only a farce. Half the places we went to eat in didn't want them. I also gave away a sugar card and butter cards.*

*I had my picture taken. The photographs would be sent to me in France. I didn't know how they would look, as I was about half canned. Carson and I met an American traveller and another tourist from Vancouver, and we all certainly had a good time. But I felt like I had a big head the next day.*

*London seemed just as busy as ever. You wouldn't think there was a war on, except for the recruiting speeches on every corner. I guess it's coming time for conscription to start. Serbia looks a little dangerous now, and, in France, the Germans keep coming over to the British lines and giving themselves up. They don't get much to eat and say they are sick of war, the same as everyone else.*

*There are two big buildings in London that were destroyed by Zeppelins. Londoners are as nervous as kids about the Zeppelins. There are big search lights all over the city and anti-aircraft guns, and an aeroplane patrol, even though the Zeppelins have only reached here twice.*

*Warneford, a British Flight Lieutenant, downed a Zeppelin by bombing it from above. The newspaper said the German pilot jumped from the flaming Zeppelin at 100 feet and landed safely in the bed of a convent, after crashing through the roof. Sounds like a lark.*

*There was another story before that in the Times about Roland Garros, the French Ace. The Times said Garros destroyed a Zeppelin by flying through its envelope. Another paper said the pictures of Garros flying his Morane Bullet through the gasbag of a Zeppelin over Paris were faked.*

*I'm sure people want to believe both these stories. They want to know that these airships can be taken down. Just like they fancy that the German army can be defeated and we can win this war. People need their heroes for inspiration, to drive them forward, forgetting about any embellishments.*

*I saw Oliver Ellwood, one of the Highgate, Ontario Boys who is married to an English girl now. A lot of the fellows are getting married* to English girls. Oliver introduced me to a girl named Doreen at the bar of the Cecil Hotel. There were plenty of girls there, and lots of soldiers for them. But Doreen was different than the other girls. Instead of talking with the soldiers, she sat alone with her father and only talked to him. Her shyness was interesting, alluring I think is the word, and she was beautiful besides. Her father, a retired Lieutenant in the British Army, invited me to sit down. He told me that about half of the girls in there are married to men who are at the front. They are not being true to their husbands. It certainly is a shame the way they carry on, running around with soldiers on leave while their husbands fight. When her father left the table to get drinks, Doreen said she will always be true to whomever she marries.

"When will this old war end?" the Lieutenant asked me after returning to the table with beers.

"This old war is good for another year yet," I said, downing some of my beer and smacking my lips. "And maybe longer. It just depends what the Russians do next spring. The amount of men lost on the Somme was awful. The part of the line I was just in is a pretty quiet place. But last spring, the French were doing some hard fighting there."

When Doreen went to the toilet, I told the Lieutenant about a town in the German's hands with about 30,000 civilians. The French sent word for them to get out, but the Germans wouldn't let them, thinking the French wouldn't attack with civilians in the town. The French, thinking all the citizens had gone, used gas.

"About a week ago," I continued, "I was taking a walk through this place and you could see women, children and Germans lying around by the thousands, dead. And the Germans have shelled it all to pieces. Just in front of our line, about two miles, is the third largest city in France, in Fritz's hands. Fritz and the townspeople there are working the coal mines and using the factories, and our people never shell it because civilians live there."

Before leaving, I told Doreen I wanted to stay. I didn't say I wanted to stay with her, but only added I couldn't be away any longer than allowed. One potential dishonourable discharge in a family is plenty.

*I walked through the city with Oliver, Doreen, and her father. We all ended up at the law courts, where we heard a divorce case. There was a lot of shouting and carrying on about everything they had done to each other.*

*As we were leaving, I smiled and said: "Let me tell you, that was more fun than a picnic."*

I spent time going to the London Tower and the British Museum as Pa had, only now, they were closed, boarded up and locked shut. The British Museum tube station was packed with squatters, like I had been so long ago.

The Strand Hotel was open, a luxurious palace in the city with beautiful piano music reverberating through the halls. I had not seen this place before and did not want to leave. After sitting on a couch for an hour or so, listening to the music in an area resembling an outdoor patio, a tidy young blonde woman, an employee of the hotel, approached me.

"Are you staying here?" she asked.

"Yes," I said. "Are you? I don't need anything, if that's what you're after. I'm fine here, thank you."

"What room are you in?"

"Room 14A. My father stayed here many years ago, and I see why. Although I figure you weren't working here at the time. Too young and such."

"We don't have a 14A, sir."

"There's a 14A at the Cecil Hotel."

"Perhaps you should return there, then."

The sirens and rumbling of overnight bombing raids near the Cecil Hotel kept me awake for countless hours, making me wish I had stayed at the Strand despite the rudeness of the staff.

After packing my belongings and descending the stairs the following morning, I found a telegram telling me to report for duty immediately. My leave was over. I was being posted to barracks in the north of England, reassigned to my old unit due to the always obscure "operational requirements."

If this was a trick by my superiors to get me into more training exercises, I would be applying for a transfer somewhere, anywhere, immediately.

After stepping out of the front door and into a taxi, I saw that the far end of the hotel was flattened. My taxi rounded a corner by a group of tenements on my way out of the city, revealing more randomized demolitions. Looking through the taxicab window at a familiar part of the Thames where I cycled in my youth, I only saw the loss of tranquillity and equanimity that once permeated these streets.

Seeing this unwarranted destruction, evident throughout the city, made me impatient to end my gratuitous holiday and get after those responsible for this mess.

After returning from leave to my old unit, I had a rank insignia which the others seem to respect; those who had previously bothered me now left me alone. I engaged in various field exercises and was assigned to command a group of twenty men and perform mock battles against other units, assaulting each other in open fields and in pre-fabricated towns at the edge of the hills. I ordered my men to proceed efficiently from house to house, leading them as we smashed imaginary windows and threw dud grenades inside to simulate flushing out life. The men appeared bewildered at my determination in the face of this illusory foe; apparently, they weren't aware that the non-existent adversary I was fighting against was the treachery of my superiors in ordering me back here for more mock battles and training exercises.

I applied for a transfer, uncertain of where I would be sent, seeking active service. A week later, my Sergeant, a tall, thin man with a grey moustache entered my tent as I was cleaning my boots with a rag.

"Here you go," he said, handing me a paper which I quickly read through.

I was being posted to Brancepeth Camp, near Durham in England.

"More training?" I asked.

"You wanted a transfer? You're being transferred."

Brancepeth Camp had huts with bunks, and everyone wore denim work uniforms. The meals consisted of boiled and tasteless potatoes, beans and tough meat that came apart in strings. We occasionally walked to Brancepeth Castle, where the stores were. I was issued with an overcoat, a respirator, two Mills Fragmentation bombs, and another pair of boots.

We engaged in drills. There was endless marching, shooting at the rifle range, weekend inoculations, bomb throwing exercises in sandbag areas, and ruminating about my father's ennui in wanting to get to the front. This war had no fighting in France and, fit and ready and eager to go, being granted occasional leave to London, my requests for transfer to Singapore or Africa were inexplicably denied, saying that I was needed where I was. I wondered why I was needed there to fight sham battles against mock enemies, to go to countless pubs and movies in town, and to generally lead a dull life.

Then, an event came that changed all of this. I was posted, along with everyone else, to barracks by Southampton in England. Something was finally happening.

# <u>26</u>

After several weeks in the port town of Southampton, firing at ranges, navigating through obstacle courses, hiking, running, and crawling through trenches covered with barbed wire, there was still no news about any impending attack. I was assigned to a battalion, though: British Second Army, Bucknall Corps, 50th Infantry Division, 69th Brigade. And then, one day, late in the afternoon, we loaded our gear into the back of trucks and moved close to Dover.

A few days passed, and there was a knock on the barrack door. There was no light outside, and no one was awake. All of England was blacked out to highlight nothing for overhead planes, yet lights must have been on somewhere inside the building. Had I missed my day on the duty roster? I hadn't checked in days. Was this all my fault? The doors opened to reveal senior Officers of the British Army yelling orders. No one shouted directly at me. I wouldn't be reprimanded; at least, not for this.

We were taken to the port in the dark of the early morning, where we were moved to tents and given a meal of hard rations: biscuits and tea. I was outfitted with a rucksack, a Mark III helmet, binoculars, a life belt, ammunition, a Bren machine gun, and a tool kit.

I was briefed along with a group of officers after we had packed into a narrow metal building. The Company Commander, Johnston, a tall officer with a dark moustache and a gruff voice, began:

"We will be moving onto boats right before dawn," he said. "You will each be placed in charge of thirty men. You will be given maps, a compass, and told where to rendezvous. The 3rd Canadian Division, 7th Canadian Brigade will be on your left flank during the landing and the British 50th Infantry Division, 151st Brigade will be on your right. You will be landing on Gold Beach before proceeding inland. That is your objective for the first day. Your ultimate goal is the same as everyone else's: to liberate Paris, before pressing on to Berlin."

Heavy with the weight of our mission, we were packed onto transport carriers that rolled into darkness. The sea was rough; the air windy, cold, and unpleasant.

Johnston, seated beside me, would not stop talking of his wife and daughter back home in Wales. He was giving a detailed account of his daughter's last visit to her grandmother's house, during which Grandma had doled out too many sweets. Afterward, his daughter couldn't stop talking until late into the night, unable to sleep. I had to put a stop to his gibberish.

"Remembering my trip across the Baltic," I said, interrupting him. "I wonder if this, too, is a distraction from what's going on somewhere else."

"There're rubber decoys, tanks, military transports and planes, set up near Dover where we were stationed," he said. "It's across the channel from Calais, France. These two port cities are closest, and Calais is the most anticipated spot for an invasion. All the rubber inflatables are diversions from the assault we're on that'll include a hundred and fifty thousand men, and thousands of transport vessels, warships and aircraft. Paratroopers and bombers are being sent in before us. We should have sent the inflatables in first, instead. That'd be quite the sight to see, all those dummy ships and planes floating on the horizon as the Germans look through their binoculars trying to figure it out. Then, meantime, we'd be moving in somewhere else—"

"I heard there were dummy paratroopers sent in to confuse the Germans: half-sized men with firecrackers," a bearded Lieutenant interrupted, shouting over the clamour of the vessel's engine as the ship rolled with the waves. "Some of the real paratroopers had trouble with their chutes opening. They were jumping too low. The planes couldn't ascend 'cause of anti-aircraft fire. But 'cause of the bombing raids, the coast'll surely be cleared, so we'll be able to advance up the beaches and into the French countryside."

"I wouldn't be so smug," I said, "If the paratrooper planes couldn't put up with the anti-aircraft fire, how could the bombers?"

Along with most of the other men from the British Second Army, Bucknall Corps, 50th Infantry Division, 69th Brigade, I was seasick on the way over. We vomited beneath the seats; the boat, a steel hull without a keel and enclosed on four sides, was thrown back and forth by the wind blustering by on the overcast day of June 6th, 1944.

We studied our maps. Gold Beach was near La Rivière, and we would pass by Cruelly, moving by two major sets of roads and a river to our checkpoint at a railway line near Bretteville-L'Orgueilleuse, northwest of Caen.

We were about 10 miles out and in rough water when, as fires and smoke rose over the beaches, shells bombarding the coast from ships behind us, a group of a dozen massive American Sherman tanks floating nearby suddenly overturned. One by one, the tanks slipped silently and serenely over the edge of the landing craft, and down beneath the surface of the water. A temporary peace descended as we sat waiting for what was to come.

As we approached the horror of that beach, the whine of bullets could be heard, along with pinging impacts of flying metal on the bow of the boat. The Company Commander told us all to get ready.

The ramp opened.

The men in front went down.

Machine guns fired. There were echoes. Yelling. Screams.

I wanted to stay, to turn the craft around and go back. Too many had already died getting out. But I was in charge; I had to get the men moving. I had to go.

"Move!" I shouted, pushing the men one by one and then following them out myself into the waist-deep water.

A beach lay before us, littered with men and explosions, fire, bullets. The temporary stillness that accompanied us in had become thunder.

The noise was deafening as navy boats fired, bombers shelled, and machine guns rattled.

More men fell.

Pandemonium. Chaos.

Smoke bombs were dropped by low flying aircraft, to disguise the advance of the troops.

The Company Commander had to shout to be heard, moving us forward.

I urged the men ahead with their heavy packs, as some of them tried to stop and help others, all of us wading forward.

"Don't stop!" I told them. "The medics will get them! Look ahead!"

There were grey blankets visible beside medics attending to the wounded on our smoke-filled Gold Beach. This area was not cleared but full of machine gun fire, enemy snipers, and obstacles on the beach's edge.

We plowed toward the shore to the whine of bullets near and far. We fired blindly into the quickly dispersing smoke.

American tanks and transport trucks rolled off ramps, with men and boats as far as the eye could see. Engineers moved in with wire cutters to clear obstructions of barbed wire, and others worked on mined metal beams offshore and on the beach.

Men dropped, and bodies littered the sand and floated all around.

There were too many men dead and alive to count, shelling and explosives causing unbelievable clamour.

The Company Commander directed other vessels ashore. Recalling navigations through innumerable obstacle courses, I waded as quickly as possible through the water, knee-high now, yelling at my men to do the same.

Then, our boots met sand.

I utilized my training in Scotland and England when leading my troops through. Taking quick inventory of those remaining, I walked at a pace not frantic, but steady. Firing into the hills ahead, sometimes blindly, not waiting for the clearing of the barriers, we pressed on. All that was on my mind was escaping that nightmare beach.

For all my rationalizations and justifications, what was I doing here?

I dropped down as low as possible, as often as I could, as my Commando training had taught me to do. Without waiting for others to get onshore, I instructed them to charge forward along with me.

Men were dropping around me. An active machine gun nest. A metal bunker.

Get them or they would certainly get you.

"Drop down!" I said, and the men obeyed.

With my rifle, I took aim at the opening. The gunner stopped firing and was attempting to reload. Metal ricocheted off metal as I fired several shots, picking him off.

Running forward, concealing myself behind bushes as I did, I tossed a grenade in that direction, and then another. After detonation, smoke emerged from the bunker.

Then, temporary silence.

My men rose up, and we proceeded.

We moved on toward buildings on the beach front, houses and hotels. A nice place, surely a tourist destination, in better days.

And now, we needed to get to the checkpoint.

Moving forward slowly, methodically, cautious with each step, we began plowing forward at a rapid pace. We ran and crawled through trenches and fortifications covered with barbed wire. Shallow trenches, not like in Pa's war.

"Another training exercise with live ammunition!" I told the remaining fifteen men in my charge, as I pushed some wire aside and moved through.

With difficulty, we were able to pass through a hedgerow, a barricade advantageous to German defenses which we had not planned for, a set of 12-foot tall bushes that caused an impediment for our tanks. Coming out scratched and bleeding on the other side, the air ripe with gun smoke, and eager for death, with planes dropping bombs from overhead in an infernal racket, I yelled as my men emerged from the greenery.

"Look out for mines or obstructions!"

We found ourselves near a dirt roadway, a short time later. I counted seventeen groups of British and American privates escorting prisoners back to the beaches before I stopped taking note. Coming upon an area that was still noisy but somewhat quieter, we stopped for a brief rest. Fifteen of my men were here.

I lit a cigarette and opened Pa's journal, as the men dropped their packs. No one spoke, although I wondered how we had made it through. We didn't want to continue, that was implied, but we certainly didn't want to go back to that beach.

*The Canadians pushed Fritz back about three miles from the Somme front, where there were a thousand Fritzs put out of their misery. There were all kinds of guns and an unlimited supply of ammunition, and we pounded Fritz 24 hours a day. Fritz was getting short of men all right, for he had Marines in the trenches.*

*The ground we advanced over was plowed up, with shell holes all over. The villages were nothing but a pile of brick dust, and the woods looked as if a big storm hit. When Thieval was taken, 2,800 guns bombarded it, each gun firing an average of 10 shots a minute. So that gives an idea what Fritz was getting. And our land Forts walked over to frighten Fritz with a quick firing four-pound gun and a bunch of machine guns. When Fritz beat it, we turned on the machine guns and mowed them down like grass.*

*We were made aware of an attack coming up where we would have to take Fritz's front line trench on a 250-yard front. We had been in the trenches 24 hours and it was hard to get rations up to us. We were all pretty hungry. The attack began, and we got Fritz's front line alright. He had some big saps dug in the ground, 20 feet, and they were all timbered up and bomb proof. Well, this German we found dead in one of the trenches was getting his supper ready, and we all chipped right in and ate it for him. He had hot coffee, bread, butter, jam and sausage. And we never lost an inch of it.*

A short time later, after eating canned meat and a peanut bar from my field rations, we resumed our travels along the roadside.

A jeep appeared in a trail of dust, and we scattered into the bushes.

Peering through the foliage, I saw a tall officer with a dark moustache driving one of our jeeps. The Company Commander, Johnston. We emerged to greet him.

He was making rounds, and, as we approached his vehicle, smoke and flames appeared behind him in the distance.

"You here to tell us about grandma's sweets again?" I asked, approaching him.

"Your orders have not changed," he said, examining a crumpled paper, "And you're heading in the wrong direction."

"Who's on our flanks?" I asked.

"The 3rd Canadian Division, 7th Brigade's on your left and the British 50th Infantry Division, 151st Brigade's on your right. That could change any time, everybody's advancing at different rates. So keep an eye on your flanks all the time. Your key objective is still a place northwest of Caen near Bretteville-L'Orgueilleuse. The 5th Battalion of the East Yorkshire Regiment, currently in La Rivère, will soon be joining you in the fun. Now get moving."

Day passed into night in a blur of small villages and towns. We had been unleashed on the enemy. Mont Fleury had endless German gun emplacements, and we went after them all. Ver-Sur-Mer, surely an inviting town in more peaceful times, didn't welcome anyone. Crépon machine guns and field guns fired back at us.

Allowing the tanks to go first, we crossed the Seulles River over a pontoon bridge. We then went through some of the villages from house to house to flush out Germans, smashing windows and tossing in grenades like we were back in training, some soldiers running out when the grenades hit the floor, others still cowering inside, beside the dead, as we came crashing through front doors.

I lost five more of my men to German fire. Good men. Good soldiers.

Passing by parachutes, countless bodies, gliders with broken wings, and craters that littered the land, we hiked and ran as full transport trucks, tanks, and artillery passed by periodically. We found ourselves stopped finally at nightfall, exhausted from the weight of our packs and from lingering thoughts of those we had left behind.

After resting for a long time and consuming some field rations, I took a few minutes to analyze my maps. We were eight miles inland, about three miles from Caen, miles yet from where we were supposed to be, and only halfway to our stated objective. Without knowing what had happened and why, we needed to get to our objective point of Bretteville-L'Orgueilleuse, what I was calling "Betty the Organist."

Once the expression caught on, Richard, one of my men with brown hair and matching eyes who spoke rapidly and was a good shot, stood over me as I lay on the ground.

"We have to get to the party to see Betty," he said. "I'm sure she'll put on quite a recital."

"I'll say," I replied. "We'll fire off an R.S.V.P. And then we'll have some swell time."

Later that night, new instructions were delivered by a runner, an American on a bicycle disguised as a local Frenchman. The instructions were to set up perimeters with guards, and so I ordered the few remaining men I had in my charge—10 out of the 30 who started—to take refuge in a wooded area beneath bivouacs, tarpaulins set over long poles, the only function of which was to keep the rain off. The runner also provided orders indicating that we were to proceed to Cruelly by 0700 tomorrow morning, as a Sherman tank would be firing upon the town at 0900 the following day.

There were slit trenches and dugouts to be cleared with grenades, and while we were dropping our explosives down, we found no Germans anywhere. There was no enemy fire at all that night, and no rain. We cooked eggs that some of my men brought back from a local farm. We alternated watch as others, exhausted, slept beneath the bivouacs, their heads resting on knapsacks in a period of temporary peace.

When my turn came, I lay there, dreaming of riding Betsy through the streets of London, and the amusements of my irresponsible days.

Late the next afternoon, looking for fresh water as we were walking down a peaceful country road while enjoying the singing birds and the lovely view on our way to Cruelly, the dirt suddenly came to life. Heavy machine gun fire from a farmhouse up the road. We had gone too close to the medieval town.

Frantically, dropping out of sight and sprinting through the wheat fields lining the roadway, bullets whining after us, we beat it out of there. I shouted at my men to follow. We ran until the bullets ceased and the wheat became weeds and bushes. We regrouped in an overgrown area, beside a tree covered with foliage. Seven of my men followed. I immediately recognized who among us was not here.

"Rodney, John, and David?" I asked, nearly out of breath. "Where are they?"

"Down," Richard replied, panting. "Not wounded. Dead. Back there, on the roadway."

"I'm responsible. I brought us too close to the town."

"None of us saw anything before the shooting started..."

My father's war letters sometimes revealed war as a contest, a game—where challenges were overcome and rewards instilled—instead of the candour of this horrendous liability.

"You didn't kill them," Richard continued. "The Germans did... so, where are we now?"

"This is our vantage point," I said, peering out through the greenery with binoculars. "There's a single machine gun emplacement at that farmhouse in a fortified concrete pillbox, and German snipers in the silos. All waiting for the party to start. Not Betty's party, but a party nonetheless. And we're the guests of honour."

I was ready to go home. The boys often talked of their hometowns. But where *was* my home, anyway? Around here, the houses which were once homes were in farm country with cattle, cows, pigs, and chickens. Up the road was the entrance to the cruelty of Cruelly, blocked and barricaded with Germans on guard. A howitzer stood at the ready. My orders indicated that a Sherman tank would be firing upon the town at 0900 tomorrow morning. We were far enough away from both the farmhouse and the town entrance, and evening was approaching.

I posted a guard and fell into an uneasy sleep.

Several hours later, I was roused, and took guard.

The hours passed looking out into a darkness permeated by searchlights and listening for noises in the distance. Men shouted, and jeeps moved.

A while later, we went over to the roadway.

We sat and waited while searchlights probed elsewhere. When no jeeps were travelling by, one by one, we made the trek to the other side of the road, closer to the farmhouse.

Then as the sun began to rise, giving us the light we needed, we made our move to get even closer to that farmhouse and protect any troops and equipment that might be coming up the road to take the town.

As the sun cast illumination over the fields, the snipers looked out from their silos. They did not see us yet.

Their searchlights, and those around the town's perimeter, were extinguished.

I alerted the men to stay low. We would have to crawl on our bellies. The wheat stalks, only four feet tall, were our best ally. We began by moving through the fields to a nearby stream in a wooded area, where we stopped for a drink and to fill our canteens. Following alongside a winding path, we emerged in an area where the water came close to the farm.

The silos were within easy view now.

The men came, one after the other, in quick succession.

Next, a gravel path led up to a wooded area next to the barn. Richard and Archie approached me once we reached the wooded area.

"What now?" Richard asked.

"This place is lit up like Christmas morning," I said. "Time to make my move. Listen: you two are my best shots. I want you both to stay here. Richard, you'll be in charge. Can you two hit the silos from here?"

"We certainly can," Richard said.

"Then when the shelling starts, I want you two to take the snipers out."

Then, turning to each in turn, I continued:

"Oliver, Sanders, George, Tom and Will, you are to spread out and focus on the pillbox. Me, I'll take that pillbox with your help. Then, we'll all go for the howitzer at the entrance to the town and take that out. Clear the way for the 151$^{st}$."

Moving quietly like a foraging jungle cat, I shifted through the brush and up to what looked like a clearing behind the barn, clutching a grenade and waiting.

When the shelling started at 0900, the timing precise, we had enough of a distraction to begin our assault. Shots rang out through the fields and then, from the pillbox. The snipers both fell 10 metres to the ground. As instructed, there was continuous firing at the machine gun nest.

Aligning myself behind the barn, I pointed my Bren gun around the corner as the firing continued from both sides. I was close enough to see the eyes of the men in the bunker as they fired without noticing me. I ran toward the bunker. My men ceased firing. The German machine gun continued, and when I was close enough, the Germans finally saw me. I tossed a grenade in. One blast. Silence. A few distant explosions. Another grenade thrown in and detonated. I walked in to find three men, none of them moving.

At the entrance to the city, the howitzer was blown apart on the ground from the shelling. The Germans shot back for what might have been an hour. Then, groups of our boys, reinforcements from the 151st Brigade, came marching down the road. Two Sherman tanks followed soon after.

We moved through the town with chickens running at our feet, and we installed snipers in the church and at the Cruelly Castle, northwest of the village. The Germans came out and surrendered, and were held in a centralized location.

A Second Lieutenant in his late fifties from the 151st, Gerard, handed us orders, instructing us to proceed to Caen.

"We were headed there anyway," I said. "So, we're glad to go. There's a party not too far from there."

"The First World War was fought on this same terrain, but it was not as fluid as this," Gerard said. "It was just stagnant. Nothing doing at all, sometimes for days or weeks."

"Before this, I wanted an end to my endless training," I replied. "But nothing doing for days or weeks sounds like a picnic right now."

We continued, exhausted, not having slept much the night before, our ammunition supplies low.

We followed a British tank for a time, chopping our way through twelve-foot hedgerows that we did not know were there, hedgerows that the Germans defended vigorously.

And then, on the fifth day, our ammunition nearly depleted, we stood down for some well-needed rest.

I was told that our Company Commander Johnston had been wounded and that additional men from the 151st, who were separated from their division, were on their way to regroup with us. More coming to join the search for Betty's party.

Supply trucks began arriving, along with jeeps and armoured vehicles. We stayed in a village near Caen that had been liberated, where we were given fresh clothes, eggs, and chocolate by local women who also showed us where we could obtain fresh water from the wells. They spoke little English.

All of this was a welcome sight for these sore eyes, including a woman from the town who reminded me of Jane. She said in mangled English that the Germans treated them well. Although these women were polite, the presence of us as an invading British force in their town, just as the German one before us, was not welcomed but tolerated. Fine, all the same.

Word from the 151st was that the fighting in Caen was intense.

"There were multiple assaults waged against the city," Gerard said. "And the 69th and the 151st continue to fight. But before we reach the place, there is an apple orchard nearby."

We stopped at the orchard that night, and I gathered countless apples before I lay down under a tree to sleep before my watch began.

My eyes opened. A loud roar. Then another. And another. Fire. Smoke surrounding me. Debris flying everywhere. I was back in the tunnels of South Leeds, in my father's final moments.

I was conscious, then fading into unconsciousness with the pain.

And in the instant before blacking out, I contemplated what I might have written if I were moving at incredible speed, or if time slowed. Although I had never done anything of worth in my life, and would be missing Betty's party, I would now repeat Horace's statement in Latin that others in my group had called an outdated lie based on the horrific poem my father once told me about, *"Dulce et decorum est"* by Wilfred Owen, but which I considered otherwise, *"Dulce et decorum est pro patria mori,"* it being a "sweet and seemly thing" to die for one's country. The photograph of my father in uniform at the British Museum, the man who survived with around seventy others from a battalion once numbering a thousand soldiers, returned to my mind along with the image of his blackened face from the mines; my father, the man with the hardened authority on the probabilities of existence and extinction and the familiarity that, in an instant of a bomb blast, or a bullet whining through the air, or a Davy Lamp crashing to the ground, either outcome was just as feasible.

# 27

I awoke, yelling, recalling how Pa was once startled from sleep after days of insomnia to a shell burst above him in the Great War. Then, I recalled our liberation of Cruelly and the intense fighting in Caen with the 69th and the 151st fighting together that I heard about but did not see. There was an apple orchard, and reclining under a tree to snooze before my watch began.

Roused by a loud roar, a shell must have landed in our midst. No possibility of escape. The rest of my men may have been killed. Debris had cut into my leg and abdomen, knocking me unconscious. The Germans had got me before I could get them. No chance for payback.

A nurse came by to comfort me, stroking my hand and then feeling my head for a fever. I patted around and found my journal, and my father's journal, which were on the table next to me, along with a small collection of my belongings.

This was some indeterminate time later, I gathered, and I was in a modern, clean American hospital in London.

The nurse departed as men came in with field dressings to be changed, and nurses poured white sulphur powder on their wounds and gave them chloroform or ether that made the men physically ill. They counted backwards from ten before falling into unconsciousness and being wheeled out into another room.

The men talked of the Allies pursuing the Germans across France, toward the Rhine and the German homeland. German troops were apparently surrendering by the thousands. There was no need for me to go back, and although I wanted to, my nerves had something to say about it; my work here was done.

Death had come closer than ever; not adjacent to me, as in the mines of South Leeds and as I stormed the beaches in France. I wanted to become Myles Farworth in the novel *Men of Iron*, a young 15th-century squire-turned-knight who became a man of valour and importance. But now I was returning to my younger self: the boy who wanted to stay in England and fight as Devon, Mum and Ian embarked on their overseas voyage, yet travelled with them to go into hiding in Canada.

"If the story of all those Germans surrendering is true," one of the men said, "We need to get out there and round them up."

"The lot of you are being transferred to an Irish hospital to recuperate," an aged orderly explained. "You're not yet fit enough to go back to your regiment. For now, you won't be rounding anyone up, except yourself for mealtimes."

"That's fine for now," I said, knowing that although I should, I did not ever want to return to the possibility of facing shrapnel falling like rain.

After travelling by train and then by boat across the Irish Sea, followed by a short ride by transport truck, I found myself in a place called Bangor in Northern Ireland. The room was close to the edge of the water and overlooked the sea. I could hear the splashing of waves through the open window as I fell into a tortuous sleep, the worst in recent memory.

I awoke to a young doctor examining my wounds the next morning. Most of the men around me were not yet awake.

"Will I be sent back?" I asked, startling him. "Or will I be going home?"

"We need to fight our way to Germany in victory," a man with a peppered beard beside me said, in a thick accent I didn't recognize. A young nurse walked up and placed her hand on his forehead.

"Don't fret, Costache," the doctor said, lifting the blanket and inspecting my bandages. "You'll have your chance. Nicholas, you have not been sleeping well. You will be sent back to the army as soon as you are fit. By all appearances, you may both be sent back together."

Months passed before I could get out of bed for extended periods. The seemingly interminable time was spent playing cards, reading letters aloud, writing letters home, meaningless journal writing about the sea and sky, discussing our lives before the war, and pondering our anticipated futures. And in this time, I reflected on my life in Khartum. I wrote a letter to Jane, to my mother and brother, and even to Uncle Devon; I imagined sitting in front of the fireplace with Jane and our baby, and talking of our future on the farm.

"My story's simple," Costache said one day as we were lying around, waiting for nothing. "I'm a married Lieutenant with a British father who died long ago. I did not know him, really. Only some memories are left that I hasten to recall. I remember him slapping me when I stepped over a newspaper instead of handing it to him. And my mother, she still lives in Romania. I used to see her a few times a year, before the war. She has a big garden and a nasty temperament."

"It's a wonder you turned out so charming," I said.

"But I did grow up with my auntie in Cuffley, so maybe that has some bearing. Like my wife, my auntie isn't such a shrew."

"I've been to Cuffley, many times," I said. "To the train station, at least. It's not so nice. Maybe I saw your non-shrewish auntie there. I wanted to move to Northaw after my pa died, but then my uncle had different plans. I made loads of mistakes trying to get my family together when my pa lived in South Leeds, and my mum lived with me and my brother in London. Anyway, we somehow landed in Canada on my Great Granny's farm in a ghost town."

"Seems your story is not so simple," he said, smiling as he rested his head back. "Tell me more."

I wrote letters to Jane and Mum, and read through my father's wartime journal where he postulated the end of his war. If the Allies were pursuing the Germans across France, toward the Rhine and the German homeland, Costache repeatedly said, he wanted to be a part of the drive to make that happen. I said nothing, simply nodding my head in agreement.

*July 21, 1916*
*I suppose you have heard about the French and English big guns.*
*Well, you can make up your mind that this old war is nearly over. About*

*two months ago when we took back some trenches the 3ʳᵈ Division lost,
we captured a German Officer, a Sergeant, and seven Privates. The
Officer said to not mind, that Germany is prepared for three more years
of war. The Sergeant said he was a liar, that it's all he could do now to
keep up. I decided to side with the Sergeant, thinking the Officer was just
feeding us a line.*

*There is lovely weather now. We have our baseball team all fixed
up, and we are having some very good games of ball. There is a hill
between the Germans and where we are, so we can play without
getting a few shells in among us. But every time we go in the trenches
after Fritz, we come out with half a team.*

Three weeks later, a telegram arrived. As with the letter instructing
me to report for military duty in Ottawa in two weeks, I was astonished at
the irrevocability of these words. I could no longer be optimistic about the
prospect of seeing Jane and Daniel again. I was being promoted to
Lieutenant and re-deployed. My doctor protested that although I was still
unable to sleep through the night, I was being discharged along with
Costache and sent to Belgium.

Comfortable in the nest I had built there, longing for home, I
reluctantly departed from those doctors, nurses, and patients who had
been my constant, faithful, and involuntary companions, for a new front.

It was March 15, 1945 and I was seated in the snow beside an outdoor fire
and a metal bunker amidst snow-covered hills. I was between Liège and
Namur on the Meuse River in Belgium, about fifty miles from the
Western Front at the German-Belgian border, waiting for nothing.

I was content to sit here with my carbine on the cold ground beside
me, without anticipating what might happen, dressed in my white over
smock with a hood and veil issued upon my arrival.

All the men around chatted over coffee or cleaned their carbines, still
others warming their hands over the fire beside the group of tents that
constituted the small encampment.

I had been assigned, along with Costache, to the 4th Squad, 3rd
Platoon, N Company, 432nd Infantry Regiment, 115th Infantry Division.

Despite orders to wait, Costache told anyone who would listen about his plan to head straight to Germany, where Allied troops were reputed to have been battling their way across the Rhine, soon to triumph.

Like everyone else here, I could do nothing but idle away the hours, barely able to sleep, until victory was declared. Fine with me.

Despite the cold breeze and intermittent heat of the fire, my eyes were closing as I sat outside with a pen and writing paper in hand. I yawned. My chin slowly fell into my chest before I was startled awake by the crunching of approaching footsteps. My eyes flipped open as Costache approached, stroking his ragged beard and adjusting his olive drab uniform, his rifle slung across his shoulder. I scratched at my own growing beard and placed the pen and paper in my jacket pocket beside my journals.

"Nicholas," Costache said, lowering his head to talk to me, fog forming with his words. "The Germans can't reach the Meuse River. This is one of the last strongholds. And here you sit, writing letters as if you're still in the Bangor Hospital. All of us could be taken prisoner, and you would be writing letters without knowing we were gone."

"I know, you're sick of waiting for orders," I said, wiping my nose. "You want us to move in to Cologne on the Rhine River ourselves. You and me. The rest of the men can stay here. Our two-man defence can become offensive to the German army."

"You are taking watch now?" he asked, smiling.

I rose from my seated position to dust the windblown snow from my pants.

"I suppose it's time," I said, bringing the carbine to my waist. "Anything doing on your watch?"

He did not respond until a few minutes later.

"Snow," he said with rotten breath. "Fog. Germans, they're behind our lines. Reported near our position now, wearing uniforms from our dead soldiers and prisoners of war. They turn signs around; damage the wires and mechanics of our jeeps and artillery. They direct our traffic the way they choose and spread gossip that we're defeated in important areas. They will not be captured. They know they'll be executed for wearing our uniforms. Some wear their own uniforms underneath, thinking they may be safe if caught by their own."

"Splendid," I said, retrieving the binoculars as I walked toward the bunker. "Any more good news?"

"Wait," he said as I began walking away. I turned around, and he gazed intently into my eyes. "You're not sleeping still?"

"No one is."

He did not reply, his stare intense.

"Not for three days," I continued. "And not much since I was wounded. You saw how much sleep I didn't get in the hospital."

"Everyone gets wounded. You need to get past it. Soon darkness will be here, and your tired mind will play tricks. We need to know that our men are rested, that they have food and water. And we need the same."

"I've had insomnia before, but not like this. My pa's lack of sleep in the trenches came from constant battles, and fear of waking up to a bomb blast, like me. His insomnia started from the time five of his brother officers were killed, all at once, when a shell hit. I can't relax either, knowing I could wake up to steaming shrapnel coming down like rain."

"Don't think of that. You need sleep."

"My body wants to, but try telling my mind that. And then when I do sleep, there are only nightmares that jolt me awake: nightmares of the apple orchard and my father crawling through tunnels with me, then us going through the trenches of the First World War together."

After entering the confines of the metal bunker with its wide window and machine gun, I watched Costache's retreating figure outlined on a sea of white against the backdrop of the encampment, the hills rolling down into the bank of the Meuse River that carried frozen corpuscles of snow and ice with its current. Above the flowing water, a narrow bridge spanned across two tracts of land. We had a few sentries posted throughout the area, and I was in one of two manned machine gun bunkers nearby. Not enough to thwart a potential attack.

I overheard a conversation between two of the sentries nearby. Our orders to move in on the city of Cologne would certainly come at any moment, and we would move out at 5:30 a.m. tomorrow morning. We would be moving east, closer to the front where the fighting had intensified. Everyone would be up at 4:30 a.m. for instant coffee and pancakes, and when the whistle was blown, we would begin to march. But for now, there were no such orders. Only talk.

The forest, forty miles to the east, was not visible. Those imperceptible trees could spew out any number of Germans, all eager to slaughter our entire platoon before they passed into Belgian territory and moved toward Brussels or Antwerp. The "Jerries," or the "Krauts," formerly the Fritz, were now using anti-aircraft fire against ground troops. My company, my commanding officer, and all those at the camp were relying on me. My position was a crucial one. There was now the safety of 4th Squad, 3rd Platoon, N Company, 432nd Infantry Regiment, 115th Infantry Division to consider.

The tree stumps outside, with the downed trees beside them, would soon begin moving again in my imaginings. The shadows on the bridge would become the outlines of German Panzer tanks, armoured personnel carriers, and Kraut soldiers with small arms, mortars and heavy artillery. These visions would dissipate into the air as I turned with my machine gun to fire, vanishing as quickly as they appeared.

I asked a Private standing nearby, smoking a cigarette, for a coffee. The boy, much too young to be in the army, promptly returned with a cup of steaming water and a palm of instant coffee, which he deposited into the water before handing the cup through the window.

"Tonight," I said to him as he bent over to return my gaze, "will be a long night."

The hills stood still. Their whiteness against the moonlight provided sufficient illumination for a hundred feet of visibility all around. There was no one on the bridge. No vehicles anywhere. No tanks or artillery, no troops or wildlife. Just the hills and the bridge standing still amidst a backdrop of white, silent emptiness: a smoking volcano that could, at any moment, erupt.

Yawning, I stood up and stretched. My wristwatch informed me it was three o'clock in the morning. Sitting down on the cold metal chair again, I read through part of my father's journal and contemplated why I was keeping my own if such record-keeping was forbidden, as I had been warned. If such an unspoken prohibition existed in the First World War, how might the soldiers have passed their time in the trenches without transcribing their own random deliberations?

"*In the Great War,*" the Chemical Lieutenant had said, "*there were diaries issued to all of the privates. Many of the men kept notes in them. I did so myself. But keeping a journal now is strictly forbidden.*"

"I am keeping a journal," I said quietly, now. "Like a lot of what my father wrote, there is nothing there that might interest the enemy."

*January 1917*

*I was transferred out of the Grenade Company and back to 16 Platoon D Company, my old Company, again. January brought a month of real winter: a little snow and freezing all the time. Just like Canadian weather. Better that way than rain. I have the Rheumatism from being so much in the wet, but I am getting treatment. It looks as if the USA might enter the war.*

*The more the merrier.*

*Mother wrote asking if I got a medal. Nothing doing. I am not a Christmas tree to hang things on.*

*I sent a picture home, and those people were having quite a time criticizing it. A Frenchman took that picture. We wear those outfits in the trenches. That was a steel helmet I had on. It protects the head against shrapnel. It has saved many a fellow from nasty wounds in the head. I was having a bit too much beer that day and looked as if I had been pulled through a knothole.*

*We are having very changeable weather. Yesterday it snowed and blowed. Today it is fine. Nothing doing for a pass to Canada till after the war, but I would like to go all right. I will take a pass to England instead, I told my Sergeant, and the man nearly belted me when I said it. The Sergeant has been acting crazy from all the constant fighting, just like lots of the fellows, me included in that bunch.*

*Fritz is certainly getting his medicine on this front. If only the Russians would give him a crack too.*

*They said that while the English and the French fight for land, the Canadians fight for souvenirs. That is about right, too. I just got three pieces of German money from the last German I ran across. I guess he must have been nearly the same as me, on the rocks.*

*There has been real fine weather lately, the kind for fighting. The Russians have made a start and if the Allies can make a start, Fritz will be all in by fall. Fritz has given us quite a bit of gas lately, without any effect, except I can only talk at a whisper.*

*One of Fritz's Aeroplanes came over a few days ago, dropping leaflets giving us five days to get out of this place. Our time is up, but he hasn't tried to put us out.*

*If he tries, believe me, he will get a warm reception.*

A group of six Privates walked by, stopping to light their cigarettes with the fire before me, drinking from their flasks. They stayed for a while, conversing and smoking with the sentry, eyeing me as they headed back to their tents.

If the Krauts came tonight, they would certainly get a lukewarm reception.

The night had been, and would continue to be, a long night.

# 28

Awakening with a start, I surveyed my surroundings. My heart flipped around in my chest like a landed fish. I had been sleeping in the bunker with two journals open on my lap. I put the records in my front jacket pocket. The sound of thunder accompanied flashes of lightning that illuminated the night sky. The noise became artillery and mortar shells exploding in the distance.

Someone was running toward me. Taking the machine gun in my hands, I immediately lowered the muzzle when I recognized Costache.

"Heavy German activity to the north," he said, reaching through the window to hand me a mug of black coffee. He shoved some pancakes through on a tin plate. "Watch close."

He paused, bending over to examine my face.

"What has you bugged?" he asked.

"This war," I replied, taking his offerings. "My nerves. But I'm at the ready."

"We received new orders to move north. We will set out in three hours. I will relieve you at 0600."

"I was sleeping for thirty minutes, maybe more. No one noticed, except maybe you. But I'm afraid of what might've happened, if the attack came here instead."

"But there's no attack here. So, let your mind relax. Keep your head with us here, now."

I examined the pale whiteness, consuming the dry pancakes as Costache retreated into the distance. Setting the half-eaten meal on the floor of snow and walking outside, I kicked the logs of the nearby fire as Uncle Devon always did. The logs protested with a flash of sparks. Stoking the fire by placing a fresh log inside the charred embers, I returned to my breakfast, sitting and eating and waiting, more awake and alert than ever before.

Costache arrived at 0600 hours in a ten-wheel truck driven by an American infantryman. The sun was rising, illuminating the nearby snow-covered hills. A sea of fog surrounded the area. The infantryman jumped out and opened the hood, a cigarette dangling from his lips, checking the fluid levels as the truck's engine continued chugging. The truck was parked so my line of sight to the bridge was cut off. I left my bunker and approached them.

"I requisitioned a two-and-a-half-ton truck and driver," Costache said as he stepped down, his breath clouding in the morning air. "We need men; I'd say ten or twelve, to remove snow and logs up the road."

He presented me with a hand-drawn map.

"All roads going north, they must be cleared," he said.

"Fine. I'll gather some of the guys who are looking for a fun time."

He started toward the empty bunker, calling back to me: "I'm taking over your watch."

"Yes, you enjoy yourself."

Stepping into the mess hall, I sequestered a dozen men who finished their breakfasts quickly and ran outside behind me.

Walking toward the truck together, I saw that a group of American General Infantry was congregating on the bridge. I recognized none of them.

The truck driver closed the hood, urging me to step inside as the volunteers filed into the back. But my attention was still focused on the bridge, and I asked the driver for binoculars.

The Americans began to traverse the bridge, visually surveying the area. Something was wrong: most of their uniforms seemed too tight, and some were soiled with blood and dirt. Thoughts began materializing as my exhaled breath crystallized in front of me in clouds.

My head began to spin, my eyes widening, when I realized what was happening. These might have been the saboteurs Costache was talking about yesterday. Germans in Allied uniforms.

If so, I would have to act. Fast.

Only through intuition, instinct, and rapidly surmising the facts could one, and one's unit, be expected to survive. My actions needed to be unpremeditated, uncalculated and instinctual. I would do what must be done. Jumping over the edge of the embankment, I would dive, bayonet first, down into the German trench.

The horn honked in the requisitioned truck, startling me out of my thoughts. The men on the bridge looked over.

There was no time to wind up the phone and call the Company Commander for instructions. Whatever these men on the bridge were doing here, whoever they were, they needed to move on.

Raising my rifle, with Costache waving his arms from the bunker and yelling for me to stop, I was frozen in place; not knowing how to proceed, except to bayonet first and ruminate later.

I fired a warning shot in front of them. Now, the purpose of these men would become clear. My lean belly flopped down into the snow.

At the onset of the noise, a few soldiers came out of their tents with rifles, some of them still in long johns, others in full gear. Having instigated this, I would wait for either retaliatory fire, or a reprimand from the Company Commander. Mistakes would have to be made to safeguard the camp. I could already hear myself explaining this to the Commander, only seconds after I had fired the shot.

Return fire did not come, confirming that I had made a grave error. Lowering my gaze, my head fell forward, limp, into the snow.

But then, as men continued running, shouting, another shot rang out through the cold air, echoing through the encampment. One, and then another. The men rushed out of the back of the truck, and from all the tents.

In an instant, the camp had erupted into life.

There was the hiss of breaking glass as bullets flew and the driver fell out of the truck, landing on the ground nearby. The shots had come from the direction of the bridge. The driver had been hit and lay in the snow, motionless. An explosion came from the furthest bunker, and I saw one of the GIs on the bridge tossing grenades at random.

I fired, and then fired again.

Jumping up, I ran, firing toward the bridge.

Now, upon reaching Costache's machine gun emplacement, the bridge still obscured by the truck, there was a loud clang of metal on metal as a grenade hit the bunker, then bounced and landed somewhere beneath the snow.

Costache and I darted toward the truck.

The grenade detonated, ripping apart the bunker and sending metal fragments flying in all directions.

Hit, bleeding from shrapnel, I fell to the ground.

Costache was on the ground too, his face mangled with a metal piece lodged close to his temple near his helmet. His chest, too, was red with blood.

There was a sudden fire of artillery shells all around. Explosives detonated and took out the bridge. The bright lights of anti-aircraft fire began flashing in the distance. Germans were everywhere, dozens, maybe hundreds behind them. All around were the sounds of injured troops crying out: "Medic! Medic!" My breath crystallized in front of me.

With my heart thumping wildly, my head disoriented and fuzzy, I looked down to see blood on my tankers jacket. My overcoat and galoshes weighed heavily as explosions shook the ground.

My legs wanted out. My head had no say in the matter.

There was blood in my eye as I grabbed Costache by his collar and dragged him toward the truck. I was my wounded father now with the Sergeant on his shoulder, walking to the dressing station... then, I was back with the muddled confusion of flashing lights and explosions from the invasion of Normandy, and the mines with Pa, and the apple orchard in France, then back in Khartum, calling out for the doctor with the darkness and the smell of burning wood and the stars intermittent with clouds above...

I fired a few shots before telling one of the Privates to get the Company Commander on the field telephone. The boy came back with the box and dialed. The Company Commander identified himself as Kent.

"We were surprised," I said. "I don't know by how many. They're using anti-aircraft guns. We were ordered to move everyone north at

0700 hours but the road's yet to be cleared. Now the other Lieutenant and I are both wounded."

"You need to stay and defend the area," the Company Commander replied. "We will send reinforcements and as many medics with stretchers as I can spare."

I repeated the orders to confirm, the Private placing the phone box in the back of the truck as injured men entered. The truck filled with a dozen wounded, some of them unconscious.

More shots, several explosions.

"We need to get these men out!" Costache yelled. "More Germans are coming into the camp!"

"We have orders to remain here," I said.

"No order will make me stay. We're outnumbered ten to one! The Company Commander doesn't know what's happening here. Look around, there's no one left but us!"

He was right. Innumerable Germans were coming in from all directions. Our men littered the snow. A dozen of us were still alive out of 50 in the platoon. We were just about done for.

Climbing up to the truck, firing at random as I did, I found the driver's seat. Costache was beside me. I put the truck into reverse.

Another anti-aircraft burst hit nearby.

The ground shook. The engine roared.

Grinding into gear. Reverse. Grinding again. Now forward. We set off down a bumpy roadway.

"Don't go south!" Costache shouted, grabbing at the steering wheel and tugging hard to the right. "The road to the north! To the north!"

Driving fast in an indeterminate direction, I had trouble keeping the truck in control through the winding curves.

We almost tipped over and fell off the road into a snowbank at a steep curve, after a short straightaway.

There was another sharp turn. The truck didn't respond, even when I pumped hard on the brakes.

"I can't slow down!" I shouted.

"The other pedal!" Costache yelled. "You're pushing the clutch! Push the other pedal!"

He pulled on my knee, attempting to move my leg over, but my foot was lodged in place. Indiscernible yelling came from the back.

Slamming hard on the useless brakes at a turn, the truck seemed to loosen its grip on the road, as though we were being launched over a pile of loose stones.

The last thing I remembered before blacking out was blood stinging my eyes, the sight of stones flying in all directions, and the truck flying, seemingly straight up into the air.

# 29

*I* saw a pretty nice attack pulled off by a Canadian Battalion. Just on our right, we were in the trenches, and a section on the flank joined the Battalion that attacked. Our trench was a little higher than those on the right, so I got a dandy view. Our artillery bombarded for three minutes and the Canadians went over. That was the first wave. Fritz was firing at them to the beat of a band.

I could see a German Officer arguing with his men as he was firing. My whole section and I were trying to shoot this German, but we couldn't hit him. When the Canadians got up to Fritz's trench, then Fritz started to beat it for the second line. But the first wave of the attacking party dropped down on one knee. The second wave then stood up and rapid-fired overtop of them on the Germans. Our artillery had such a barrage of fire on Fritz's second line that the Germans couldn't get through, so they threw down their arms and gave themselves up.

Some of the Germans who were captured said they were going to make an attack the next morning, and they had a lot of men in the trench. So, we made the attack first, and our artillery certainly played hell with them. They certainly don't like the tanks, for the body of the tanks are strong enough to resist the shells of field guns. The shells from the bigger guns that fire up in the air, Howitzer movement, would put the tanks out of order. But they couldn't hit a moving tank with a Howitzer gun in ten years.

Afterward, there were hundreds of dead Germans lying in the trench.

Our battalion moved from the Somme to a place where Fritz didn't send over a dozen shells a day. At the Somme, they sent that many over in a second. I shook hands with myself that I got out of that place.

The truck I was driving was found by reinforcements from the 106th regiment, sent our way to assist in defending the area. When I awoke the following afternoon, my head bandaged and on fire with fever, I shook hands with myself that I got out of that camp. I initially remembered nothing of the incident that brought me to Liège Hospital except that I had instigated the fighting, and that doing so was not a mistake. The error I made was disobeying a direct order to defend the area, driving away from the scene of the fighting in a two and half tonne truck with wounded men in the back while being seriously wounded. I panicked at a time when I should have been rational. But rationally, if I had not done so, this war would have been over for the lot of us, before the reinforcements arrived. Or would it?

Still, this war was over for me. It had to be. My nerves would not allow me to be sent back again as soon as I was fit. I might never be fit again. Although I should go back to set things right, French Leave would be my only option.

Costache was in the next bed, sitting upright, his head bandaged on one side. Upon seeing me awake, he said he would soon be sent back to the front.

"Maybe we'll beat it back there together," I said.

"No, you'll be sent home," Costache said, tilting his head back. "You are fortunate."

"What are you on about, home?"

"Take a gander at your chart."

I reached down to the foot of the bed and retrieved the clipboard hanging there. Reading through, I discovered that I was scheduled to be discharged from the hospital. Shrapnel was removed from an area near my left eye, and the metal fragments had been pushed deep from the impact with the truck. The reason for the discharge, according to the chart, was septicemia: blood poisoning. Potentially lethal.

My father spent time in and out of the hospital and went back to the trenches time and again. One time while in the trenches, he had lots of company with lice and was scratching himself raw. A lot of sores started where he scratched. It went on for three weeks and, compounded with the discovery that the water they were drinking was bad from some dead Germans in the stream, his blood got in a bad condition and he went to a clearing hospital for non-life threatening injuries. Soon after, though, he was out and fighting again.

"I don't believe this diagnosis," I said, calmed at the possibility that this could be true. "I won't be sent home."

"You will," Costache said. "Regardless of what you believe. Good that you're not a doctor. Or a taxi driver. You were pushing the clutch, you realize, and not the brakes."

"I'd never driven a truck before. Or an automobile."

"Unfortunately, that was quite apparent. Lucky we were not all killed."

"Ya, lucky."

As we were served Christmas dinner that evening, I envisioned walking down the main street of Khartum, having to face all the townspeople with my head down like the Frances family upon their return. They had failed in their endeavours outside the town, just as I had. Walking through town, looking at no one, shamefully having to return before the imminent end of the war, I would return as a lesser man than my father—a boy whose panic in a moment of confusion might have cost him the ability to fight the rest of the war and to engage the Germans on their own territory, to be emboldened and made brave through the example of my father in the previous war, to smash everything I ran across in a bid for unconditional German surrender...

Back home, I would be unable to share my secret ignominy of being discharged from the war, the same as Devon. We would both have been discharged, not for wounds sustained during battle, but from running in moments, not only of panic, but of cowardice. My wartime career would be equated more with my Uncle Devon than with my father.

The doctor in Liège Hospital did not ask about the circumstances surrounding my injuries, and I was grateful. Later that afternoon, I recalled the words from my father's war journal, passages such as "*I am glad to do my duty,*" and "*I have never felt better or happier in my whole life...*" As I reflected on the last entries in the journal, I wondered how I should conclude my own war journal, and what my future son might think of his father if he read these words. Meanwhile, Costache recounted contented memories he had of being stationed in Tripoli in North Africa between the wars, and his desire to return there after this one.

"The time I was there was among the best of my life," he said.

"My time in Khartum with Jane and Daniel was the best of mine," I replied.

"And you'll be returning for more of the same."

During my father's first Christmas outside of Canada, in Bustard Camp, England in 1914, the men were delirious and restless to get to the front. They were having a pretty good time, considering where they were. There were long tables set up in the big YMCA tent, and everything was all decorated inside. The privates sat down, and the officers waited on them. The privates had a chance to order the officers around for a change and they took it. The privates had all the turkey and dressing they could eat, along with roasted potatoes, tomato soup and lots of plum pudding. The people of England gave them all a box of cigarettes apiece, and the Duchess of Connaught gave them each a box of Canadian Maple sugar.

As Pa's Mum would say, like when she got a jar of jam for Christmas one year, it was glorious.

Christmas 1915 and 1916 were spent in London. 1916 was the year Pa, Tommy, Carson, and some other men went to London for a week of Christmas holidays, and when he met Doreen. They had a big chicken dinner on Christmas Eve, turkey on Christmas Day, and another chicken dinner on New Year's Eve. All welcome time spent out of the trenches.

In Christmas 1917, Pa received a pass. He could have gone to Paris, but he wished to get as far out of France as he could. So he went to Edinburgh, Scotland, with Doreen and her father, who elaborated that they were walking the streets where John Knox spearheaded the Scottish Reformation, the last great Protestant victory in Europe, where Catholic trust in works for salvation was ousted in favour of the original gospel message of belief credited as righteousness in Romans 4:5. Christmas was the best one since he had been in the Army. For dinner, they had all kinds of turkey and dressing, plum pudding with brandy sauce, salad, celery, mashed potatoes, vegetables, nuts, candy and plenty of liquor.

All of that was immensely preferable to the cold, dry turkey on crusted rolls with powdered potatoes and instant gravy we were served that night which was, I realized, the single worst meal of my life.

# 30

I was sent back to Canada a week later, and welcomed back into Khartum with a festival of lights in the town square. Mum began crying upon seeing the extent of my injuries, the long scars on my right cheek that the doctor said would never heal bringing symmetry with the same type of scars on the left side of my face from the mines. A patch still covered my left eye and the bandage wrapped my left hand. She hugged me for a long time without letting go, saying she was thankful I was here again, adding the perplexing remark that she knew we would not be together for long.

The Mayor shook my hand firmly, congratulating me for being home and thanking me for my service. I was given a wooden key to the dying town. Men gathered around and commented on my wounds, a few boys asking how I was injured in action. Their requests were met with silence.

"Maybe he doesn't want to talk about what he saw," my mother said. "Would you?"

The boys, along with the men, slowly dispersed.

My uncle, a cigarette dangling from his right hand and a sombre expression on his face, had an appearance reminiscent of my father's photograph from the British Museum. He wore a dark, buttoned jacket, matching trousers, and laced shoes.

"Your Mum and I were married two months past," Devon said.

"You're part of our family then," I replied, smiling. "As you always have been."

"You must have been hit hard," Devon said, eyeing my bandages.

"Harder than you know."

He grimaced, nodding his head and shaking my hand. Mum hugged me as he walked away.

I sighed and glanced up at the lights above and the snow beneath my feet. This powder was not the same as in Belgium. Even the smell of the wood smoke was different. The snow here was almost grey, flecked with stones that jutted in places. I was so used to gazing at the whiteness, checking for any motion even in my exhaustion. Here, I no longer had to stare. Any activity was not my concern. For all I cared, the snow could be undulating like the sea.

I saw that nothing had changed, except that I didn't see Jane or our baby, or any of the Frances family anywhere in the crowd. I expected, with my newfound predilection for the rigidity of army precision, that I might be welcomed with a parade; that my dinner would be set out on the table by 1800 hours; and that Jane, baby Daniel, and her family would be here.

"Where's Jane and Daniel?" I asked Mum.

She sighed.

"The Frances family has moved again," she said. "Jane and the baby went with them."

"Where?"

"They've gone to Stratford. Ontario. Not England. We will be going back there—to England, I mean—once the war's over, which seems quite close at hand. We'll get along without you, of course. We'll live with Devon, in the countryside. Your great-grandmother has finally agreed to go after years of our bothering her. We will care for her during the trip. Ian will help, as he's done here. Of course, I want you, Jane and Daniel to move back to England one day, too."

I made no reply. She seemed to know that I would be staying in this land that my father was from, the land my father fought four years for, through hell and back, an experience I now shared through my own limited vision. And I had a family to start. I would return to my wife, even though my actions in the war made me afraid to face the woman with whom I once talked at length, and so often, about my father's wartime activities.

That night, I told everyone that I would be leaving Khartum the following morning. They all whispered sullen goodbyes. Mum gave me directions to the Frances family home, left by Jane.

"The bus goes part way," Mum said later, after everyone was asleep. "The Frances family had to walk most of the time to get there, as you will. I asked the Mayor to help, I said he owes you, but he said his motorcar is kind of on the pork. Same as when the Frances family left. That thing is good for nothing. Regardless, I will pack you food, drinks, and a blanket."

"I acted disgracefully, at times, while I was overseas," I said. "And I didn't make it to the end of the war."

"Sometimes," she said softly, her eyes widening, "the details are not what matter. Fighting part of the way is still fighting, giving to the cause of victory. You are a hero to the people of this town, and to the people of both your countries. Your father said people need their heroes for inspiration, to drive them forward. And he was right."

And with those words, she kissed her eldest son goodbye.

# <u>31</u>

I rose out of bed early the next morning, before anyone was awake, and peered into the cracked mirror as I shaved with a straight razor for the first time in months. My face had been shaved by the nurses in the hospital and now my stubble fell off in short auburn and black flecks.

Looking out through the broken window, past the cobwebs which now seemed to hold the plates together, early morning light cascaded in through the glass and reflected off the fields in floating dust rays. I asked myself the same questions I had asked over and over since I left the hospital in Liège: the parades I imagined that would take place to welcome the troops back home, when would they all happen? When would the war be over, and would my dishonour end with the declaration of peace? I would not have the unbelievable joy that my father certainly experienced when his war concluded.

*November 11, 1918*

*Armistice was signed today! Fritz was near Haudroy and went to Paris to sign the terms of the surrender, which I heard are very bad for them. The civilians in this village, and I am certain everywhere else, are the happiest people you have ever seen.*

*Thousands were killed on both sides in the last hours of the war. As the Fritzs retreated, the Yankees beat it after them and didn't let up.*

*We will march for Germany and cross the Rhine before we go back to England. I plan to marry Doreen in London, and after that we will board a transport boat back to Canada together for a time. Doreen doesn't want to live there. Her father insists that we live with him. So we'll just go for a visit, maybe a month or two, before we come back to England.*

*I will ring off now, as it is near Parade Time.*

After saying goodbye to Mum, Ian, and Devon, and departing from their waving hands, I walked out of the town with a knapsack and some items she packed for me in a large canvas bag.

Overlooking the parking lot of an abandoned store just outside of town, the birdsong of the morning reverberated in my ears. Shadows unfolded over the snow-covered parking lot as the sun began to rise. I boarded the bus, exhausted already.

I had been on so many trains and buses and cargo planes recently. These methods of transport took me away to places where I lived for a time among those from whom I concealed things. These buses and trains and cargo planes, and once a British cargo ship, seemed the thread that connected, and then provided the distance that obscured my secret humiliation.

Arriving at my destination as the sun was beginning its descent, I stood outside a tiny shack with no lights inside, which the driver said was the Havelock bus station.

It was nearly dark, and a sodium vapour lamp flickered above my head. I would continue until I could no longer walk.

A while later I fell, exhausted, into a thicket a hundred yards from the road. The blanket Mum packed for me, a heavy woolen one, the same as my heavy wool hat, would get me through the night. Yawning, stretching, and dusting some snow off a fallen evergreen tree, I set the blanket out. After wrapping myself up, I succumbed to the world of restful sleep.

## <u>32</u>

After awakening and scratching at my side, I consumed a breakfast of bread, cheese, apple juice, and cold coffee from the supplies Mum had packed. For a moment, I was a child in London again, eating my lunch in the schoolyard, trading food and dirty poems of Petronius while dreaming of Violet, my head still hurting from Glen and the other boys I had fought outside the Duke and Duchess Theatre.

I walked unabashedly through several towns, without stopping in them, having to endure the confused stares of those pausing to observe this daytime apparition in their midst, this man who once had a home and a wife and child, a man who now seemed to prefer abandoned places and overgrown railways with rusting railcars. I was a daytime phantasm wandering through Havelock and Canifton and Wireton, thinking all the time of how a place was only as inviting as its inhabitants, only as good as the people residing within, the same as in the village Pa resided in during the closing weeks of the war, sheltered from the final flurry of killing before the end. Here, friends and family lived together in these towns, people whose relationships were based on trust. They neglected this dodgy man, and I did the same in return, thinking only of my destination, specifically of Jane and Daniel.

*1918*

*The Yankees gave Fritz a slap and took 20,000 prisoners, so while Fritz was on the downturn we had to keep at it till we finished and got back to the land of milk and honey. Fritz was burning every village around his lines. He certainly had ruined Cambrai.*

*In late October, our company was having a little rest in a village just captured from Fritz. The civilians, after four years in Fritz's hands, were the happiest people. The way Fritz used the French people was certainly terrible. The fellows said they would take no more prisoners after seeing what the Germans had done to them. And these civilians thought the Canadians were the good boys. They would do anything for us. One old lady and man offered me their bed, but nothing doing, that was too much for me.*

*Fritz used to take the beds and make people sleep anywhere they could find.*

*I got a bed one night but was lost between the white sheets. It was more comfortable sleeping on the floor.*

*We advanced nine and a half miles the first day and captured umpteen villages before Fritz beat it out of there. While he was leaving, Fritz took the civilian's horses, cows, chickens, and anything of value. He even took the young men and girls back with him. Believe me, if I ever get into Germany, there will be something doing. I, for one, will smash everything I run across. Nothing now, but an unconditional surrender, then Fritz will be where we want him. Fritz is trying to make a stand, but his men have lost heart and don't fight half as well as they used to.*

I was fighting as though across the German terrain, pressing on to Berlin, when I reached Wireton, the last of the towns before Stratford. I was growing oblivious to the stares of those I was liberating, and I saw, in the structures surrounding me, only old memories of places my father and I had been, indistinguishable between the trenches and the snow of Belgium, the exploding shells, and the German fortifications.

Stopping to look through a window at a hotel's fireplace while consuming my remaining apples and sandwiches, I remained there for a long time. Watching that fire, I experienced the same serenity that I always had during fireside conversations in Khartum, and in my childhood home in London that now seemed a lifetime ago. Now, I was alone, wandering the earth as when I had flipped through Mum's *Grand Tours of Europe* travel guides as a child, meandering through the various countries of the world.

Continuing, dead trees and blackened stumps populating the swamps of yellow-white muck mixed with snow made me feel queasy, as though all around me was death. The surface of what was once water was now only a plate of jagged, blackened ice. Moving on quickly past the swamps, recalling the smoke and the wounded soldiers in Belgium, I began to feel nauseous.

I walked for hours before reaching Stratford and finding the home identified on a hand-drawn map. The façade of the manor was flat and unobtrusive among the surrounding trees, the place uninviting with its high, black rust-iron fence. The odd assemblage of naked vines and leafless overgrowth that attached itself to the grey brick only allowed a small portion of its face to be seen—one which might have once possessed the pretence of wealth. But such a building could be renovated, updated, and made new.

The front gate creaked open and I ascended the staircase toward the entrance. My feet dusted their way across the snowy porch. As I knocked on the front door, I had the thought that I had always, until this moment, been forced into action; and because of my desire to conceal so much from others, I had also been led to my own dishonour. But now, of my own volition, I was choosing to begin a new life.

I saw before me an open door and Jane, with a stunning smile. My beautiful bride had her hair pinned up as at our wedding, looking more striking than ever before, with baby Daniel in her arms. Our sweet child stared up at me with bright, brown eyes, a smile creasing his tiny face.

She embraced me with one arm and then kissed me, baby Daniel squirming between us.

"I never thought I'd see you again," she said, sniffling.

"I couldn't let you two wither away in this place alone."

She released me, stroking Daniel's hair and standing in the open doorway. Stepping away from the door, she invited me in.

Later, after a warm meal of chicken and dumplings, after playing with Daniel until he fell asleep, and after the shock of our meeting had subsided, I sat with Jane by the fireplace, our slumbering baby on my lap. The words of contrition, locked for so long within me, poured out.

"You are my only true love, Jane. But I left you just like I once departed London, enlisting without telling you, the same as I once left without telling Mum I would be working in the mines. I was not able to reunite the family there, as I thought I could. I felt responsible for the death of my father, although now I realize it was his time. And while his death was meaningless, his life was not. I once told my brother that liars are sometimes those who sit idly by without refuting a lie, and those who lie have the makings of a coward. The same as the Ottawa Valley *voyageurs*, who went from Alexandria, Egypt up the Nile and couldn't rescue a British war hero in Khartoum, Sudan, I had failed in Belgium by leaving, despite orders to stay, during an important battle which we might have won. I was wounded in an apple orchard in France before that, and didn't want to go back. I was far too fearful, and later misled others about my actions. My father had no such concerns in the mines or in the war, and only thought of the desired outcome. But listen to me; I'm on about myself and my father like a maniac! Please know that I love you and Daniel so much. I'm so grateful to be back here with you. As I told Costache, one of the men in my platoon in Belgium, my time here in Canada with you and Daniel, although brief, was the best of my life."

We sat for a while in silence as snow began to fall outside. I stroked Daniel's hair, and watched as the fireplace drew wavering outlines along the subtle, lovely features of Jane's face.

"I understand why you didn't tell me about enlisting," she said. "I wouldn't have let you. But now, I realize how selfish I was in wanting to keep you here. Maybe your uncle realized his self interest in wanting you to remain, too, although I'm pleased I didn't incite the same anger you had toward him."

"I fought against my uncle without understanding that my anger at his cowardice was actually resentment at my own; as I didn't have the nerve to stay in Europe and go off to war. I wanted to hide in Canada but didn't admit that to anyone, even myself. In England, I saw the bombs and the panic in people's eyes, and that became my fear: dread of seeing others hurt, of my own death, and fright when I saw the destroyed house I grew up in, a home for which my father and I had spent years paying. The once vibrant city I knew had become a ghost town, and the place we moved to in Canada was a constant reminder of this."

"But then, you and I met," she said, and we both smiled.

"And I married my beautiful bride, and we had an adorable son before I went overseas. Then when I got to the war I was fighting as I should have been all the time. My father was a hero and taught me what that meant. For a brief period in the invasion of Normandy and taking the town of Cruelly I did my best, in instances of courage, something of great worth. Fighting in the war is something I can never beat for the rest of my life, whatever I do."

"Apart from marrying me," she said, still smiling.

Now I needed to lift the veil of illusion and imagination, disgrace and shame, insolence and egoism, estrangement from those closest to me, and focus on what was real, to show baby Daniel what it took to become a man. Mum was right: *Fighting part of the way is still fighting, giving to the cause of victory. You are a hero to the people of Khartum, and to the people of both your countries. Your father said people need their heroes for inspiration, to drive them forward.* Sons often deem themselves unworthy when contrasted against their fathers—that was the finest assertion I could offer my son.

Jane gazed into my eyes as we sat there together, the snowfall intensifying all around.

"I was angry with you for a long time," she said. "But I eventually forgave you for leaving us. The problem was me. I know you had to go. You didn't betray me, or Daniel, or anyone else. It was our duty to our country to let you depart. You were honouring us, honouring our country, and honouring God. I'm sorry for insisting you stay."

"I once lived for myself and all that I wanted," I replied, "justifying that this is what others needed as well. This had led me to become selfish; but now, I realize that living for myself is no longer possible. Now, here is our family, together. A new start for all of us. A new life. No turning back."

I reached into my knapsack and found my diary and that of my father, placing these transcriptions of affectedly rapid maturity, the growth of two boys into the hardship of manhood, in the sleeping Daniel's arms.

Earlier, Jane had invited me into her house unreservedly. She now stood, closed the grate on the fire, picked up Daniel and the diaries from my lap and took me by the hand, putting Daniel to bed before leading me into her—our—bedroom.

*-End-*

# <u>Acknowledgements</u>

I have had the great honour, privilege and blessing to know Gordon Schottlander who, at the age of 19, fought bravely with the 5th Battalion Royal Berkshire Regiment as a part of the D–Day invasion on June 6th, 1944. Gordon was trained as a British Commando and as a commissioned officer, and some of his story is incorporated into this novel. As with the main character, Gordon's father fought in the trenches of WWI. Prior to talking with me in multiple interviews, Gordon seldom talked to anyone about his war experiences. He reports that he has been much more open with his family and other people since then. Thank you so much, Gordon, for your service to our country. And thank you so much for fighting for the freedom we have enjoyed our entire lives.

John 15:13—Greater love has no one than this: to lay down one's life for one's friends.

After the war, Gordon came to Canada with his wife Colleen, building a family that includes four sons, 16 grandchildren and 18 great grandchildren. His many accomplishments include President of the Junior Chamber of Commerce, Chairman of the Burlington Planning Board, serving with the Knights of Columbus for many years, Chairman of the committee that raised over $1 million for the local YMCA, and being named Burlington's Citizen of the Year in 1968. Gordon was awarded the first Key to the City for 2020. He lives in Burlington, Ontario and is 96.

My great–grandfather Wilfred Littlejohn fought with the First Battalion, First Canadian Regiment in the trenches of the Great War. He was one of 70 out of 1000 men in his regiment to have survived. A series of 85 letters sent home from the trenches, hospitals, and camps during World War I was recently discovered in a family attic. I would like to thank my Uncle Darrin Canniff, Mayor of Chatham–Kent, for supplying photographs and copies of these valuable letters, which form a portion of the novel and were very helpful with research.

During my initial research, I corresponded with George Sharp, who lived in London, England between the world wars and helped with some of the details of life in those times. He passed away in New Zealand. http://adplus4.20m.com/catalog.html

I would like to thank the Humber School for Writers, especially Antanas Seleika who retired in 2017 as Director and has always been very supportive. As of June this year, he told me he was working on another novel and continuing to read other writers' works, so he is staying busy in retirement!

I would also like to thank my Writing Mentors David Adams Richards and MG Vassanji for their wisdom and guidance. I thank David for providing valuable feedback on earlier versions of this manuscript, and for agreeing to provide a quote for the book.

And I thank Steven Heighton for his encouragement and support; I recently traded his novel *Afterlands* in exchange for my novel *Poor Man's Galapagos*. In a note, he indicated that based on the jacket description, *Poor Man's Galapagos* is in some ways a very similar book. I initially read with Steve at the Draft Reading Series in Toronto. Steve keeps busy these days and recently published/released five projects!

I would also like to acknowledge the book *For Freedom and Honour?: The Story of the 25 Canadian Volunteers Executed in the First World War* by A.B. Godefroy, which assisted with research into James Wilson and other facets of Canadian deserters in WWI.

To my editor Shane Joseph, I would like to thank you for improving the manuscript immeasurably through your detailed, insightful and thought–provoking comments. And thank you to Blue Denim Press for publishing this work.

I would like to thank my wife Roxanne, the love of my life. We just celebrated our 20–year anniversary. Twenty wonderful years of love and laughter that started with me stopping to ask her for directions, and later proposing to her on a snowy bench. God had a wonderful plan for us that led to two amazing children, Colin, the intrepid explorer and outdoorsman, and Abigail, the wonderful artist, reader, and fitness enthusiast who have consistently taught me the value and enjoyment of fatherhood.

I would like to thank my parents Craig and Barb, my brother Ben and his wife Leigh-Anne, for their continued love, support, and encouragement throughout the years. Also Dave and Fiona (and Charlotte and Mabel too!), and Monica, as well as Mary of course, thank you for your love and friendship.

John 3:16—For God so loved the world that he gave his one and only Son, that whoever believes in him shall not perish but have eternal life.

# <u>Author Bio</u>

Christopher Canniff is the author of *Poor Man's Galapagos* (Blue Denim Press, 2015, submitted for the 2016 Scotiabank Giller Prize) and *Abundance of the Infinite* (Quattro Books, 2012, a finalist in the 2012 Ken Klonsky Novella Contest). Christopher has been mentored by two of Canada's top writers, MG Vassanji and David Adams Richards, at the Humber School for Writers. David Adams Richards was his Writing Mentor for *Intervals of Hope* and *Poor Man's Galapagos*, and said of Christopher Canniff's writing: "...your description is as powerful as any writer I have ever had in this course." Christopher is a Past President of the Canadian Authors Association Toronto Branch. Christopher's short stories have been published in Descant Magazine (Issue 152, spring 2011) and in a Tightrope Books anthology (2006). He was shortlisted in the 2012 Ken Klonsky Novella Contest with Quattro Books, and in the 2010 Matrix Litpop Awards for Fiction. He won LWOT Magazine's 3-Hour Novel Contest in 2007.

He wrote two radio scripts for Falcon Picture Group in Chicago, Illinois, USA for a nationally syndicated radio program. Christopher lived in Ecuador where he read over fifty books of world literature, learned a new language and culture, and taught English at an Ecuadorian university for WorldTeach, a non–profit and non–governmental organization based at the Harvard Institute for International Development. Christopher obtained a Mechanical Engineering degree in 1995 from the University of Toronto, and he is a registered Professional Engineer in the province of Ontario. He is married to the love of his life, Roxanne, and has two amazing children, Colin and Abigail.

He trusts in the Word of God as truth. Please find more information at www.christophercanniff.com.

# End Notes

[1] https://poets.org/poem/dulce-et-decorum-est (From the poem "Dulce et Decorum Est" by Wilfred Owen. This poem is in the public domain. Latin phrase is originally from the Roman poet Horace, 13BC.)

[2] https://www.iwm.org.uk/collections/item/object/80033695 (Catalog number 33040)

[3] https://www.iwm.org.uk/collections/item/object/80033693 (Catalog number 33038)

[4] https://www.iwm.org.uk/collections/item/object/80033694 (Catalogue number 33039)

[5] The following essay indicates "the majority of the publications that the BUF had were published on leaflets and sounded like this." Quote within the essay:
https://www.ukessays.com/essays/history/fascism-and-anti-fascism-in-great-britain-history-essay.php?vref=1
This is also Quoted in Martin Walker, The National Front, Fontana/Collins, np, 1977, p. 25, as noted in the essay
https://www.scribd.com/document/56764159/British-Fascism

[6] Courtesy of Guardian News & Media Ltd.,
https://www.theguardian.com/world/2009/sep/06/second-world-war-declaration-chamberlain

Printed in the USA
CPSIA information can be obtained
at www.ICGtesting.com
JSHW011913281023
50806JS00010B/117